The Indies Enterprise

The Indies Enterprise

A novel

Érik Orsenna

Translated from the French by Anthea Bell

Ouvrage publié avec le soutien de Centre national du livre.
Published with the support of the Centre National de Livre.

First published in France as *L'Entreprise des Indes* by Editions Stock, © Editions Stock 2010

First published in Great Britain in 2011 by Haus Publishing Limited

HAUS PUBLISHING LTD.
70 Cadogan Place, London SW1X 9AH
www.hauspublishing.com

Copyright © Érik Orsenna

ISBN 978-1-906598-93-8

Typset in Minion by MacGuru Ltd
info@macguru.org.uk

Printed and bound by CPI Group (UK) Ltd, Croydon, CR0 4YY

A CIP catalogue for this book is available from the British Library

The seaman's profession makes those who follow it
want to know all the secrets of this world.

Christopher Columbus,
The Book of Prophecies

I was not expected to be telling this story.

In our family, it is the elder brother who dreams, and his dream is considered sacrosanct. One way or another, Christopher took us all on board with him.

He had given each of us a part to play.

Mine was to help him, day and night, and to keep my mouth shut.

I never thought of protesting. There is no point in rejecting a law when the law is part of your own heart.

And it was just as well that I went along with the dream, because that is how it came true.

In this new city of Santo Domingo, the Alcazar Palace is intended to remind one of Seville. However, it is only a large block of grey stone set on the banks of the little river Ozama. Come closer, never fear, come through the gateway. It is not very likely that the guards will trouble you; they sleep most of the time, and their snores show how unstintingly they devote their best efforts to the noble art of slumber. Turn left and go through two chapels, one large, one small. Open a door, also on your left. The room is so empty and so dimly lit that you will think you are stepping into a tomb. Such is the magnificent and gloomy apartment assigned to me by the Viceroy. The Viceroy is my nephew Diego, Christopher's only legitimate son.

I am often asked: Bartholomew, what incomprehensible force makes you stay here on this island? Why choose Hispaniola as your final earthly abode, rather than those other parts of the world that are blessed with greater charms, more obvious comforts, and without

1

a shadow of a doubt better doctors? Why not your beloved Lisbon, or the incomparably mild and gentle valley of the Loire in France?

Depending on my inclinations from day to day, I cite one of the countless reasons that make me love this island so much: the variety of its bird life, the nine colours of the sea, the nearby mountains, the violence of the storms, the strong perfume of its women, the boldness of its little girls and its flowers alike, going everywhere and adopting the most immodest of poses …

I never give the main reason.

On this island, contrary to our youthful ambitions, Christopher and I did not discover Paradise itself, the Paradise of Holy Scripture; but we came as close to it as possible. My mind is still clear enough for me to know that my choice of Hispaniola as my home will not protect me from Death, whose swift approach I feel. I know only that this place, rather than any other, is where I shall best be able to resist the other ills of old age: a sense of perpetual cold in spite of the heat, the pain that afflicts old men's joints, the torments of memory.

On Hispaniola you might think that every night effaces the memory of the day before; every dawn breaking over the sea, still calm at this hour, is new, pure, light. No past weighs down on the island, by which I mean none of the mistakes of the past.

As there are deeps on earth where life does not follow the same laws as on the surface, so time has gulfs in it.

I miss scientists, who could have explained that phenomenon to me. I think it must be that the hours slow down in relation to our distance from the sun, situated as we are on the borders where it sets.

Dare I confess that, in what might be called my permanent present here, I live more at peace with myself than ever before? Rid of the trouble of dreaming, now that Christopher has left this world, but also free of the remorse that my multitude of sins ought to make me feel.

That Sunday in 1511, the first Sunday in Advent, the city and I woke together. I love this palace for its coral stones that let sound pass through. First I hear the birds welcoming the return of the light, then men coughing and spitting, horses snorting, the creak of cartwheels, the first screech of the saws. A caravel is coming in. I can tell by ear what sail she is furling, where in the port she will moor. Dogs are barking. They will go on, louder and louder, until they have been fed. A new day is breaking slowly, like a ship moving away from the quay. On every one of these new days I express my gratitude to it for taking me on board.

And with no premonition of the assault about to be made on my soul, ruining my peace of mind, I set off for church.

Mass began.

Praying was difficult, seated as I was in the front row, between Viceroy Diego and his wife Maria of Toledo, where all eyes were turned my way. May God forgive me, instead of addressing myself to Him and Him alone, I was constantly returning the greetings I received. Suddenly I gave a start of surprise. A Dominican friar had stepped up into the pulpit and was beginning his sermon:

I am the voice of Christ crying in the wilderness of this island ...

Such was his text. Then he launched into the sermon itself:

I am the voice of Christ crying in the wilderness of this island [...] a voice that says you are all in a state of mortal sin, because of your cruelty towards the innocent and your tyranny over them.

Sentence by sentence, his voice grew stronger, his words were more clearly articulated. You might have thought they were changing into stones flung in our faces.

Tell me, by virtue of what right and in the name of what justice do you keep the Indians in such cruel and dreadful servitude? Who has authorized you to wage terrible war on peoples who were living at peace in their own countries, where now they have perished in such vast numbers? [...] Why do you keep them in such a state of oppression and exhaustion, without giving them food to eat, or caring for them in the illnesses from which they suffer, worked to death by all the labour you demand from them? You kill them solely to get gold out of the land day after day. Are these Indians not men? Have they not minds and souls? Are you not bound to love them as you love yourselves? [...] Why have you fallen into so dull and deep a sleep? In your present state of mind, it is certain that you will be no more able to find salvation than the Moors and Turks who reject the faith of Jesus Christ.

3

Such was the tenor of the sermon preached that day by Brother Antonio de Montesinos before all the authorities of Hispaniola and all the *encomenderos*, those Spaniards who had been given the Indians' land, as well as the Indians themselves to cultivate it.

The astonishment of the congregation soon gave way to anger.

Glances passed back and forth, from the preacher uttering his terrible words to the Viceroy trying to maintain an impassive appearance.

The officiating priest had to exert all his authority to ensure that Mass came to an end without a revolt on the part of the faithful.

Once back in our palace, the Viceroy immediately summoned the Dominican, of whom no one had ever heard before, and spoke to him in paternal tones as follows: Each of us, if he is ill-informed, can be induced to say what is not true. How can a man be blamed for falling into error because he has had inadequate information? More specifically, said the Viceroy, the work of the Indians was necessary for the good management of the island and thus for the greater glory of Spain. Consequently the preacher, whose talents, incidentally, all admired while they also understood his strong emotion, would have no option, now that he was better informed, but to deliver a sermon of a very different kind next Sunday – a sermon that would restore, to the population at large, the peace by which His Majesty the King set particular store ...

And without giving him time to reply, Diego introduced me: My uncle Bartholomew, the Admiral's brother, first governor of this island in the years 1496 to 1500.

Montesinos started in surprise. He looked me straight in the eye and said a single word.

"Why?

The Viceroy was already showing him out.

"I count on you, Brother Antonio. The equilibrium here is very fragile. We must all observe our rightful stations."

As Montesinos opened his mouth to reply, the door was shut in his face. Every member of Spanish high society looked forward to next Sunday's Mass with confidence, sure that the incident was now closed

❧

All that week the single word "why?" haunted me. Every time I put it out of my head it came back like an angry wasp, always preceded by the same vision of the preacher's two penetrating eyes.

And at night, behind the familiar noises of the port, I heard a sound that I did not recognize, like the friction of a wheel on the road, or the turning of a mill.

I felt sure that Montesinos – curse him! – had turned back Time. I was going to lose my refuge. And the torments of memory, which I feared so much, would not be long in returning.

Next Sunday, well before Mass began, the entire island, or I should say the entire Spanish population of the island, gathered outside the entrance to the monastery. Many had come from afar, from remote corners of Hispaniola, from the province of La Vega, from the mountains and even the north coast and the Samana peninsula. Rumour had done its work. No one wanted to miss the sermon.

Some were just dismounting from their horses. They splashed themselves with water from the fountain so as not to enter the House of God all dusty and travel-stained. Why, they cried, we haven't seen one another for ages! We thought you were dead! There were exclamations, embraces, you would have thought it was a family party. People exchanged the latest bad news, spoke of deaths and births, the severity of the climate, the disappointing harvest, the poor yield of the mines.

After two or three such exchanges, conversation was about the Indians and their indolence, bestiality, imbecility and cruelty. Then talk turned to the deranged priest, who within a few days had become the most famous man on the island. Do you know this man Montesinos? What in the world got into him? Well, it seems that the Viceroy received him, brought him to see reason. If that's not so, he'll have us to deal with. Their faces were ferocious. They had come armed.

The Dominicans were at their wits' end. Unless the walls of the church were extended it would take no one else. A good three hundred of the faithful, to their fury, had already been turned away. And more kept on coming. Even before Antonio de Montesinos had said a word, the atmosphere was at boiling point.

At last, amidst much discontented grumbling, Mass began. It seemed to me – although I had no instrument with me for measuring its rhythm – that the first part went faster than usual.

And suddenly a strong voice rang out above all heads. There was Montesinos, having climbed into the pulpit no one knew how. Perhaps his friends the Indians had taught him their own ability to move about unseen. The pulpit rested on a large, carved wooden serpent. Some among the congregation were muttering that this accursed preacher had made a pact with the creature to protect him from the crowd.

Why do you keep the Indians in such cruel servitude? Why do you wage such cruel and abhorrent war against peaceful people? Why do you kill them by making them work at a pace that none of you would survive? Why do you not regard them as men, when God has given them souls just as he has given souls to you?

Far from intimidating Montesinos, the precepts of the Viceroy had confirmed him in his views. The authority of his words asserted itself. On the previous Sunday his voice had been shaking, not with fear but with indignation. This time his words passed through the air as hard and accurately aimed as missiles.

The congregation reacted at once. Voices rose higher and higher. Twenty, thirty of the *encomenderos* had risen to their feet and, forgetting where they were, were pointing menacing fingers at the preacher, telling him to be quiet.

Montesinos took no notice of this exhibition. Not content with continuing his sermon in the same equable, clear and determined voice, he sought the eyes of the most vociferous among the crowd.

This provocation almost lit the fuse. A group more determined than the rest was on the point of mounting an attack on the pulpit. A dozen Dominicans intervened to prevent them. They must have anticipated this offensive, and had gathered at the foot of the little wooden flight of steps.

· ❧

That same afternoon a man arrived at the palace and had himself announced to me as the son of an old comrade of Christopher's, one of those who had accompanied him on his second voyage in 1493. Could I, in spite of my weariness, refuse to open my door to him? He was a man of fine bearing, and could not have been much older than thirty. He told me that his name was Las Casas, and his first name, like mine, was Bartholomew. He wanted to know my true opinion of the sermon.

He had arrived on the island in 1502 with the new governor, Nicolas de Ovando. He was still under eighteen at the time, and was one of the many who had come from Spain hoping to make a fortune fast. Like others, he had been given a plot of land and the Indians who lived on it. He had prospered. But a life of accumulating wealth had soon seemed unendurable to him. Some years later, he left it all, became a priest and joined the Dominicans.

We spent the rest of the day in discussion. Had not the discoverers corrupted their own discovery? How did God view our cruel practices? We promised each other to seek replies in Holy Scripture.

And so I returned to the habits of my younger days.

Every Sunday, in Lisbon, my brother and I used to read aloud in turn a chapter from the Bible. A man who wants to know the world, Christopher often said, cannot ignore the Book.

When Las Casas came back a couple of days later, I got him to read what I had found in *Ecclesiasticus*: the implacable reply to our questions.

"For if the needy curse thee in the bitterness of his soul, his prayer shall be heard of Him that made him." (IV, 6)

"Whoso bringeth an offering of the goods of the poor doeth as one that killeth the son before his father's eyes." (XXXIV, 20)

Las Casas did not allow his face to show anything. But I looked at his hands and they were trembling. The sermon delivered by Montesinos had affected him as much as it affected me. But being younger and more courageous, he was not content with a sense of devastation; he wanted to fling himself into the breach. What use was his life, he said, if from now on he did not devote it to the truth?

He had not come alone. There was a boy with him, a tall lad with round cheeks who had yet to grow any hair on his face. Yet his white robe showed beyond all doubt that he was a Dominican. Was the sudden growth in the size of the world forcing the order to recruit children so young?

"Let me introduce Brother Jerome," said Las Casas. "He has

only just joined us, and he will help me in the enterprise that I am planning."

At that word I gave a start. The Enterprise. The Indies Enterprise, so Christopher had called his voyage.

Las Casas had a different ambition: not to explore, like Christopher, but to tell a story. The story of the Discovery, so that no one would be ignorant of it and all could learn its lessons.

He looked deep into my eyes. His gaze was almost as intense as the expression in the eyes of Montesinos.

"Your experience at your brother's side is of incomparable worth. Given your great age, sir, you will not be long for this world. You cannot refuse me your aid."

I did not hesitate. I knelt without delay.

"In the name of the Father, and of the Son, and of the Holy Ghost ..."

"But what are you doing, sir?" Brother Jerome, the Dominican boy, was looking at me, baffled. "You are beginning already? But ... it's so late."

His eyelids were closing. I know the young; they can't resist their weariness. I did not take pity on him. I had been waiting so long, without knowing it, for the moment to tell our story.

Las Casas was smiling. "Listen, Jerome, listen. Christopher's four voyages will belong forever to the history of mankind's curiosity. He traced a route across the sea that superseded all others. He went all round the world; he populated the horizon."

In the usual way, all we remember of voyages is their destination, forgetting their beginning. But that beginning is the tale I am about to tell. My fingers are too painful and twisted by age for me to take up my pen. So I shall dictate the story of the truth to you, my dear little scribe Jerome, and you will record it well, with absolute fidelity and down to every least detail. On certain days, when you hear some of my secrets, I am sure you will cross yourself and the colour will rise to your cheeks. I shall not feel sorry for you. You can offer up your suffering to the Lord. Your place in heaven will be all the more certain.

Seaports are not the only point of departure for ships, Jerome; it may be a dream that sends them out to sea. Many historians have

8

written and will write accounts of Christopher's discovery, arguing about its consequences.

Being his brother, the only man who knew him all his life, I saw his idea born and his fevered obsession with it grow.

I am going to tell the story of that birth and that obsession. Perhaps the seed of our future cruelty had already been sown in his feverish desire for knowledge?

To your post, Jerome, and let us put out to sea!

We shall soon be in Lisbon, where it all began.

I

Curiosity

I was born in Genoa, which is a natural prison. You come up against mountains on three sides, so there remains only the fourth, which is the sea. It is by sea that the people of Genoa make their escape, each in his own way, some as merchants, others as navigators. I think my brother's very first steps took him down to the harbour.

It took me longer to get away.

※

"So why would I hire you?"

This was the scornful but legitimate question that welcomed me to the kingdom of Portugal in the spring of 1469. I was not yet sixteen. I had simply followed the flow; for people from all over Europe were making for Lisbon. Some came after being expelled from their homes, like the Jewish scholars of Majorca suddenly branded undesirable by the King of Catalonia. The knowledge of others interested the Portuguese monarchs, who had the means (in the form of cash paid down) of attracting them. I obviously fell into a lesser category. I had heard one of my father's customers, a knowledgeable man despite his heavy drinking, say that there was a large colony of Genoese on the banks of the Tagus these days, working as cartographers.

The information opened up new horizons to me. At last I could free myself from the family business. I didn't yet know that no one escapes his God-given destiny, or that far worse servitude lay in store for me.

※

And that was how I found myself at the door of Master Andrea, the most famous of his guild.

"So why would I hire you?"

"Because I want you to."

"Good answer, but not good enough. Seeing you look so pale and thin, I'd guess that you have never been a sailor. Am I wrong?"

"No, sir, you're not wrong."

"And you're too young to have heard many seamen's stories yet."

"True, sir."

"So what do you know about the sea?"

"Nothing."

"What, in your opinion, is a cartographer?"

"A man who ... who draws the borders of the land."

"And thus the shape of the sea. Are you that man?"

"No."

"Then if you don't know anything, what use do you think you could be to me? Off you go, lad."

I went on my way, fists clenched, tears of anger and humiliation in my eyes. But just in time, I remembered my origins. I was Genoese after all! And a Genoese doesn't lose a battle without even putting up a fight.

I retraced my steps and went back to the cartographer's studio, where I said, "I can ... I can ..."

In those moments when the kind spirit of Illusion takes pity on me, whispering in dulcet tones: there now, Bartholomew, your life hasn't been such a disaster as you think – in those rare moments I hold my head high. I think again of my proud reaction that day in 1469, and I tell myself that it played a part in the history of the world. But for that moment of self-assertion I would have missed my way and would never have benefited from Master Andrea's vast store of knowledge. And my brother Christopher, later, would not have had that advantage either. Without it, would he have thrown himself into the unlikely venture of his voyage?

So to return to myself as a Genoese lad, little more than a child, standing with my fingers clutching my little woollen cap, shifting from foot to foot in front of the greatest cartographer in Lisbon. "I can ... I can ..." How was I going to finish that sentence, since there was nothing I *could* do?

"I can ... I can write very small."

The idea had come to me all of a sudden, in much the same way as, just before you sink at sea, you may suddenly see a vision of the rock that will save you between the breaking of two waves. I had remembered my one and only talent: ever since I could first hold a pen, I had been able to write minuscule but perfect letters.

"Show me!"

Master Andrea told someone to bring me ink and a pen. He picked up the scrap of a map that had been abandoned and was lying on the floor, handed it to me and crossed his arms.

I hadn't finished writing *Ceuta* and *Algiers* before I felt a tap on my shoulder. I was hired. One task was entrusted to me immediately: to write in all the names on a chain of tiny islands off the coast of a part of Africa called Senegal.

Over the next few days, my new comrades' jealousy grew. It filled the studio, as palpable as a thunderstorm brewing before it breaks. They were, after all, older than me and a thousand times more experienced. But they could not bear the way Master Andrea, their master as well as mine, kept coming back again and again to watch the play of my fingers. Particularly when he spoke to me. Even so long afterwards, I can remember our conversations word for word.

"Where did you get such skill in writing tiny lettering?"

"I've been practising it forever."

"But why practise it?"

"Because I'm afraid."

"Afraid of what?"

"I'm afraid when things are too big. When they're bigger than me."

"Why did you want to work with maps?"

"Maps live by being small."

"What do you mean?"

"Maps are small compared to the world they describe. A map as big as the real world wouldn't be of any use."

"Undeniable! Do you know about the woodcock?"

I confessed to my ignorance of that subject as well.

Master Andrea nodded. "Soon you will have no more faithful friend than that bird."

෨෬

I was about to discover many other strange things about the world. For example, our neighbour's was a very noisy trade. He often came round to our studio to give his eardrums a rest and marvelled at the silence there. While half-naked men spent their days in his workshop, blowing the bellows of their forges, hammering away at pieces of iron or bronze, all you heard in the cartographer's studio was the faint scratch of pens on parchment.

Sea captains always went to this affable man and his deafening forge to stock up before they put out to sea. Their purchases were always the same: cauldrons, large cooking pots, bowls and improbable quantities of barbers' shaving basins.

I was surprised: what use were all those basins? Did beards grow faster and more densely at sea than on land?

He was happy to tell me, not without a hearty laugh at my ignorance. "Everyone knows that, Bartholomew! We trade with African chiefs, and they're crazy about all such metal containers, particularly shaving basins. They chuckle with delight as they try gazing at their reflections in them; they use them as lids to keep the flies off food; they put them on graves in honour of their dead. God knows what goes on in the heads of those African tribesmen. But it's a fact that the most ordinary household items, as we see it here, are enormously valuable out there, worth much more than other trading currencies such as textiles, glass jewellery, brass rings. For one basin you can get up to three slaves or fifty grams of gold!"

I still wonder today about the strange mechanics of trade involving goods sent from one side of the planet to the other. Why would we rather have gold and slaves here? And why do they fight to get their hands on shaving basins in Africa?

What was my outstanding characteristic at that time?

Not timidity, painfully shy as I was. I had only to hear someone speak to me to find my forehead and the palms of my hands breaking out in a sweat. Some ten times during my first weeks in Portugal, I almost went back to Genoa. I felt sure that the Atlantic was too vast and open an expanse of water for me. Why, oh why, I kept saying to myself by night as I sat on my straw mattress, arms around my knees, why did I ever leave the Mediterranean, which is more like a lake and suits me so much better?

Nor was my main quality that permanent concern with fornication that was to remain with me all my life, even now as the end approaches, although the climate here makes the least hint of a salacious thought exhausting. There is nothing new about the obsessive wish to copulate felt by male creatures of sixteen, which was my age at that time.

No, my outstanding characteristic when I arrived in Lisbon was sheer *ignorance*. An ignorance quite different from anyone's inevitable lack of knowledge at the beginning of his life. A resolute ignorance. A *taught* ignorance, although the association of those two terms is far from adequate.

Logically, knowledge is what you are taught, so how can you be taught its absence?

Our mother Susanna was responsible for that paradox. A very devout woman, she had only one ambition for her children: to see them firmly established in the love of God.

What was the point, she used to say, of wasting your time in human cogitation when all you need to get to heaven is an understanding of the divine will? As a result – by means of womanly wiles such as blackmail extorted in bed – she contrived to get us sent to the worst of all the schools in Genoa, a school preoccupied first and foremost with ignorance, and that is where we were educated: I, Bartholomew, my elder brother Christopher and my younger brother Diego.

One day our teacher, an old priest, unrolled a scroll of parchment and pinned it to the wall. "This is our earth," he said. "Praise the Lord for its creation!"

We praised the Lord in chorus.

"That circle represents the inhabitable world," he said. "It is divided into three by an ocean shaped like the letter T."

ASIA

EUROPE   AFRICA

"Why is Asia on top of the other two continents?" one of us asked.

"It is a choice, children, a choice imposed by logic. All good geographers show *orientation* on their maps. Asia is in the Orient, is it not? And what about Jerusalem? Who can tell me where God has placed Jerusalem? Where the Orient begins? Excellent. You wouldn't want the Holy City to come lower than any other part of the world, would you?"

We applauded this demonstration. How had we ever gone so long without guessing that "to orientate" meant to place the Orient above everything? I put up my hand.

"Why are there only three continents?"

"You haven't been studying your Bible, Bartholomew. Listen carefully to this commentary, written by the learned scholar Isidore of Seville in the year 600. Our planet was divided up between Noah's three sons. Shem received Asia, the name of which goes back to one of his descendants, Princess Asia. Twenty-seven nations live there. Ham was given Africa, where there are thirty different races and three hundred and sixty cities. Japhet received Europe, with its fifteen tribes and one hundred and twenty cities."

"Only a hundred and twenty? My father told me that he passed through seventeen large and very beautiful cities on his journey to Rome alone."

My lively recollection of that lesson derives not from my memory but from my behind, which got a severe beating for my remark. How dare I cast doubt on the sacred truths revealed by Isidore?

I kept quiet in the next lesson, shifting on my bruised buttocks.

"Children, do you know what the pagans believe?"

We vigorously shook our heads, making the sign of the cross. In the name of the Father, the Son and the Holy Ghost, amen!

"They believe, and this will show you how lacking in intelligence they are, that there are living beings in the Antipodes."

We burst into roars of laughter. How grotesque, what idiots, what ignorance those pagans showed!

The priest looked at his class with satisfaction.

"You are good little boys, but do you at least know what 'antipodes' are?"

Our silence gave him the reply.

"Well, it's true that you haven't learnt much Greek! Antipodes are people who walk about on the other side of the earth, with their feet (*podos*) opposite us (*anti*). And thus they walk with their feet above their heads."

This time our laughter must have set the whole city shaking.

"What fools the pagans are! Do they have any brains at all?"

At this point the dunce of the class, a boy who was always falling asleep – little Johnny Daydream, we called him – woke up. He suffered from some kind of disorder of the stomach or the eyes, no one knew what, and spent his days slumped over his desk. At this, however, he sat up straight, exclaiming, "But then the earth is flat!"

The whole class replied, in unison, "Well, of course the earth is flat!"

≫

Another memory. Another lesson in ignorance delivered by our old teacher.

"When Saint Augustine was faced with a difficult question, his custom was to get up and go for a walk. On the day of which I speak, he was trying unsuccessfully to disentangle the mystery of the Holy Trinity. How was one to understand a God who is clearly One and yet is divided into Father, Son, and Holy Ghost?

"He decided to walk on the beach, for the vast presence of the moving sea often gave him good ideas. As he walked along, he met a child busy with a strange task. He had dug a hole in the sand; he carried a sea shell in his hand; and he was going back and forth between his hole and the shoreline on which the waves broke.

'What are you doing?' asked St Augustine.

'I'm going to empty the sea.'

'With that shell? Why, you'll never do it!'

"The child just looked at St Augustine with a smile. Then he disappeared. And the saint thought, once more, of the Trinity and understood the message: our intellect will not help us to understand the mysteries of faith, any more than we can empty the sea with a shell. The essential truths are to be reached not through reason, but through faith and love. And that is all that I can wish for you."

The old priest had finished his lesson, except for one final recommendation. "My children, I adjure you never to depart, never, from your state of holy ignorance."

In these conditions, how could I enter a cartography and cosmography studio, that temple of knowledge, without fearing for my soul?

≉

I have often thought, since then, of the holy ignorance that the Muslims also teach in their schools.

No doubt that is why, among the few books I brought to the island of Hispaniola with me, there is a copy of the *Confessions* of St Augustine.

Yesterday I was re-reading Book X, Chapter XXXV, *Of the second temptation, which is curiosity.*

There is, in the soul, a fickle, indiscreet and curious passion which, by adopting the name of science, leads it to employ the senses not for the sake of the pleasures of the flesh, but to carry out experiments and acquire knowledge through the flesh. And because this is a desire to know, and sight is the first of all the senses where knowledge is concerned, the Holy Spirit called it the concupiscence of the eyes. [...] It is this malady that leads us to seek for hidden secrets of nature that are none of our business, for to know them is useless, and men wish to learn them only for the sake of knowledge.

If a great desire to taste the unknown is a sin, then you must condemn me, but not me alone: you will have to consign the whole of Lisbon to hell.

I was born in a seaport. I know how curiosity gets blunted when ships are always coming in from sea carrying the same cargo. In Genoa, hardly anyone celebrated such arrivals, because no one was expecting anything out of the ordinary.

There was no such apathy in my new country.

I hadn't been in Portugal a week before one day, in the middle of the morning, I looked up from my work on the miniature lettering to see my comrades suddenly rushing headlong out of the studio. I ran after them. Someone must have called "Fire!" I thought, and in spite of my growing passion for cartography I had no desire at all to burn alive along with the maps.

Out in the street, everyone was running. I joined the flow of the crowd without any idea what it was all about since no one deigned to answer my questions.

Houses were disgorging their inhabitants. People who never usually went out emerged: cooks with tousled hair, ladles still in their hands; mothers with their bodices undone, babies attached to their breasts; dribbling old folk in their shirts, looking half dead; lovers taken by surprise in the middle of their amorous raptures, adjusting their clothing as best they could while they ran; not forgetting the cats, dogs, chickens and other poultry. The crowd was growing all the time; everyone was shouting.

Soon we came out on the quayside, and with one accord our arms went up in the air, pointing to the horizon as if to show each other what we all saw there.

I have watched the same scene a hundred times, in the company of a similar crowd.

And each of those hundred times, my heart has beaten just as

strongly. Every time, I have felt that the voyage now approaching its end and about to deliver its fruits has expanded my mind and made me grow. Every time, I have had to struggle to keep myself from plunging into the waves and swimming out to meet the ship as she comes in.

This immutable ritual is the breath of life to Portugal.

A caravel slowly sails in on the rising tide. Her sails are mere rags patched together; it seems that only a miracle keeps her masts upright. What war has she been waging, against what enemies? Several boards in her sides are stove in and her stern-castle is only a ruin.

A rowing boat goes out, flying the king's flag.

A black silhouette gets down from the caravel into the rowing boat. This black-clad figure is the notary.

Since the time of Henry the Navigator, every caravel has taken a notary on board. His job is to keep a detailed account of all incidents that take place during a voyage of exploration. He is the man who describes the discoveries made in detail. It is he who keeps the gold brought back from Africa in a purse.

And now the whole city, gathered on the quay, watches the rowing-boat and its eight oarsmen gliding up the river. The notary stands upright. No other notaries, landbound notaries who never go to sea, will know such glory. Everyone is aware that the king is expecting him.

Once the black-clad notary has disembarked, all eyes turn back to the caravel. Now that she is closer, the crew come into view. They look like old men, their skin tanned to leather by the sun, their hair bleached by salt or perhaps turned white by fear. No doubt time passes more quickly at the other end of the world. Moorings are cast out and at last the caravel comes to a halt. The sailors scrutinize the crowd on shore: which of all the women waiting on the quay is my wife? And the women scrutinize the sailors: which of those men is my husband? How can they be expected to recognize each other after an absence that can sometimes last six years?

Master Andrea was getting impatient.

"Keep your eyes peeled, for God's sake!"

Two of us, more agile than the others, had managed to clamber up part of the harbour wall and we were now describing what we saw on the deck of the caravel. Gathered at our feet, the others were jumping up and down with excitement.

"Red and white cloth …"

"We're not interested in that. Carry on!"

"Wait while I count – ten, eleven … yes, fifteen blacks, six women among them, none of them pretty, and five children."

"Why would I want to know about them?" asked Master Andrea

"Strange plants, tall and green. With two kinds of giant pineapples growing on them, each as big as a man's head."

"And then?"

"Ah, here comes something different! The sailors are beginning to bring out cages. Looks like birds in them."

"What colour?"

"Some bright green with red heads, others grey with white heads."

"How about their beaks?"

"The first set have grey beaks, the second have shiny black beaks, very hooked."

"That's better, much better! Parrots!"

Master Andrea told us to follow those parrots until they reached the market where they were to be sold.

"And keep your ears open! Those birds sometimes talk in a language that's easy enough to translate, and they may let slip not just certain comments on the customs of the savages, but also useful information such as the frequency of storms off the coasts of this or that cape, or the presence of bright metals in their native forests."

Unfortunately other master cartographers had had the same idea. So much so that if we were to get anywhere near the parrots, we had to launch ourselves into a fist-fight that went on until evening.

I gained a certain reputation at this sport, along with an equanimity that was never again called into question. Writing very small never prevented anyone from hitting very hard.

I will admit it: telling the story of my youth brings me happiness that I have never known before. It cannot be said that much attention has been paid to me in the course of my long life. Christopher wasn't interested in anything but his Enterprise, and no one else was interested in anyone but Christopher.

And now, suddenly, two persons of quality come to see me every day and hang on my every word. Las Casas never takes his eyes off me, or his ears either. And Brother Jerome writes down everything I say as if his eternal life depended on the accuracy of his records.

So many old men end up in a state of indifference!

How could I fail to relish the unexpected curiosity that I arouse?

It seems to me that my intellect is reawakening.

Ideas come to me, ideas of which I would never have thought myself capable. This one, for instance: there are two kinds of trade. Genoa and Venice dealt in goods or materials already known, transporting them at the best price and highest speed. Lisbon, at the same time, was sailing blindly into seas still unknown and bringing back curiosities.

My dear Las Casas, my dear young Jerome, before condemning me too harshly, ask your hierarchy what its doctrine is. Why would God look more favourably on the first kind of trade, dealing in goods that are known, than on the second, trading in what is unknown? Indeed, it seems to me, although my theological knowledge is slight, that the latter does greater homage to infinity and the mystery of God's Creation, blessed be its name!

One January day, I remember, Lisbon was shivering from the onslaught of a terrible north wind. We worked muffled up in warm clothes. I kept blowing on my fingers, usually so skilful in tracing minuscule, almost invisible lettering, in my attempts to warm them up. Master Andrea tapped me on the shoulder.

"Leave it for now. Not even you will get anything done today. Let's take this opportunity for a little talk. What, fundamentally, do you know about our planet?"

I confidently told him that it was flat, consisting of three continents and the ocean around them was shaped like the letter T.

Astounded, he heard me out. Around us, my comrades were beginning to chuckle.

"Who taught you that?"

"My schoolteachers."

"And you never tried to find out any more?"

"I don't need to. I only draw details, parts of the coastlines. And anyway, the three continents and the T-shaped ocean are truths. It says so in Scripture. Why – don't you believe in them? Are you a pagan?"

The hilarity around us was increasing. I saw no good reason for this excessive merriment, particularly in such cold weather. Master Andrea sent all the others away. And it was in the now deserted studio that I was introduced to a new country, the country of the intellect.

"Bartholomew, I am going to tell you a story. Once upon a time, two and a half centuries before the birth of Christ, there was a man whose name was Eratosthenes. He lived in Egypt, in the city of Alexandria, which attracted all who loved knowledge because it had the finest library in the world. Eratosthenes himself was the head librarian. He was a mathematician and a geographer, that's to say a mathematician who loved to walk along streets and through fields. Algebra and geometry were not just abstract sciences to him, not just a source

25

of intellectual pleasure: those two branches of knowledge, as he saw it, ought to help us to solve questions arising from daily life.

"One day he heard a traveller saying that at noon on June the 21st, in the city of Syene in southern Egypt, the rays of the sun shone down the shafts of wells at an exactly vertical angle.

"Eratosthenes thought to himself: here in Alexandria, everything casts a shadow, even at noon. If I can calculate the angle of that shadow at the precise time when there are no shadows in Syene, then I shall know the size of the earth.

"He waited for the 21st of June. With three young men who worked in the Library to help him, and watched by a crowd of bystanders and no doubt a number of interested dogs, Eratosthenes traced lines in the sand. Then, transferring them to papyrus, he came up with the following result: there in Alexandria, the sun stood at an angle of 7°12' to the vertical."

As he spoke, Master Andrea was drawing a diagram to help him explain it to me. In that freezing cold, a strange warmth was breathed out by his story of summertime and June, sun and shadows.

"A circumference is a figure of 360°. 7°12' is one-fiftieth of it. Therefore, thought Eratosthenes, to work out the circumference of that globe the earth, he had only to multiply the distance between Syene and Alexandria by 50. Do you understand?"

I was far from that sudden sense of peace and flooding light that accompanies true understanding. But I did think I saw a faint light in the distance. I made up my mind to do all I could to keep it in sight, for then, I thought, I might one day be able to find it.

Unperturbed, Master Andrea went on. I heard him although I could hardly see him, so dense was the mist of vapour coming from his mouth.

"And now he had to calculate the distance between Alexandria and Syene. Eratosthenes resorted to camels. According to travellers, it took those useful animals 50 days to make the journey. Every day a normal camel, neither very slow nor very fast, can cover a distance of 100 stadia. So there were 50 × 100 = 5,000 stadia between Syene and Alexandria. That distance being one-fiftieth of the circumference of the earth, it should therefore measure 5,000 × 50 = 250,000 stadia."

26

I will be honest with you. If my story sounds fluent, that is because I have been thinking of it over and over again for more than forty years. I tell it now as you might recite a poem, the poem of the intellect at its peak. But that day I soon came down from the peak again, even though I kept vigorously nodding my head at each new step in the argument – the conversion of Egyptian stadia into Portuguese units of measurement, the final multiplications. Master Andrea concluded his demonstration without me; I was lost. And I had other preoccupations. There were angry questions on my mind. Why had people told me falsehoods for so long? Why had no one ever before mentioned that man of Alexandria who could measure the size of this earth, with the aid of nothing more than shadows and camels? Why did the priests go in such terror of the truth?

But I must have managed to pull the wool over Master Andrea's eyes. Before wishing me goodnight, he told me how happy he was to have hired an apprentice like me, capable of both writing very small and thinking on the grand scale.

This undeserved compliment soothed me and kept me warm until next morning.

You will have realized that Master Andrea placed cartography very high in his personal hierarchy, only just below God the Creator. And it was not hard to get him to admit to some extremely heretical ideas, very dangerous in those early days of the Inquisition. Without the support of cartography, he thought, God was not fully God. What would man know of the Creation without maps? And without man's knowledge of the Creation, how could God the Creator be worshipped? What was a God worth who was not worshipped or was poorly worshipped, by those he had created?

Master Andrea would indulge in such philosophical arguments in his few expansive moments, on evenings when he had taken a small glass of wine, which did not agree with his digestion, in celebration of some profitable transaction such as making a good sale. Then, suddenly alarmed by the words he heard coming from his own mouth, he would stop short and look at us one by one.

"I hope you didn't believe me? You must forget all that folly at once!"

We could tell, however, that he had said what he really thought.

Then he would return to more prudent ways of expressing himself. "To make maps is to describe the Creation. Making maps, then, is a form of prayer."

His troubles began when, after Mass every Sunday, he invited those who wished to come, young or old, to visit his studio and listen to the tales he told about cartographers.

"There was once a man called Hipparchus of Nicaea. Two hundred years before the birth of Christ, he thought of drawing parallel circular lines around the earth, some horizontal, others vertical. That meant that everywhere in the world belonged to a certain square and could be located."

"There was once a Majorcan Jew called Abraham Cresques who, in around 1375, compiled the Catalan Atlas, a masterpiece before which we all bow down."

Andrea would never listen to our warnings: how could we keep our secrets if such a crowd overran the studio?

As for the Church, who could suppose that it would tolerate such gatherings for long? Above all when Andrea made frequent reference to the "Golden Legend of geographers". For the real *Golden Legend* contained stories of the lives of the saints; and how could the Church allow a man who called himself a believer to claim that a cartographer was the equal of a saint?

The tragedy had already been written, and every day brought us closer to it.

꙳

Listen to me, my dear Las Casas.

My confession will not be as amusing as you expected, I accusing myself of sins, you blaming me for them and then, in the name of God, absolving me.

It is true that the story of my life will soon venture into dark territory. Before long I shall have to admit to the inadmissible. And you will find it easy to require stern penance from me.

First, however, it is for me to interrogate you. I have a question to put to you as a Dominican. Do not the Dominicans claim to be the Christian order that devotes more attention than any other to logic and knowledge? For two millennia the Greeks first guessed and then demonstrated that the earth was round. So why did Christianity wish to believe, and force us all to believe, that it was flat? Why such a hatred of knowledge among priests?

I am beginning to know my confessor.

When something in what I say troubles him, he looks at me with a smile that is half distressed, half indulgent – the insufferable smile of an adult speaking to a child, a smile that says: talk away if you like, I know things that I can't explain to you, you're too young, you will understand later.

Perhaps I shall murder Las Casas one day for that smile of his!

Meanwhile I relish his uneasiness.

I shall owe him a good night.

Chickens, lambs, calves, rabbits, fish, woodcock … when I entered the profession I did not know that we cartographers owed so much to our brothers and sisters of the animal kingdom. As I was the last apprentice to arrive at the studio, it was my job to make contact with these creatures.

Let's begin with chickens.

Never fear, I am not about to digress upon the dozens of concoctions used by painters and cartographers to bind, dilute and dry their paints. That is an activity with something about it of alchemy to which I have never really applied my mind.

And I have so many stories yet to tell, so many universes into which you must venture.

I am only warning you; I will go on.

You should know that there is nothing like egg, whether a whole egg, only the yolk or only the white, for binding coloured powders of mineral or vegetable origin. Hence my frequent visits to the henhouse.

And as I was still, so to speak, a virgin, I found myself blushing as I stroked the bellies of lambs, choosing the one that would provide the best surface on which to draw a map of Africa. The job was not so pleasant when it came to putting the animal, whose most tender parts I had just been caressing, to death; and it became a nightmare when I had to take its freshly removed skin to the tanner, and help him to treat it with substances that gave off a terrible stench.

Thinking of unpleasant odours, I remember the pungent smell that filled the studio every morning. It seems that human urine has wonderful qualities of dilution, so whichever of us had not drunk too much wine the previous evening was called upon to piss into a can.

Nor will I forget my friends the rabbits and the fish. Their bones provide the glue with which you coat vellum and parchment before drawing on it.

I haven't finished yet. When I think back to those days, I feel as if I passed all my time with animals.

What is a cartographer?

A man who goes in search of woodcock.

The finest feathers in all creation grow on that bird's wings. They are known as pin feathers. Without such a finely pointed quill, all the names of places that have to be written on a map would never fit in, however large the map itself.

Fowlers themselves knew the value to us of those rare feathers, and asked a very high price. It was better to track the birds down for ourselves. And it was always Bartholomew, whose chest had been weak from birth, who was sent out in winter to get lost in the woods, or even worse, splash about in icy marshes.

Does the woodcock guess at the hidden but vital part it plays in the depiction of the world? I am inclined to think so. At the moment of death, it gazes at you with a look that seems to say it consents to its fate. And with its last spasm, it stretches out its wings to you.

❧

When I think back, Lisbon as I knew it then was teeming with animals of every kind. The city was not only fed, clothed and drawn thanks to animals, but *spellbound* by them.

That day, immersed in a particularly detailed piece of calligraphy (fitting twenty-seven names of ports, villages, capes and anchorages on the tiny disc that represented the island of Minorca), I resisted the general mood of curiosity and refrained from going to watch a ship come in. Master Andrea had me summoned to the harbour because I was missing a remarkable spectacle, and a good cartographer ought to know everything.

I abandoned my woodcock quill and ran down to the sea.

When I arrived, two hoists were trying to raise the enormous stone that lay on the deck of the caravel. What a strange cargo! It looked like a grey rock, broader than it was high, and an unusual rock at that, because it had two eyes, a mouth, four paws and a tail. This rock appeared to be bringing forth other rocks, an unheard-of phenomenon. A horn, short but broad at the base, grew from it,

31

pointing to the heavens as if – what sacrilege! – to threaten the Most High.

To loud applause, the living rock was raised. It hovered in the air for a few moments, and was then set down a little roughly on the quayside.

And now, while children pelted it with stones, in spite of the soldiers who were trying to defend the monstrous visitor, delighted to see them bounce off the tough skin, most of the adults, trembling between horror and fascination, were shouting, "Throw it back into the sea!"

"It will bring bad luck!"

"It's the Devil incarnate!"

"It carries the plague!"

"Or even worse diseases!"

None of all this affected the creature. It stood there in its stony immobility, which was interrupted only at curiously regular intervals by the ejection of a greenish substance that turned to mud as soon as it fell on the quay.

At the end of the day, to put an end to state of disorder that looked to be getting even worse, a whole troop of soldiers dragged the animal off to a safe place.

⁂

Debate did not die down, however. Far from it. Now removed from public view, the creature was at the mercy of the popular imagination, which ran wild. Every day the animal grew larger, more demonic, more terrifying in the descriptions of it. Two priests contradicted one another in their pronouncements from the pulpit.

The parish priest of the church of St Mary Magdalene delivered his sermon at the second Mass on Sunday. Gone were his usual tedious homilies to his flock, diatribes against the evil thoughts of women and the intemperance of men. His attacks on the monster had suddenly swelled his usual congregation tenfold. People fought to hear his denunciation of the baleful creature.

He had two lines of argument, which he cleverly either alternated or combined from Sunday to Sunday.

The first line of argument ran thus:

"My brothers, let us instantly do away with this insult to God! What was the Creator's wish? He wished for a well-ordered world, with a place in it for everyone. Now picture that foul and, moreover, insolent creature. You can see for yourselves that it dares to flout the divine will by mingling the animal and mineral kingdoms! Only the Devil can have sent us that unnatural hybrid to confuse our minds!"

And the second line of argument ran as follows:

"Dearly beloved brethren, do you know where that dreadful creature came from? Out of a hole! Yes, my brothers, out of a hole in time. Did you see its shape, its skin like something before the beginnings of history? The animal is not of today, nor even of yesterday. Not only has it come from far away, it has come from the very depths of the ages, and it does not come alone. In time, scourges even more terrible will follow it out of that hole to afflict us, epidemics, deluges, the Four Horsemen of the Apocalypse ..."

Whichever argument the preacher chose, it always led to the same conclusion: let us burn this poisoned gift and the ship that has brought it here from Hell. And let us close for ever the opening through which misfortune is attacking us!

The crowd refrained from applauding, since the Bishop had forbidden any such thing on pain of excommunication, and went around the corner to the church of St Nicholas.

"Let us praise God," the second priest responded in the same vehement tone. "Yea, verily, let us praise the Lord in all his works. Let us raise our voices in gratitude to those who venture into lands far away! Thanks to those bold captains we are daily extending our knowledge of the Lord's creation and its inexhaustible diversity. And let us denounce as heretics those who would pick and choose from among created things. Who are we to discriminate between the works of the Most High?"

The congregation nodded and murmured in low voices: he's right, who are we to pick and choose? A few of the more determined turned back to the church of St Mary Magdalene to nip heresy in the bud. Here deacons of the opposite camp were waiting for them and brawls broke out.

It was in the hope of calming and distracting the minds of the populace that the municipal authorities decided to organize a fight.

Pillory Square is one of the most popular places in Lisbon. The civic authorities fasten such criminals as they have managed to apprehend to wheels in the square and from time to time executioners come along to break their limbs with heavy clubs. Women faint at the sight, men applaud, children amuse themselves by spitting on the sores of the tortured malefactors. The place provides a great deal of entertainment.

On the day of the fight, however, Pillory Square offered a different kind of spectacle. Privileged persons crowded the balconies, others thronged close together outside the walls of buildings, standing on crates as they tried to get a better view. Palisades had been erected, turning the square into an almost perfectly oval arena. And in the very middle of it, instead of the bloodstained wheels, stood a colossus with a nose almost as long as its tail, legs like four trees, ears bigger than a parasol, testicles the size of a man's head, and its droppings were larger than molehills. In short, it was an elephant. An old acquaintance, of course, ever since the startled Romans first left descriptions of the animal, and many paintings and drawings of it had been made. How did the caravels manage to bring such massive creatures to our shores without capsizing? Yet again, we had to pay tribute to the skill and courage of our sailors.

Soon the elephant's adversary, the live rock, appeared on the other side of the arena.

Two horsemen, armed with long spears, tried to prick the lethargic animal's rear end in an attempt to speed it up. They failed; their spears bounced off its hide.

The crowd, which had begun by uttering loud cries of amazement and terror, was getting impatient. Instead of the sanguinary spectacle we had been promised, nothing was happening. The two animals were reluctant to move at all.

More and more missiles – stones, bits of wood, also hats, shoes and a few daggers – were soon flying in the direction of the combatants who showed such scandalously pacific inclinations. The rhinoceros was still facing the elephant without moving, the elephant took no notice of the rhinoceros, busy as it was in exploring the nature of the various projectiles now littering the cobblestones of the square with its trunk. Finding nothing edible among them, it flapped its enormous ears.

In the end the rock with the single horn got annoyed with being ignored, raised its right foot, struck the ground with it twice, and to general applause, the beast charged.

The elephant, despite its gigantic size, took fright. It stood motionless for a few seconds and then uttered a raucous cry. Its ears were waving about like clapping hands. Just before the horn of the live rock could pierce its chest, it pivoted on its hind legs and, with astonishing agility, ran for it.

It broke down a balustrade, crushed a dozen or so spectators, galloped away into Goldsmiths' Street to the sound of booing and disappeared. The most surprising part of the whole incident was that no trace of the elephant was ever found apart from its two recently severed tusks, which were to be seen the next day on a stall at the back of Terreiro do Paço Square. They did not languish among the lettuces and turnips lying there for long. The clock of the Church of St Julian was just striking nine when a man sent by Lazaro the jeweller took them away. A single question – "Amazing! But where on earth did you get them, my dear fellow?" – had been enough to enable the jeweller's envoy to buy them from the stallholder at a ridiculously low price.

As for the rock, the victor in the fight, it was taken back to its cage amidst loud cheering. Its glory cost it dear. One morning its horn was found to be missing, sawn off by someone in the night. No doubt the man with the saw had remembered the chuckles of the ladies when its glorious excrescence was first seen. A certain powder was discreetly offered to the richest – and consequently the oldest – men in town. Evidently the seller was guaranteeing that it came from the famous rhinoceros horn and could make the limpest of male appendages equally rigid. It is said that soon afterwards a young woman, amazed and still breathless after her old spouse's unusual performance in bed, asked him what the cause was.

Lisbon is a city of open secrets. Next day the entire population wanted some of the magic powder. To supply demand, the seller stepped up production, mingling more and more other ingredients (pounded shells, ox-bones, gravel) with ever decreasing amounts of the powdered rhinoceros horn. The day came when lovers of both sexes had to acknowledge the fact that the mixture had lost its powers. The man selling it was arrested and ended his lying life, beaten to death, in the same Pillory Square that had seen the triumph of the horned monster.

Ship-owners instructed their captains to bring back not slaves from Africa but more of these horned animals, as a more interesting commercial prospect. Unfortunately the creatures, warned no one knew how – perhaps by one of the many migratory birds that choose to stop off in Portugal on their flight – had gone into hiding. Only one was brought back, five years later, a young rhinoceros with its horn still too soft to give anyone of either sex hopeful dreams, not even those parsimoniously endowed by Nature in that respect.

Living as they do in a country with a temperate climate, a place that often seems too tranquil for them, the Portuguese were bound to love wildlife. Like children, they marvelled at all the strange and more or less monstrous specimens of the animal and vegetable kingdoms brought back from Africa.

In what other churches in Christendom could you see giant crocodiles hung up above the altar? There were fashions in this love for wild animals. After the ultimately disappointing rhinos came great enthusiasm for giant tortoises. I saw these large, strange creatures on the Cape Verde islands on my one voyage along the African coast. The local people are happy to eat them, liking the flavour of their flesh; and they burn the oil they extract from it to give light.

What doctor, I wonder, first claimed, and on what grounds, that these tortoises could cure leprosy and many other serious diseases? He must have based his argument on the longevity of the creatures, which can sometimes live for over two hundred years.

I have witnessed several of these medical treatments. The method is simple, if disgusting. The creature's shell is cut off with a knife, whereupon it bleeds so freely that it soon dies. The blood is caught in the tortoise's shell, which now becomes a bath tub. The invalid is plunged into it, and the blood is left to dry on his skin. It seems that this red coating treats the disease, and so does the meat of the creature's flesh, so long as it is eaten daily. After two years of this treatment, they say that cases of leprosy are cured.

I do not know why I have come to feel affection for these lumbering animals. Perhaps because they cannot decide whether they are animal or mineral? The giant tortoise has a bird's head and a body like a huge stone. Similarly, here in my beloved island of Hispaniola there are plants so powerful that they might almost be animals. This mingling of the natural kingdoms gives me confidence in the strength of life at the very moment when I must soon leave it. If all life is one, appearing sometimes in one form and sometimes in another, then perhaps death is only a momentary matter, a phase in the eternal and general metamorphosis.

Be that as it may, I could not shake off my anxiety over the fate of these poor creatures. I learned from a Breton merchant by the name of Kermarec, a bustling man who often came to our port with a view to selling the white wine of Burgundy, that King Louis XI of France himself took an interest in the unfortunate animals. His physicians could not cure the various disorders that afflicted him and he had given orders for the miraculously medicinal tortoises to be sought out in their native land. An expedition to Cape Verde was in preparation and command of it had been entrusted to the famous corsair George the Greek.

I was still saddened by that news when Kermarec next came to Lisbon, but he told me, all smiles, the verdict of the divine tribunal: King Louis had died on the eve of the day when the corsair George was to put out to sea. We celebrated the tortoises' stay of execution in the most suitable way – in white Burgundy wine.

๑๛

There was a price to be paid for this love of natural science: the smell.

In Lisbon, and later in Seville, you had to name your new discoveries quickly. I remember a moment when delay was making the stench unbearable. One morning, when the wind had changed direction at the same time as a hot, humid, sultry atmosphere set in, the King of Portugal wrinkled up his nose on waking. At least, the entire city saw that wrinkling up of his nose as the beginning of the story.

"What," he asked, "is that foul stink?"

"Sire," replied his chamberlain, "I have made inquiries, and it's all the fault of the warehouse."

"What warehouse?"

"The warehouse where cargoes are stored once they have been brought ashore and are waiting to be properly named."

"Take me to this place!"

The closer you came to the warehouse, the stronger the stench was. The faces of the courtiers disappeared behind their handkerchiefs. Only His Majesty strode briskly on with his nose uncovered.

"I want to know about this, I want to know! People keep too much from me in this kingdom of mine!"

When the warehouse doors were opened the smell was almost enough to suffocate you. The stale odour of decay took you by the throat.

On one side of the warehouse were plants of all kinds, shapes and colours, from peppers to flowering shrubs, placed on hurdles or heaped up on the ground. On the other side were animals, a picture representing a wide variety of dead creatures. Some had been eviscerated and then clumsily sewn up again; no doubt their guts had been removed on shipboard so that they would keep better. But others had been brought back alive, and it was their corpses that were now poisoning the air of Lisbon.

Wooden billets, more or less flat, had been placed on many of these animals and some of the plants, with words scribbled on them. Apart from the smell you might have thought you were in a market, but a deserted market where there was no one to buy or sell.

A group of figures emerged from the dimly lit back of the warehouse, a dozen or so grotesque apparitions. They wore large, pointed masks, like those used to protect wearers from the miasma that carried the plague. A guard shouted at them to take their masks off – the king was paying them a visit, a great honour. At once a startled white face came into view, followed by other faces, terrified and black. Those with the black faces were slaves who made haste to kneel down and beg for mercy.

"What's going on in this inferno?" asked the king.

The white man bowed and then straightened up, standing to attention in a comical way, for there was little to suggest a military uniform in his clothing.

"Sire, we are trying to name all these things that have come ashore," he said, and pointed to the slaves. "And these fellows are helping me. They are the only people who know the flora and fauna of their part of Africa. They point out a plant or animal to me, they give me its name in their dialect, and I write it down."

The king resisted the attempts of the mayor of Lisbon to lead him outside. Absorbed in his questioning, he did not seem at all inconvenienced by the smell, but expressed his great satisfaction at the work that had been done.

The namer of names raised his arms to heaven.

"We'll never come to the end of it, sire! Too many of your ships go exploring, too many of your ships come back. How can we be expected to give names to everything brought ashore here fast enough?"

The king took hold of a minister's arm and pressed it firmly. "Give this man all the assistants he asks for. And get the warehouse cleared within five days!"

The slaves had understood none of this conversation, but observing that the king was pleased they began to sing. In spite of their accent, you could guess that they were offering thanks to the almighty God of the Christians and to King Alfonso V, his prophet.

As the king's coach moved away the namer of names, ignoring protocol, ventured to run after it and catch it up.

"If I may allow myself to say so, sire …"

"What is it this time?"

"There's another reason for all the delay."

"You are going too far!" said the mayor.

"It's on account of the Christian names …"

At this point the bishop coadjutor, a man whom the king liked and respected, and whose function it was to assist the diocesan bishop, put a word in. "I have a good idea of the problem on this man's mind. It is too delicate a matter to be discussed here."

"I'll receive you at court then," said the king.

And to the great relief of the courtiers, many of whom, prostrated by the terrible smell, would stay in bed for several days to come, the king returned to the palace.

❧

The bishop coadjutor was a shrewd diplomat. He knew the flattering turns of phrase that please the powerful.

"To sail the seas is to kneel before God, and making discoveries is a form of prayer." With these words the prelate launched into his plea. What better way could He have found of telling the king, without actually saying so, that His kingdom was the Lord God's favourite? "Thanks to your sailors, the glory of Our Lord increases with every voyage they make. But sad to say …"

Like all good clerics, the bishop was also a story-teller. For what, after all, is a cleric if not a man whose task is to pass on the word of God? And what is a story-teller if not a man who can always rekindle interest in his narrative by waking his audience up?

Sure enough, the king woke with a start. "Sad to say? What are you talking about?"

"I am saying that God, if He takes pleasure in seeing the whole of His creation gradually revealed to humanity, cannot like to hear it so poorly described."

Here the bishop coadjutor conjured up the dissatisfaction that the Lord must feel every time He heard any of His works named in one of the African languages.

"What pleasure can His ear take in the dialect of these savages?"

"Yes, I can understand why He doesn't like it. What can we do to appease Him?"

"We can translate. We can translate the names of all inanimate objects and all animals that come to land on Portuguese soil into Christian language."

The bishop coadjutor carried his point. An academy was set up consisting (chiefly) of poets, but also of gardeners, musicians, ecclesiastics and physicians. To gain more time they stopped bothering with native names. Artists drew the novelties brought on land in detail as precise as possible, and they were named.

At first the meetings of this academy were public, and I never missed a single one.

You would have thought that plants already withering and animals in an advanced state of decomposition came back to life by virtue of receiving new names. That resurrection lasted only long enough for the clerk to record the designation allotted to each – after that, death could finish its work.

Soon the audience started meddling with the choice of names. From crowded benches, the spectators addressed the authorities of the academy.

And so a tree with dark red-brown wood, said by the natives to be called *zaminguila*, became known to us, don't ask me why, as mahogany.

In the same way, a kind of large seal with a heart-rending cry, brought back by the sailors in a huge basin of water, was called a manatee.

Further delays followed. A decision was made in very high places, and much to my regret, that from now on meetings would be held in camera. I consoled myself (not very successfully) by regularly looking through the dictionary listing these new discoveries as it grew ever thicker.

Now that you are well and truly embarked on my real story, I will venture to reveal the fact that it fed on lies: as we practised cartography, our fingers produced two kinds of maps.

The first were ordered by the king, reserved for his sole use and the use of his fleet. That is to say, they bore as close as possible a relation to the truth.

Every captain who had just disembarked came to tell us about his voyage, even before he went to greet his family. Our maps therefore had the benefit of recording the latest state of knowledge. You almost felt that they smelled of the sailors' sour breath, so quickly did we add the latest information as they gave it to us. "Watch out for a line of reefs just beyond Cape Juby." "Level with Cape Blanco, a fierce current runs into shallows ..."

When two sea captains had different opinions on a certain section of the coastline, Andrea summoned them and they came running. They were terrified of being struck off the king's list of licensed captains. They would explain what they meant, and the facts of that part of the map were established on their joint responsibility. Such methods helped to foster good understanding.

No one of my profession would ever cast the first stone at a seaman who doesn't fully understand what he has seen. He is drawing on his memories and doesn't grudge the effort; he shows us his shipboard log; he keeps nothing secret and does his best, because that's what the king requires. But the reality that he is asked to describe is more changeable than any other. How can we expect him to be precise and certain? His observations are made from on board a ship which has had his head spinning for weeks on end. He is blinded by sea-spray and mist, deceived by the tides, hallucinations plague him, savages threaten him. It's a miracle that he can bring us back any reasonably solid facts whatsoever.

All credit to the navigator's genius for observation!

There is no more peaceful occupation than reading a map. As you follow the lines traced on it the world seems so simple, so firm, so certain … who can imagine what lies on the other side of the map, what's behind the scenes, what's at its heart, what efforts have been made to establish those simple lines, what questions and inquiries, what deductions and adjustments have been carried out?

The other maps were equally and perhaps even more meticulous. Those were maps made for our enemies, our rivals in the exploration of the world. I am speaking first and foremost of our Spanish neighbours.

It was in Lisbon that I found out how closely related lies are to the truth. How can you tell the least little lie without recourse to the truth to help you? You have to lean heavily on the facts.

Lying calls for the most careful attention to your skill as a liar. If you give a lie too long a rein, if you let it go wherever it likes, what guarantee do you have that by pure chance it may not come close to the truth?

A genuine lie – I mean the only useful sort of lie – is the opposite of fantasy. The smallest inattention to detail destroys it.

You should have seen and heard the way we went about lying. The sparkling delight and cheerfulness that enlivened the studio at such times would have made you tremble, my dear La Casas. What evil spirit possessed us, you would ask, when we dared to modify creation, what demon made us enjoy inventing falsehoods so much?

The real map was spread out on the longest of our trestle tables – I almost said laid out, like a corpse in a mortuary. We never took our eyes off it, and one by one we suggested changes. Minor changes at first, but audacity soon took over. We moved sandbanks, we shifted the position of reefs, we flattened capes. The cartographer whom we called "the Liar" sat alone and impassive at one end of the table, writing in a little notebook. Master Andrea fanned the flames of our enthusiasm.

"What's the matter with you all today? Are you afraid of reality? Come along, come along, don't forget we want to deceive the enemy! A good shipwreck can avert a naval battle!"

Ah yes, I remember!

The youngest of us – that was me – was told to watch the hourglass. When the final grain of sand dropped through the narrow neck of the glass, I would raise my hands. Our fun was over and we all went back to our real work, making maps that told the truth.

The Liar would disappear for days on end. He had asked, and had been granted, permission to work in a little room on his own. "False-hood is the child of truth, but a child must leave his mother one day if he is to live his life to the full" – that was the way he used to talk, or rather mutter, in enigmatic phrases.

It seems that once, before I came to the studio, he had been known as "the Forger". Then someone had pointed out that a forger is the most scrupulously exact of copyists: he tries to reproduce the original as closely as he can. We, on the other hand, producing genuine maps, were authentic forgers.

And so a new name had been found for him: "the Liar". What term could have fitted him better?

I had timidly asked him whether he felt wounded by the name. He shrugged his shoulders.

"Well, look at you, see yourselves for what you are: slaves, a lot of sheep! You follow the lines. I invent them. Lying is a noble pursuit."

❧

It takes a certain cast of mind to be a good liar; imagination and discipline don't often go hand in hand. As a result, mendacious cartographers are few and far between. The studios pounce eagerly on them, and they can ask fees that those of us who work at the real thing will never get. In the same way, so it is said, good poisoners make more money than good cooks.

❧

Once your lie was constructed, you had to get people to swallow it. I don't suppose I need specify that the Liar himself never condescended to concern himself with this final stage. Nothing would have induced him to leave the glorious realm of falsehood. Anyway, by

44

that time he was already devoting himself to another work, another deception.

With the passage of time, Andrea had perfected a two-pronged strategy. Both parts of it had proved their worth. He would choose between them at the last moment, depending on signs and omens that must have been present in the air of Lisbon, although only Andrea could spot them. Whichever option he chose, it began by setting a rumour going.

The first rumour was known as *the old and perfect map.*

It worked extremely well, but it had one weak point: it called for collusion with a sea captain. Once he was back from his voyage, and the formalities were completed, the seaman would go to celebrate his safe return in various taverns, in the usual way of captains. And as one round of drinks followed another, he would praise his cartographer's work. "With the document he provided I navigated with more certainty than I'd walk along a road on land. Apart from two or three details, which I have noted down, we may now consider that the right route has been found."

You will say that a sea captain, even one who is colluding with a cartographer, never talks as clearly as this, particularly when strong drink has been taken at the time. And you will be right. I just wanted to explain the origin of the first rumour as clearly as possible.

It is in the nature of rumours to swell and grow, just as the action of yeast makes dough rise. A few hours after the captain had uttered his enthusiastic if inebriated remarks, everyone wanted to acquire, by any means possible, the miraculous map, which I need hardly say was the work of our Liar.

A good rumour never takes effect unless you are scrupulously careful with its subject. The map concerned had to show all the scars of a long voyage: torn places, grease spots, corrosion by salt, the effect of strong sun burning down, etc. The Liar's assistants specialized in providing this fancy dress.

The second rumour was known as *the ultimate state of knowledge.*

This rumour had to be our own child – I mean the work of those employed in Andrea's studio. By dint of our dogged silence, which was even more silent than ordinary silence, as well as our refusal to talk when in fact no one had asked us to say anything ("I promised not to say a word") and our disclaimers ("No, no, nothing out of the ordinary, I assure you, we're not working any more or any less than usual, and taking no more and no less care"), we had to implant the following idea in other people's minds: "At this very moment they are making THE MAP OF MAPS in Andrea's studio, the map that unites all the knowledge we have today, the key to all the gates of all the new worlds."

Both rumours culminated in either loss or theft.

Any day you can see a sailor or apprentice giving Fate a helping hand by dropping a valuable document from his pocket, or accidentally leaving it on a table after drinking freely. But doesn't the man who picks it up, or rather the man who buys it from the man who has picked it up, start wondering about the extraordinary ease with which he came by this treasure? And doubt of the method whereby it came his way inevitably goes hand in hand with doubt of its veracity. So it is better to opt for theft, which means protecting the false map so conspicuously that no one can resist a wish to snatch it and take it away. And protecting it in such a way that if a man really desires that treasure he will find flaws in the system protecting it.

You never saw more soldiers posted on guard outside our studio than when we had just finished work on one of these misleading maps. And you never saw so many soldiers suddenly overcome by an irresistible urge to drop off to sleep.

Some of us couldn't bear this constant pitching and tossing between Falsehood and Truth. It gave them a kind of sea-sickness. One morning, with his face even paler and his bearing even less assured than usual, such an apprentice would go to see Andrea.

"I'm leaving the studio, Master."

"That's your right. But it's my right to kill you if you reveal a single one of our secrets. Unless you'd rather I cut your tongue out here and now."

"I understand, master."

Later I would meet some of these penitents (what else can I call them?). They all chose to work as agricultural labourers because of the regularity and undisputed reality of that way of life, subject as it is to natural cycles that have tirelessly recurred for thousands of years, unaffected by the human imagination.

As for me, I couldn't have found a trade I liked better. For no one, not even Christopher, navigates as constantly as a cartographer between falsehood and truth, with a marked preference for the former.

I remember the dates of all the events in Christopher's life.

Between 1469, the year when I arrived in Portugal, and 1476, the summer of his shipwreck, all through those years that he spent at sea, my brother put in at Lisbon only once. Or at least, it occurred to him only once to remind me that he was still in the land of the living. As he must have been sailing up and down our coasts all the time and the port of Lisbon is incontestably the best on the Atlantic as far as Bordeaux, it would have been odd if he did not come into harbour here more often. It therefore seems to me most likely that I was a disappointment to him on the day when he did come to see me, and the idea of visiting his younger brother again entered his head only at the dictates of necessity.

Be that as it may, one morning in the spring of 1473 Christopher walked into the studio without knocking. He was taller than I remembered him, his hair redder and his eyes greyer. He asked for Bartholomew Columbus. I was right in front of him and he didn't recognize me. I made myself known to him. He congratulated me on having left childhood behind at last and gave me a hug. I said I was very sorry that Master Andrea, who was detained in Sagres, wasn't there to welcome him. He shrugged his shoulders. Then, to my increasing discomfort, he walked up and down between our tables, glancing at our work with arrogant contempt, sometimes even laughing out loud. My comrades, some of whom were hot-blooded young men, were beginning to give him nasty looks. I prudently took him out of the studio when he started making scornful remarks.

"You're wasting your life, Bartholomew!"

"What could be more useful than making accurate maps and charts?"

"You deserve better!"

My mouth dropped open in surprise. What was special about me, something so well hidden that no one, not even I myself, indeed more particularly I myself, had ever seen it, something that deserved to be better rewarded?

He put a protective hand on my shoulder.

"These scribbles of yours are all very well in their way. I'm sure they're needed by those who claim to be navigators but tremble with fear at the idea of losing sight of the coast. But for others, the real sailors, the only sea-charts that matter are provided by the sky, the currents and the winds."

"What do you mean by a real sailor?"

"A man who crosses the high seas. The others only hug the coasts, scraping over the pebbles near shore, like horsemen with someone holding their horses on a long rein."

I tried to change the subject and ask him about our family. Did he have any news more recent and less sad than mine?

It was no use. He wouldn't talk about anything but the Pole Star, the height of the sun, the secrets of the *volta* …

And it was so many years since I had seen him.

The upshot is that I cannot tell you exactly at what time in his life the temptation of the open seas began to haunt him.

How long did he stay in Lisbon? Two days, three days? I don't remember now. All I remember is the way he blew in on a gust of wind, a talkative man holding forth in an interminable and feverish monologue. All this time later, I still have the sound of his voice in my ears. He wasn't trying to talk to me, he wanted to indoctrinate me. And recruit me.

I was just asking him what he knew about the *volta* when the church clock of Saint Mary Magdalene, striking twelve noon, brought him back to reality. He had to catch the tide.

He hurried off to the harbour, never once looking back.

So I had to wait another three years before I heard him give his own version of the famous phenomenon of the *volta* and explain why it would be the great ally of his Enterprise.

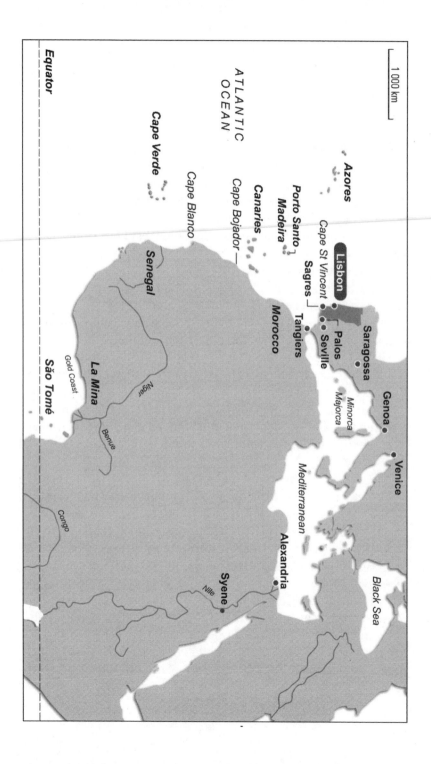

Master Andrea thought of his cartography studio as a ship.

"We are navigators ourselves," he used to say. "We sail seas just as rough and treacherous as the Mediterranean and the Atlantic. We have to watch out for our own reefs, the Charybdis of credulity, the Scylla of incredulity. We too have to make progress even when we are becalmed. I mean we must resist the drowsiness born of repetition. We have storms to face as well: our stormy winds are permanent, in the shape of our competitors."

When he began riding this allegorical hobbyhorse Master Andrea, usually such a cool and deliberate man, waxed lyrical.

"And the daily destination of our voyage is the Truth. So hoist all sail!"

He had chosen the crew for his vessel with the greatest care. I would like to pay tribute to its members here, although I see that Las Casas is getting impatient.

"Governor, you are free to speak as you like, to take your life as a drama of major importance and tell me all about it, character by character. I would only remind you that time is passing, and your days are numbered."

There, there, Dominican! I understand you.

Just let me mention Arnaldo Spindel, our principal spy, a wonderful thief of the best-kept secrets; Antonio Carvalho, who was a bitter enemy of the sea that had drowned his three brothers and therefore regarded cartography as single combat against the deceitful oceans; and Baptiste Cozinheiro, a worshipper at the shrine of Geometry, who took scrupulous care with correct proportion, something so often trodden underfoot in the work of our rivals. There was Felix Sagres, a magician with colour and a master of indelible inks ... and never mind your impatience, I will also salute Samuel Toledano. But for him Master Andrea's studio would not have reached such a high degree of excellence, nor would Christopher have had such knowledge at his disposal.

Samuel claimed to be a descendant – whether this was true or false I don't know – of the illustrious Abraham Cresques, father of the great Majorcan school of cartography and the assumed author of a masterpiece regarded in our profession as impossible to surpass: the Catalan Atlas of 1375.

This atlas was the yardstick against which he measured our own work. Before leaving the studio for the royal palace, each of our maps had to undergo the test of comparison. Any judged "unworthy of the Catalan" for any reason at all (patchy information, irregular line, colours too pale or pointless decorative touches) was mercilessly rejected.

Outside his daily worship of the Atlas, Samuel thought of nothing but his children. As he talked, thought and read, he let his right hand sketch their faces. He already had a large number of offspring, but he still didn't think he had enough.

His wife went into labour every ten months, at such regular intervals that you could have used them to measure time.

One day, as he was announcing a ninth birth, or perhaps it was a tenth, I asked him why he was so set on having children. He said it was for the same reason that made me love islands. I looked at him blankly.

"Islands are stepping stones in space. Children are stepping stones in time." And as I can't have looked as if I understood, he added, "When you sail from island to island, you cross the sea and move from one continent to another. When you have children you move through time and link the past to the future."

Clearly I did not share Samuel's preoccupation with paternity.

I was just short of twenty years old, and as a result I was obsessed with a single idea: who was I going to sleep with?

Unfortunately for me, I had missed the Golden Age.

Of an evening in the taverns, enthusiastic fornicators kept calling to mind the good old days when crowds of wives would climb the hills almost every day to look out to sea. All you had to do was sit down with them, express sympathy for their fears and do them a few small services. It was not unusual to be secretly rewarded, sometimes even there and then in the nearby pine-woods.

But the wives finally realized that the ocean seldom gives back its prey. After that they just left their windows open. When the usual noise coming up from the harbour rose to a roar, there was no doubt about it: a caravel had come home. Then a woman would make herself walk at a leisurely pace down to the quay, trying to slow the beating of her heart. "Calm down, my dear, calm down," she would tell it. "You know you'll be disappointed. What are the chances that your husband, who left so many years ago, will be on the ship coming into harbour?"

Rather than strain their eyes gazing at the ever-empty ocean, they decided it was better to turn to the captain of all captains who rules the movements of all the shipping in the universe: God himself.

Churches once again became the places to visit if you wanted to find as many women as possible gathered together. You did risk cruel disappointments; a figure who looked promising from behind might show, on turning round, a sallow face like parchment, ravaged by old age. But having made enquiries, I knew that these sad eventualities were not as common in Lisbon as in the rest of Christendom. Since ships were always leaving from that seaport, carrying away young sailors, there was nothing for their equally young wives to do in their spare time but come to church and pray, joining the company of other wives who had also been left behind at earlier times, ever since it took the fancy of a certain Prince Henry, accursed be his name, to make a people that had never left home before into a nation of navigators.

So women of all ages mingled in church; you had only to go to church too and look for the one who suited you.

It was at the church of St Mary Magdalene, a place where many women went to pray, that I met Master Júdice. What was the man's secret? He certainly carried himself well; his features were noble and his full lips suggested that he enjoyed all the pleasures of the flesh. But how could his improbable attraction be explained? No sooner had he knelt at his prie-dieu than most of the women present did all they could to attract his attention in a variety of ways: winking, coughing, dropping their missals. And when Mass was over, out in the forecourt of the church, they were falling over each other to take his hands, brush past his shoulder, even touch his cheek. They simpered: *Don't you remember me?* They took a tone of playful reproof: *You naughty man, you've forgotten me!* They begged: *When can I come and see you, oh please, when?*

He caught my envious eye, smiled, disengaged himself and came towards me. He must have liked the look of me – and the paint on my fingertips.

"You must be a cartographer, I think? Well met! I may have an additional career to suggest to you."

And taking my arm he led me towards Infanta Square and the inn at the sign of the New Wine, where he seemed to be a regular customer.

I could restrain my curiosity no longer. "With them ... I mean women. How do you do it?"

"I make myself useful to them." My eyes must have been shining, because he added, "Not in the way you think. Or at least not directly. I'm an attorney, specializing in absence. And what about you, young man? Is your mind bent on fornication or exploration?"

I looked at him blankly. With good humour, patience and care he explained that in his experience, men who love women fall into one of two categories: they are fornicators or explorers. Obviously there are fornicators who don't always ignore the charms of exploration, and vice versa. But in essence the two groups are distinct: fornicators enjoy the body alone, while explorers relish first and foremost intimacy with women. They take extreme and ever-renewed pleasure in discovering the way women look at life, which is as different from ours as those of the Antipodean savages – we make children together, yes, but otherwise we are like day and night. For himself, he said, he definitely belonged to the second category, taking extraordinary pleasure, for instance, in finding out how women cut their toenails and perfume their private parts, and above all how they talk among themselves about us, men, that other species of human being.

"And now, my dear new friend, which category do you belong to?"

I confessed to suffering from such terrible diffidence that I would certainly need centuries of exploration before I ever dared to sleep with a woman who wasn't a prostitute.

"Well said! So you're of my own way of thinking, you're for exploration. I was looking for a companion. The few men still left in Lisbon take advantage of their good luck to go from bed to bed, without stopping to think that we have a better opportunity than ever before to explore the kingdom of women. Now that's a real voyage of discovery – and you don't need a caravel to embark on it!"

And so began both my friendship with José Miguel Júdice, known to me as Ze Miguel, and the treatment of my malady of shyness.

≈

Our master Andrea was a man incapable of tranquillity. He was obsessed by a conviction, perhaps as a result of watching the movements of the sea for too long, that nothing in the world was permanent; as he saw it, everything was changing or about to change, usually for the worse. The only use of calm waters was to herald a storm. Good health was nothing but the antechamber of sickness. And the present prosperity of his cartography studio was the clear sign of its inevitable decline in the near future. Soon Portugal's passion for discovery would die down. All of a sudden, just as it arose. One morning light would dawn on the sailors: why suffer so much to go exploring distant lands, they would wonder, when God has given us the sweetest land of all? They would therefore refuse to go on board ship, and what use would our maps be to sea captains becalmed in harbour?

This philosophy of transience, far from making him gloomy, fed his inexhaustible energy, giving him the kind of feverish joy that I have seen in certain people in the very middle of disaster. He lived cheerfully with his obligation to keep finding ways to ward off these threats of his own invention.

Some ten other businesses, entirely unrelated to sea charts, were the outcome of his constant worrying: a tannery, a herb garden, a shop selling sandals ... he regularly went around inspecting them and came back with his mind at rest.

"However the world turns out," said Master Andrea, "I shall always have the means to keep myself in my old age."

I therefore had no doubts as I went towards the studio with Ze Miguel. The idea that he had explained to me was sure to appeal to my master. What nobler ambition can there be than to come to the aid of women deprived of their husbands by Portugal's voyages of discovery?

Many of them, it's true, would not for the world have abandoned the uncertain status that was theirs at present. They had quickly found compensations for their sadness; in replacing an absent husband as head of the household they tasted new responsibilities, and relished the liberty of being on their own more every day.

Some, however, wanted to be widows – for all kinds of reasons, the most usual being a strong desire to form a close relationship with another man. They also professed an interest in the term *widow* itself; they would rather be known as widows than as nothing at all, since there is no word for a woman whose husband has not come home for decades, and is thus nowhere, neither alive nor dead. And the law in Lisbon clearly stipulated that for such a woman to be declared a widow, she had to have reached the age of seventy.

Unless her husband had been declared dead before that time, and there was evidence to support the claim.

It was here that Ze Miguel came in: his business was widow-making. He got together all the requisite evidence, real or more often invented, to establish that the husband was definitely dead. It was said that, in making his maps, a good cartographer owed it to himself to acquire the knowledge of all the navigators. In doing so he had built up an unparalleled store of facts about happy and above all unhappy

55

moments in the history of navigation... all he had to do was dip into this treasure to construct a case for his female clients.

As I had expected, Master Andrea welcomed this idea with alacrity.

"Children!" he announced, addressing us all. "Here's a new line of business suggested to us! Who would like to lend his aid to the very useful mission of this honourable attorney?"

My comrades shrugged their shoulders. They considered it beneath their dignity to act as notaries. A cartographer is a cartographer, he will be a cartographer all his life and will never have any other mission in life but to serve the cause of discovery. Who cares about weeping women?

Master Andrea and Ze Miguel were looking at one another in dismay when I raised my hand.

"I don't mind trying."

It was a timely offer. Reducing all the stories of voyages that I had picked up down by the harbour to one little line left me in a daily state of frustration. I had heard dozens of tales about every bay, the least little cape, the most dismal lagoon on the African coast. They seemed to be a dead loss, but they stuck in my memory. And something told me, and still does, that the stories would have their revenge some day.

Tracing the lines of the map was not enough for me. I wanted words as well, their precision, their freedom, their villainy and impudence, their double meanings, their hypnotic power.

I needed words, above all, because they reminded me of my brother. Where was he sailing at this moment, the enchanter of my childhood, a brother who had had no peer in conjuring up dreams as spell-binding as the horizon out at sea, and just as capable of attracting you, all the better to swallow you up? I heard that he had become a notable seaman, with all the ship-owners after him. But that was all I knew.

Those first two reasons may conceal a third, my principal reason for lending my aid to the project.

Ze Miguel's example and his amazing success showed that a widow-maker is never short of women. He necessarily meets a great many of them. And these women who were turning to the law to be made widows were less intimidating than happy women. A woman's happiness is a sure defence. Her grief is a door standing ajar.

Such were my real hopes as I engaged in this new trade, although I could not admit to them. Modesty allows me to say only this and no more: my expectations were not disappointed.

Another advantage of the work was that I was apprenticed to the trade of a story-teller.

All my life I have drawn foreign shores more than I have written about them. And I have spent less time in drawing shores than in trying to pacify the peoples who live there.

But I liked the work of writing, related partly to fine joinery (you fit the words together like so many pieces of wood), and partly to ship-building. Once a ship is well made, it will skim the waves of its own accord; once a story is well put together it will fly over the paper or parchment by itself straight to the eyes of readers.

I expect that most of the stories I wrote in order to make widows have vanished, burnt in house fires or gnawed by rats. And far be it from me to seek notoriety of any kind as a scribbler.

However, I did keep a copy of one of my pleas, because the idea came into my head easily and was easily transformed into a series of evocative phrases.

And because it originated in my friendship with a Frenchman, a master forester to whom I would like to pay tribute.

So here is the tale to which a certain lady called Gilberta owed her widowhood – and after that it was up to her to make what use of it seemed good to her.

In consideration of the fact that to get fresh water, two members of the crew of the caravel *Nostra Senhora de la Fronteira* came on land just south of the Equator on that day, the twelfth of September in the year 1472, one of them being the lady Gilberta's husband; that they set off into the coastal jungle; that after six hours of waiting, when the captain did not see them reappear, a volunteer was sent in search of them, but did not succeed in finding them; that this man, miraculously escaping the jungle himself and trembling all over, described the huge size and impenetrability of the vegetation that he saw, the darkness all around, the noise of beasts of all sizes, and all the noxious biting, stinging, strangulating creatures teeming in that perpetual night; considering also that it was once again confirmed that recently discovered worlds shelter ferocious creatures unknown to this day, where the vegetable kingdom outdoes the animal kingdom in violence and cunning; and considering that as a result of this incontrovertible relationship, reinforced if need be by the evidence of three witnesses worthy of belief, being of sound mind and able to appear before the tribunal at a moment's notice should the judge think it necessary, the lord Marco, husband of the lady Gilberta, can only have been entirely swallowed up by the tangled mass of trees, creepers and bushes that is described as a forest in our regions, but there might better deserve the name of monster, or Leviathan …

As always, a story when told feeds on the truth rather than respecting it.

Here is undoubtedly the main lesson in my apprenticeship to the art of narrative: falsehood and the facts are an inseparable pair. Even better, and my brother's adventures have provided the most irrefutable evidence of this, it is through falsehood that we enhance the truth.

I met the Frenchman who gave me the idea of this man-eating forest at the harbour, where he called himself Guy, Guy Pietresson, but a certain brusqueness in his pronunciation suggested, just as an awkward movement betrays the fact that a man is wearing a borrowed or stolen garment, that it was not his real name, or rather was incomplete. Tricks of fate must have driven him off the usual course his life was taking, and others had made him take ship for Lisbon. Others again had brought him face to face with the ruling passion of his life, to which he also owed his death: the immense forest. When I met him he was so weak that he was staggering. Apparently those wooded regions never leave you, but enter into you in the form of tiny creatures as harmful as they are set in their wicked ways.

He had been recruited to prospect for gold on the coast of Africa. But as soon as he went ashore he took no interest in anything but its inordinate wealth of botanical life.

"Bartholomew, if God grants me enough time I will compile a dictionary of all the trees that I saw there."

I supported him as best I could in his last moments. God, who sometimes sweetens his inexhaustible cruelty with a little kindness, did not allow his illness to carry him off until the dictionary was finished, the last tree in it as meticulously described as the first.

"Lisbon – ah, Lisbon!"

On hearing the refrain of my love song, Las Casas shrugs his shoulders or makes a face, depending on his mood. My passion for the city is getting on his nerves.

One day, when I was waxing nostalgic again for the calm of the river Tagus, the great and always busy square that is its neighbour, the Terreiro do Paço, for our beloved cathedral of the Lisbon See and the odours of the alleyways around it, he exclaimed, "What is it about Lisbon that makes it so special?"

"Its islands," I replied without a moment's hesitation.

Forget the lazy notion that the only islands worthy of our attention and respect are islands surrounded by water. You can never have travelled anywhere or looked around you properly to ignore the fact that islands are dotted about on the mainland just as much as at sea.

So my dear city of Lisbon is, in itself, an archipelago bearing comparison with the Azores or the Canaries in diversity and mystery. Each of the different peoples living there is an island. The main island, the island of the old stock of Portuguese, has been joined by others over the centuries. The island of the Arabs is covered by irrigated gardens of edible plants; water has been their passion for thousands of years and they never tire of hearing its song as if it led them to Paradise.

There is the island of the Jews, the Mouraria Judiaria, where mothers love their sons as nowhere else, to such a degree that the aforesaid sons never find wives who will be as dazzled by their merits, and where from a very early age the men argue endlessly about questions that cannot be answered, with the result that male Jewish brains acquire incomparable agility.

There is the island of the Venetians, who think themselves so far above the rest of the universe that they might seem to be always perched on tall piles like their palaces.

There is the island of the Genoese, where they deal in all kinds of merchandise, if possible trading with the Flemish, whose industrious placidity makes them profitable allies for Mediterranean cunning.

On the island of the Pisans they are forever hatching plots to crush the Genoese.

More modest, but only in size, is the island of the Germans; coming from places without any shorelines they are so impressed by the sight of the sea, that great and deserted expanse, that some of them go mad because until now their minds have relied on the trees in their forests.

On the island of the British they like nothing better, to refresh themselves after facing so many rough seas, than drinking strong mead and dancing with their little fingers linked.

On the island of the Greeks one might suppose they expected an imminent Second Coming as they tell their amber beads.

And there are certainly many other islands that I have not distinguished from each other because they contain too few individuals, or are well hidden away in remote corners.

Each of these islands is a universe with its own language, cookery, way of praising God, marrying off its children and burying its dead.

As there are climates that are inhospitable, even fatal for certain plants but good for others, the atmosphere of Lisbon, at the time when I knew the city, was the most favourable of all to the human race. Men and women came here and found it a good place to live when they were not allowed to live almost anywhere else in Europe.

You will ask how I, a nomad who was to travel so much for the rest of my days, never resting anywhere, always about to leave again, could be satisfied with a single city, how it could nurture me so well that I never felt any wish to leave it, and I would be living there still if Christopher hadn't snatched me away. The reason is that I was always moving from one of those terrestrial islands to another, one day with the Arabs, the next with the Jews.

As soon as I left the studio I chose a destination, a universe only a few steps away. It's as good a form of navigation as sailing on the seas; it takes less time, but has its own dangers, and gives you as many amazing experiences.

Oh, Father Confessor!

The man who hears confessions reveals himself just as much as the man who makes them.

I know you.

When your eyes burn so brightly it's because your obsession with the flesh is coming over you again. You're longing to ask me about the real reason for that frenzied exploration of Lisbon. I hear that little voice in you. I don't know what miracle of will-power you work to keep it silent, but I hear you begging me to tell you all the details – those details without which a conscientious priest cannot grant absolution: where is the sin if not in the details? – all the details of the way in which each of the women on each of the islands made love.

My namesake Bartholomew smiles, carefully choosing, out of all the possible smiles, the one that will torture his good little scribe Jerome most cruelly. In fact it is a masterpiece, made up of three smiles.

A smile of acquiescence: it is obvious that I was exploring the city and its islands with a view to expanding my experience of different ways of love.

A smile of reminiscence: ah, how that girl Djamila swayed her behind! And oh, how can I forget the smell of fresh bread about that other girl, Gerta was her name, I think, with pubic hair so blonde that you could see the little lips beneath it as if through clear water? And so on, and so forth.

And the smile of a wise old man: I had better stop at this point in my salacious descriptions; the man making confession gains nothing by sending his confessor mad, does he?

So I continue describing my walks through Lisbon.

One day I found myself by chance on the heights of the city, not far from the cathedral, as night was falling. From this vantage point I could see a great many people moving down below. Men and women were hurrying some in one direction, some in the other. An old man close to me was watching the same strange spectacle. I asked him why there was all this agitation, and why it happened at this precise time of day.

He turned to me.

"Where have you sprung from? The Arabs are going back to the Arab quarter and the Jews to the Jewish quarter. They don't have much time left before curfew. That's why they're running."

"I never noticed before."

"That's because you're a Christian. You don't have to run."

"What about tomorrow?"

"Tomorrow they'll all be back in the same city again."

I remembered my father Domenico. When he didn't like the fabric made in his workshop, he called two or three of his employees, depending on the number of threads making up the fabric. Each of them pulled out his thread, winding it into a ball, and the fabric came apart.

Lisbon was the same. Each ball of thread in the fabric of the city slept separately. But in the morning the city wove itself together again, using the same three threads as the day before.

I asked the old man beside me what the point of these nocturnal migrations was.

"I suppose they keep people from cutting each other's throats! It's said that Lisbon is the European capital of tolerance."

"Then why do they all part and go their own ways home every night?"

"Because fear grows by night, and fear is a bad counsellor. It leads you to cut the throat of anyone who isn't like you. You think you see a monster in his face."

※

Why do different peoples have such different tendencies? What origins and influences can explain those inclinations?

Master Andrea regularly met Jews, whom he thought far superior to himself in the craft of map-making. One day I asked him where this supremacy of theirs could come from. He raised both hands.

"No doubt because they have no country of their own."

"So?"

"Someone with no native land is at home everywhere. That's why there are no more skilled translators and no better-informed merchants than the Jews."

"But why this passion for maps?"

"Anyone who loves knowledge loves maps. A map is the most visible part of knowledge."

"Is knowledge a country, then?"

"I hardly think so: if they take such care over their maps it must be nostalgia for a tract of land."

"What land?"

"A land of their own."

"Are you Jewish, Master Andrea?"

✾

And what about the Arabs? I knew them only as pirates, scouring the Mediterranean, specialists in the slave trade. What is the origin of their other field of excellence, the creation of gardens? I often used their services when I wanted inks made from vegetable matter.

In the time when Lisbon was still Arab, that is to say before the twelfth century, a rich merchant of the city had an only daughter who was born blind. He set about describing what she could not see to her. Could words make up for the void before her eyes? He flung himself body and soul into this mission, spending hours and hours, like a scrupulous notary, drawing up lists of things, of the animal and vegetable kingdoms and the children of God living in the city at that time.

The little girl felt sorry for her friends who could see; what pleasure could compare with the almost constant presence of a father who makes you a present of the whole world?

And then the father who told her about everything died.

The sudden silence in the air sent his daughter mad. And in the attempt to cure her deranged mind her uncle, the dead man's brother, had the idea of a garden for the blind. A garden which would not take account of the view, like other gardens, or harmonious colours, but would concentrate on scents. He entrusted its creation to a master botanist. Like human beings, certain aromas get on easily together, while you have to keep others apart or they will clash.

Somehow, the garden for the blind survived the passing of many years. There was always some good soul who would look after it. It died only once, when the coalition of crusading countries succeeded, in the year 1147, in taking the city from the Muslims. Bad news for the gardens of Lisbon, for the skill of the Arabs as gardeners had no equal perhaps because to them, every garden is a new chapter of their book, the holy Quran?

63

The story of the garden for the blind goes on.

A cleric from the Lisbon See Cathedral who happened to pass that way at the beginning of the last century, the fifteenth, wondered about this deserted tract of ground invaded by brambles and chickens in the heart of Lisbon. A little quick research told him what it had once been.

He was amazed to think that such a charitable idea could have entered the hearts of the infidels. He got together the necessary funds to restore it, a man to run the project was appointed, and a new garden was born, not on as lavish a scale as the first, it is said, for its scents were less subtle, but quite enough for the deplorable practices that soon began taking place there.

If, from wherever he is now, that unfortunate holy man can see the garden for the blind, he must be constantly cursing himself for his good deed.

I first went that way by chance, and then I went back often, attracted by the spectacle to be seen in the garden.

The blind came to soothe their sorrow because they could not see the flowers. They breathed in the air as they walked. Their fingers passed over the flowers, and the smile that suddenly relaxed their weary faces was the image of happiness itself. They named the scents appreciatively, carefully pronouncing the syllables: lemon balm, dill, savoury. Sometimes they argued. "How I love the scent of angelica!" "How can you confuse angelica with artemisia?"

All credit to the gardeners. They had the good idea of putting the plants in raised beds, and so close to the visitors' noses the scents were not lost in the air so much

Sad to say, most blind people went to the place solely to wait for a stroke of good luck, and the only aroma that cheered them was the scent of a dress approaching. So long as it wasn't raining they did not have long to wait.

A female figure would come walking through the shrubs.

The figure came and went, turned and turned again, apparently ignoring the voices calling to her, the hands reaching out to brush and touch her. The woman's figure went on walking. All at once she made her choice. I have no words to describe the surge of emotion that ensued, all I know is that other perfumes were drowned out. There was nothing in the air but the musky scent of two human bodies. Perhaps the other perfumes were watching, like me? The embrace did not last long. The woman's figure moved away. Often the blind discussed the incident; they had no greater variety of terms for these things than the sighted.

The scent of the human bodies, in turn, gradually disappeared, no doubt going down to the Tagus which would carry it out to sea.

One by one the other perfumes came back, first fennel, then bay, then the bitterness of orange. It was as if they were shaking themselves awake, as you do on waking from a bad dream. But another silhouette would soon appear, and it all began again.

I must have come back a hundred times to watch this drama. I need hardly say that my brother did not understand my repeated visits to this garden. Unlike the admiral, whose mind was on nothing but wide horizons, I had a taste, as I have already told you, for small things. I will add that I was also strangely fascinated by the spectacle of intimacy.

How can we fail to be interested in the prime concern of us all, living our lives?

How can we refrain from learning all the strategies humanity finds for resisting despair?

Clearly a blind man was the favourite consolation of a wife whose husband, obsessed by the voyages of discovery, had gone to sea and left her at home. With two eyes that could not see, he would never know who had offered herself to him. A sighted man would always end up by boasting. A blind man cannot link a name with these wild emotions. A woman could therefore give herself to him quietly, with no fear that any rumour would stain her reputation.

What is the point of sitting in judgement on such things? We are so close to each other, all engaged in similar struggles.

But no, I'm not fooled by my own justifications. That's enough beating about the bush. The spectacle of human beings copulating has always pleased me, giving me, in fact, such transports of delight that I have no words to describe them.

65

I have found some notes that I wrote at that time.

On some days sadness and the rain seem to be in league to fall on Lisbon together. Which comes first? Does the rain make us sad? Or does sadness, feeling lonely, call on the rain to keep it company?

The sadness reaches such a point that Lisbon can no longer bear it, so it takes up the only weapon against the rain that it has, music.

You hear melodies rising from all quarters of the city, on all kinds of instruments: bells, drums, viols, psalteries.

The first odd feature of those melodies, whether they are Christian, Jewish or Moorish, is that they are even sadder than the sadness. This is the strategy employed by music to vanquish sadness, it produces something sadder still.

And the second and if possible even more inexplicably odd feature is that this strange remedy is not slow to take effect. No doubt the sad people of Lisbon, on seeing that music surpasses their own capacity for sadness, suddenly feel better.

❧

Why are words carved more deeply on memory if they are accompanied by music than if they are naked, mere words on their own? Do the musical notes have little hooks that cling to those parts of the brain where memories are stored?

I heard this little song many years ago and I could not get it out of my head even if I wanted to.

To the sea my eyes go down,
Looking at Portugal,
To the river my eyes go down,
To the rivers Douro and Minho ...

I know that it will be with me for the rest of my old age.

And I must ask forgiveness of whatever priest administers Extreme Unction to me. It could be that at my last hour it will be this simple-minded quatrain that comes to my lips instead of more elevated thoughts.

⁂

What is the point of navigating?

Wouldn't playing music be enough?

Suppose music were a superior kind of sea? Both are fluid, both link worlds. But unlike the sea, music is not grandiloquent; it does not need to show its strength in storms or its cruelty in floods.

⁂

I have an idea, an idea that is all the more pernicious because it is clear and simple. An idea pregnant with danger in these days of the Inquisition. It is an idea that I shall have to keep hidden in the depths of my mind, never uttering it. I know that words are not reliable, they are little creatures that escape from the brain, if only at night, through the door of the groans or cries that often accompany our dreams. According to my idea, all that God ever wanted, really wanted, was the sea and music. The rest of his Creation – in particular the mainland, humanity and its languages – are only rough drafts, unsuccessful variations or mechanical couplings, ideas that he regretted, failures.

⁂

Our mother, like most of the women of Genoa, had a personal enemy: the harbour. That was because the ships carrying husbands and sons left from the harbour, and many of them never returned.

She made the sign of the cross every time she had to go along the quayside on her way to market, and she could be heard murmuring our names: Christopher, Bartholomew, later Diego too. She called on the Virgin: "Mary, Mother of God, I entrust my children to you if ever, like the rest, they put out to sea."

67

Only too late, after her death, did I understand why she always turned her head towards the mountains when she walked through the city; I thought at the time that she didn't want to honour the sea with so much as a glance. Now I know that she was really trying not to attract its attention. Such are the instinctive tactics of the weak: do anything to avoid looking the one you fear in the eye, hope to pass unnoticed.

The finer the weather, the more our mother balked at walking by the seashore. Our father sometimes almost had to drag her there by force. And while the rest of the people of Genoa were enjoying the sight of the clear water of the Mediterranean, azure blue with glints of silver, she would shake her head, grumbling, "Credulous fools, all of you! Blind fools! Don't you know the sea looks so calm and pretty only to deceive you?"

One day I'll tell you about the hatred women feel for the sea. For it is in the nature of men to leave their homes. Why did God feel He needed to add another malady as well, the permanent temptation of the sea? Why did He create both men and women together? Why did He command them to procreate children, when at the same time He made the accursed sea, the most powerful mechanism there is for separating couples?

If you were to open the heads of women who live in seaports you would find anger and blasphemy inside. I can well understand why surgeons don't risk such an operation. The Inquisition always has its eyes open.

Once, just once, my mother took us down to see her enemy. There was such a strong wind blowing that we could move only bent forward and clinging to each other, for fear of being carried away, and step by single step because the air resisted us like a wall. Grey sea-spray was breaking over the quays. Green waves taller than houses kept battering the rocks along the coast. The jetty no longer protected ships, and they were moving in all directions like a terrified flock of sheep. She reached out her arm and pointed her forefinger.

"Do you want to see the true face of the sea? There it is! All the rest is false!"

Poor Susanna, her lesson bore no fruit. I remember Christopher's smile. I had never seen him so calm. He turned his head slowly from right to left, so as not to miss any of the scene. And he smiled. He breathed in the salty air and he smiled. He moved forward to feel more of the spray in his face, he closed his eyes. And he smiled.

I can tell that my two Dominicans are getting impatient.

They are waiting for the main character to come on stage. Like everyone else, they consider me a negligible quantity in this story. I can read their minds: they are concentrating only on Christopher. Who does this Bartholomew think he is, telling us all about his insignificant self? When is he finally going to tell us about Christopher and his Enterprise?

Well, never mind that!

Given the chance to speak for once, I'm keeping it a little longer. They won't dare to show their dissatisfaction too obviously. They don't forget that I am the Viceroy's beloved uncle. And that, decrepit as I may be, I still have precious memories to impart to anyone who wants to write the history of the Indies.

Don't worry, you won't have to wait for my brother much longer.

The hopes we had placed on those talking birds came to nothing: their repeated phrases, always the same, gave us no interesting geographical information. With a gesture of magnanimity, Andrea opened their cage. The parrots flew around for a little while before coming down on the one place that they were not to know was sacrosanct: the very middle of the work in progress, our final map of the Gold Coast. Our cries of horror were followed by roars of rage, for the birds left their droppings on the lines we had been tracing with such meticulous care. Miraculously, and by Andrea's express order, they escaped strangling and were forcibly returned to their cage.

Thus began two days and two nights of confrontation. No doubt to show how much they hated captivity, the birds repeated only a single phrase, always the same, *nan nga def, nan nga def*, which was no use to cartographers at all, since it simply means *How do you do?*

In tones varying from the most cajoling to the most menacing, we told the parrots they could have their freedom in return for a wider range of their accomplishments. Then, in view of their bad temper and the tedious nature of their conversation – *nan nga def, nan nga def* – Andrea gave orders for our little aviary to be sold.

I got a good price from a lady called Elizabeth who traded in birds. She had three children and no husband any longer; he had gone to sea seven years ago and hadn't been seen again. She had found a way to feed her family by going into business.

In fact widows, or future widows, having more patience than cartographers, went on seeking the company of these talking birds. It is all very well for cats, dogs, cheetahs, tortoises and tigers to show affection in their many different ways by growling, caressing or giving melting looks, but to cheer a lonely woman there is nothing like human words, real words pronounced in a human manner, never mind if they are always the same words repeated over and over again. Anyway, when the woman's husband was still there, it has to be admitted that he never said anything new either.

Among these unfortunate women those who clung most doggedly to their feelings, unable to admit that their sailor husbands had gone for ever, hoped that one fine day, interrupting their everlasting litany of *nan nga def, nan nga def,* how do you do? how do you do? one of the birds would come out with a few words in Portuguese that must therefore have been picked up from a white man who wasn't yet dead, thus re-opening the door to a hope as faint as it was lively, and perhaps even livelier than it was faint. Suppose the man whom the birds were imitating were still alive on the other side of the world, preparing to return?

Unfortunately, if they did decide to use the Portuguese language, the wretched parrots spoke in filthy terms that no delicate ear in good Lisbon society could understand. It was not unusual, in the better parts of town, to hear such expressions as *you dripping cock, lick my arse* or *mother-fucker* flying through the air, linguistic gifts from members of the ships' crews.

Old seamen liked these remarks. They brought back the good old days. You sometimes saw them asleep with their ears up against an aviary and a broad smile on their lips.

Other neighbours, however, complained of all this bad language ringing in their ears. And the lady Elizabeth of Lisbon deduced that a school for birds would be a good idea, a school where they would

71

recover their self-confidence and acquire a minimum of good education. All that remained was to find a teacher able to carry out an educational mission of this unusual kind.

As a clever and prudent woman, at least in her daytime avocations, Elizabeth sought the support of the diocesan authority before launching herself into the business of educating birds. After long and extensive discussion on the part of the theologians, she was granted permission in principle. On mature thought, to give the birds the gift of language was a mark of respect for and confidence in the Holy Ghost, the white dove who was a member of the divine trinity along with the Father and the Son.

Although this story seems to fascinate my young and charming friend Jerome, whom I see blushing and fidgeting on his chair when I talk about women, I will cut it short. If I gave it its head, it would take us too far from my main subject, into the very banal realm of unrequited love.

All you need to know is that this school for birds prospered. Mynah birds brought by the land route from India were added to the African parrots and soon proved superior in their ability to reel off long phrases.

The lady Elizabeth had a passion – where it came from I don't know, but as I told you, all the treasures of the world arrive in Lisbon, like water running down a gentle slope – a passion for Persian poetry, and in particular the poetry of a Sufi master who died in 1273 and was called Mawlana Jalal-ud-Din, known as Rumi.

Become a ball and roll when you are struck by the mallet of love.

It was as I listened to this poetry that, uncouth as I was, I conceived first the idea, then the audacity and then the evident necessity of loving this lady and helping her in her hopeless attempt to teach her birds poetry, so that they could be brilliant company for abandoned wives.

He said: "No, you're not mad,
Not worthy of this house."
I went away to run as mad
As you see me today.

He said, "No, you're not drunk,
That would not be your way."
I went away to come back drunk
As I am here today.

He said, "No, you're not dead,
You are not stained by joy."
Dead of his looks that gave me life
You find me here today.

He said, "Ah, cunning one,
You're drunk with doubt, I'd say."
Ignorant, alone, afraid,
I have come back today.

He said, "You are a candle
To which the faithful pray."
I am no lighted candle,
But only smoke today.

As you can imagine, none of the birds, not even the mynah birds, although they are from near Persia, managed to recite a single complete verse, not even when it was about the birds themselves.

He said, "You have feathers and wings,
I give you neither, go your way.
Desiring his feathers, his wings,
I am stripped of them all today.

Only we were intoxicated by the words of Rumi.

The women who owned birds wanted to hear other songs from them, plainer words to accompany their actions when the need to caress themselves became too urgent, either with simple encouragements ("Go on," "I can see you," "Don't stop now."), or with much more explicit and quasi-medical instructions that I would prefer to keep to myself if it was not my obligation to tell the whole truth: "Open your mouth," "And suppose I put my tongue in yours?"

Ten times I asked the headmistress of the school for birds, I begged her, I pleaded with her to make use of the services of my friend Ze Miguel the widow-maker. Once she had her decree, we could be united.

Ten times she refused. Her husband visited her at night in her dreams, and the country of dreams was more real to her than any other. (But for that belief, would she ever have begun on so improbable a project as the school for birds?)

One day her sailor husband did come back, I don't know where from. Perhaps some distant land? Perhaps from those recurrent dreams she had of him?

He took back his own place in Elizabeth's heart. The place that had been mine for seven years while he was away at sea. And so, since you wanted to hear it, ends the story of my one true love affair.

Among our favourite sources of entertainment was the slave market. To give our eyes a rest from books and maps we often went down the street to it. Once there, all you had to do was prick up your ears. Before bidding began the society ladies who were the principal customers endlessly compared the qualities of their latest purchases.

"I've trained mine well. The moment he snored the dog bit him. He doesn't snore any more."

"Mine doesn't lie down. I can't bear to have people sleeping in the same room as me. I feel as if they could get into my dreams. Don't you think there are bridges from one sleeping person to another?"

In this contest of secret knowledge both true and false, the prize of victory regularly went to a certain Dona Leona, a client of Ze Miguel the widow-maker. She collected Africans as others collect vases or paintings, and told her women friends all kinds of marvellous tales.

"You'll never guess what happened to me recently ... the one I bought last month – you know, that very small man – well, just think, he has phosphorescent skin. What do you make of that? It could be because he spent his childhood near the gold mines. Imagine my surprise, my surprise and delight, on his first night at my house. I have only to make him sit in a corner of the room and he acts as a nightlight. I shall never be scared of the dark again."

That morning, however, the ladies were not relaxing. They arrived in a state of high indignation, absorbed in their own anger and unwilling to say what it was about. Their silence did not last long – what woman's silence ever does last long in Lisbon?

Leona was the first to speak out, "My confessor is out of his mind."

The other women, relieved not to be alone in what troubled them, joined in with their own complaints.

"What's he saying? Mine has run mad as well."

"Imagine what my confessor told me yesterday evening! He threatened me with the fires of hell if I didn't amend my way of life."

And now confidence followed hard on the heels of confidence at lightning speed, like stitches in a piece of knitting.

"I walk about naked in front of them."

"So do I, of course. I even wash while they're in the room. They see all of me."

"Whatever does it matter?"

"One day we'll be expected to cover ourselves up in front of cats!"

"Or canaries."

"What strange fancy have the priests taken into their heads?"

We went back to the studio without really understanding what had upset the ladies so much. What was this new attitude adopted towards nakedness by the Church? My comrades and I were young at the time and the thought of women's bodies haunted us. All we could think of doing was to consult Ze Miguel, that great expert in the magical continent of women.

"I'm afraid I can't tell you." He frowned. "But perhaps ... perhaps my report has been delivered."

"What report?"

"I know that as cartographers you are sworn guardians of great secrets ... I would like to talk to you, but it must be under the seal of the utmost discretion."

And so I heard, for the first time, about the question which was to occupy my mind for all the years I have spent in contact with savages, without ever really understanding the mystery of their natures: "What do the blacks see when they look at something?"

"I must tell you that three months ago I was summoned to the arch-diocese ..."

He had been taken by guards along a labyrinth of long corridors towards a small room as dark as the sacristy of Our Lady of the Holy Sepulchre. Three men arrived a little later, the archbishop and two other clerics. They sat at a desk without inviting Ze Miguel to sit down. Anyway, there was no chair for him. He stood before them, trembling slightly.

"My son, the Church needs your help."

"My poor services are entirely at the disposal of the Church, of course."

There followed a long account of a subject only too well known to

Ze Miguel: the decline of female morality since the arrival of so many black men in the city. The archbishop did all the talking, while his companions only nodded their heads at frequent intervals. Perhaps some sickness or vow kept them mute, for they conversed only in nods.

"We hardly need to say that we do not believe those who speak of cases of carnal intercourse. Can anyone think of the daughters or nieces of our mothers coupling in such unions?"

The heads of the assistant clerics suddenly changed course. Instead of nodding up and down, they began moving from left to right and right to left, as a sign of vigorous denial.

"Our uneasiness is different, and it concerns you, my son. According to credible information, a growing number of the female faithful allow these savages to see them naked, and feel so little embarrassment about it that they do not even think they should mention the fact when making confession."

Ze Miguel could only confirm that this practice was increasing at breakneck speed.

The prelate smiled. "You are, it appears, the best defender of women. They will therefore not be able to oppose your conclusions."

"What conclusions?"

The archbishop lowered his voice and leaned over the desk, imitated by the two others. Ze Miguel did the same. All four heads were almost touching.

"As a prelude to any campaign of purification we need knowledge. Consequently, you will kindly call together a committee comprising all those whom you consider wise enough to keep a secret. Once your enquiries are finished, you will report to us on the following important question: what do the blacks see when they look at something?"

And after much more deferential nodding, the three clerics disappeared with a swishing of precious fabrics to go about other business.

The eye doctors instantly recruited, although they were the most famous in the city, were no use at all. They examined, discussed, argued, decided to carry out more examinations, could not agree and asked permission to cut out the ocular orbs of five blacks who had recently died of fever. Permission was granted. Since no clear conclusion could be drawn from this first experiment, another request was presented. Once again it was granted: this time it was to dissect, having first delicately removed it from its socket, the ocular orb of a living black. In that way they might hope for an exact observation of the mechanism of vision. A waste of time; the practitioners went on arguing.

Some took the simplistic view that the blacks, coming from the other side of the earth, had antipodeans' vision and saw everything the other way round from us. Others, more imaginative, swore that the eye of a black was the gateway to Paradise; when he looked at us, therefore, his gaze was purified by an innocence deriving from the time before the sin of Eve. And God, in His infinite goodness, had wanted that innocence to return to black men by way of the same channel that, in whites, was filled with tears. That was what gave the gaze of the blacks their expression of perpetual joy. Therefore the modesty of women could only gain by contact with the aforesaid innocence.

As for the third kind of doctors, who were in the majority, they spent hours presenting the innumerable reasons why one could never come to any certain conclusion.

The exasperated Ze Miguel finally sent them all packing. He decided on a radical change of method.

The following months were among the best ever enjoyed by our friend the attorney. He chose ten slaves of all ages, men who had come to Lisbon long enough ago to be able to express themselves well in our language.

He showed each of them three prostitutes selected for the abundant curves of their anatomy.

The detailed study that followed is famous today among all the professors of the universities of Salamanca, Paris, Montpellier and Louvain as a model of scientific experiment.

He told the ladies to undress, and then summoned each of the slaves.

"Describe her to me."

"What, everything?"

"Everything you see."

Ze Miguel had decided to note down what he heard himself,

while an artist drew the woman's body not from life but as the slave described it.

Four of them, either hypocrites or genuinely terrorized (who can tell, with the Catholics of recent times?), began by closing their eyes and crying that the Devil had come to tempt them. To avoid wasting time with lengthy explanations, they were whipped. This treatment calmed them down, and they described the spectacle of flesh and hair on display to them item by item, frequently making the sign of the cross.

At the end of four weeks of work. Ze Miguel went back to the arch-diocesan palace. He thought all he would have to do would be to hand in his report. But his Grace the Archbishop wanted to talk to him. The same guards led him along the same corridors into the same window-less room, where the same trio were waiting for him, the prelate and the two nodders.

"Well, my son, what conclusion do you draw from your studies?"

Ze Miguel tried to play for time and retreat behind the written word. But the insistence and impatience facing him were such that he had to make up his mind to tell all.

"Bad news."

"What bad news?"

"Bad news for modesty. I consider that the blacks see exactly what we do,"

"I thought so," muttered the archbishop, crossing himself.

After this study, orders were given to the confessors not to be satis-fied with sins confessed but to carry out interrogations of their own.

"My daughter, whom do you allow to see you?"

Even when the reply was "No one," he was recommended to press harder.

"By no one, do you meant that the room is empty whenever you remove your clothing?"

This time, on pain of lying, the penitent was obliged to reply that well, no, one or two slaves were in her bathroom to massage her or assist with her ablutions, and even shared her bedroom to avoid any attack on her by night.

"Sad to say, my daughter ..."

The revelation, drawn from Ze Miguel's work, that the Africans brought back in caravels had eyes just like ours did not always have the expected effect. Some good women, once they were warned of the visual abilities of their slaves, trembled in retrospective shame and banished their bodyguards from their bedrooms for ever.

To other women, and it must be admitted that these were in the majority, the news opened up disturbing prospects. Until now they had never thought about the curiosity of their slaves, any more than the glance that a piece of furniture or even a dog might cast them. Once they knew about that curiosity, all kinds of games were possible – and Ze Miguel gave me a faithful and precise chronicle of those games for our entertainment every Sunday evening.

But that is not the subject of my story, which is told primarily for moral purposes.

When I think back to those five years on my own in Lisbon, I see them as an island, my only time of freedom in the middle of a life in chains.

Before Lisbon there was Genoa and my childhood, and childhood is a prison in itself.

Then my brother took me over, and I was in more of a prison than ever. I could never escape Christopher's dazzling light, not by night or day, not in the most remote recesses of my dreams, not even when the whole ocean separated us.

So I relished my Portuguese freedom all the more because I knew it was under threat. Those who blame me, beginning with you two, for my depraved conduct at that time with all the dozens of widows or future widows whom I consoled in my own way, should remember that I did much worse things under the influence of Christopher.

My brother hadn't yet knocked at the door to let me know that my days of leisure were over, but I sensed that he was prowling around.

It was useless for me to stop my eyes and my ears, to escape conversations in the port whenever there was news of an "exceptional young Genoese navigator". He was there, hovering like a bird of prey, waiting for his moment to fall on me. If he left me alone a little longer, it was only to give me time to prepare myself. All that I learned about cartography could come in useful to him in his Enterprise.

I still didn't know what the enterprise was. Maybe he didn't yet know himself? All I knew for certain was that it would exceed my abilities, because Christopher had always exceeded me in everything; age, height, strength, intelligence, dreams and the love of women.

It was God's will for me to be born in my brother's shadow.

And it was also God's will for me never to come out of it, not even today, when he has been dead for seven years.

I almost forgot Ursula, and no one deserves to be celebrated more. Too bad if her profession upsets our Dominicans.

Although no one ever wanted to recognize the fact, particularly not

81

cartographers, who undoubtedly owe them the most valuable part of their information, prostitutes played a crucial part in our city. After long years away, with only their comrades and the ocean for company, as soon as most seamen set foot on land they thought of nothing but getting inside a woman. From port to port they had known the local women, but to their discredit, because of the skin colour and brusque manners of these women, they had regarded them more as a kind of animal than as human beings.

The navigators' relief at having survived, therefore, was mingled with a desire to prove, by means of much vigorous fornication, that they had indeed attained the miraculous state of survival.

With a few exceptions, whose names circulated all over Lisbon, most wives were not prepared to satisfy those needs. The interminable time they had spent waiting had changed their memories into dreams growing more distant and lethargic as time went by. The bodies of husband and wife met without remembering each other, astonished to be face to face and naked. Even in the happiest instances, the two spouses still had to learn about one another again, and this new learning process took time that was incompatible with the impatience of the home-comers.

Sometimes one or the other partner, or both, were not even tempted to embark on a new apprenticeship. At first sight it appeared with distressing (and repellent) clarity that love was dead, and nothing could ever bring it back to life.

Prostitutes pounced on the ruins of these marriages like wild cats. And business was good for them as never before or since.

Take care, my dear Dominicans! Do not be too quick to despise your fellow human beings. Try to distinguish subtler needs behind the animality of these women, and you may find a touching fragility.

The moisture of their thighs, the softness of their skin and the agility of their mouths were not the only reasons for their success. Once the seamen's first frenzy was satisfied, it was not those parts of the body that they preferred.

Will you believe me if I say that first and foremost the sailors sought out their ears? Not to indulge in some unnatural practice imported from Africa with those organs – I know your dirty mind under that apparently impassive expression, Brother Jerome – but simply to have someone to listen to them.

What is an ear?

I was already passionately interested in those large, flat seashells stuck to each side of the human skull.

I had begun my enquiries with my brother when I was only ten years old. How can we explain that he perceived everything relating to the sea and sea voyages, heard the most distant conversation whispered at the other side of the port, when he was deaf and indifferent to everything else? For instance to the ideas, sometimes intelligent ideas, put to him by his younger brother Bartholomew?

One night I took advantage of his sleep to hold a candle close to those mysteries, his ears. I spent some time inspecting the strange sea-shells, taking care not to let any hot wax run. In the end I gave up. Neither the two dark (and not very clean) ear holes, nor the pink folds around them had told me their secrets.

And here were these strange sea-shells questioning me yet again. What particular quality did the woman Ursula possess to attract the sadness of all the sailors as she did?

She was neither beautiful nor young, she had none of those plump curves that men like, and showed no inventiveness in making love; she caressed you without any rhythm, sucked as if she were yawning, and hummed tunes from the Mass as she opened her legs.

But she loved to listen.

"Well, big boy, what have you got to tell me?"

And she would offer her left ear, for the right ear, as she liked to recall, had been torn by her brute of a father who used to beat her black and blue, curses on his name, may he be tortured for a thousand years by ten thousand demons!

Word soon spread of this rare quality of hers, and her clientèle kept growing. A certain friendship developed between us. For I was the first to suggest the opposite of her usual practices to her: to pay her (at a high price) for listening.

Her left ear attracted men so much for a single and very simple reason: they found nothing like it on the conjugal pillow. Their wives attended only to good news: the joy of reunion, promises never, never to go to sea again, pride in having increased Portuguese and Christian territory. Not forgetting the main point: the precise list of the advantages in terms of money, social status and in kind that they would get from their husbands' long absence.

Female ears were deaf to all else, especially when a seaman conjured up the horrors of his voyage. He had hardly opened his mouth to describe the reverse side of the coin, all the anguish and suffering, before his wife consigned him to silence again.

"So?" said the wife, crossly. "And what about the horrors of *my* life all these years, on my own with our five children? Did you ever think of that?"

Let us note, by the way, that the stories Ursula told me of marriage presented so dismal a picture that they gave me an aversion to it, one that I was never able to shake off.

Once back on land in Lisbon, the sailors who had been on voyages of discovery behaved well, despite their ragged appearance. They told only the tales that people wanted to hear, accounts of marvels and conquests. They had endured too much for too long not to accept the price of their sufferings: fame and its companions, admiration, fascination and respect.

After tasting these sweet things to their full, they felt another wish, indeed a necessity which is still mine today. A sensation like a wave that comes over you one fine day, starting in the pit of your stomach it rises to your tongue, sets it moving and opens your jaws. And suddenly, while elementary prudence implores you to keep quiet, you hear yourself telling the story of your whole life, including its darker parts. Most of all its darker parts.

Once upon a time a storm arose, the most ferocious and malicious of tempests ever devised by God for his own amusement. With its first gust it swept away our mainmast; then, as it shook us, it also swept away ten members of the crew who were not firmly secured to the deck; one by one; then the hearts of the survivors and then their reason as, day and night, it mingled day with night, high with low, the sky with the sea, life with death ...

Once upon a time there was a great calm. Perhaps God was tired.

Nothing moved, not the air or the flying fish or the sand in the hour-glass, we had fallen into a hole in time.

Once upon a time there was a whale that thought our ship was an anvil and hammered on us with its tail.

Once upon a time there was starvation, once upon a time there was starvation, once upon a time there was starvation.

One upon a time there was heat, once upon a time there was heat, once upon a time there was the kind of heat that broils the inside of your head and overcomes you with weariness; how can anyone sleep for so much as a minute? Night is a furnace and so is day.

Once upon a time there were fevers; our bodies shook so violently that the ship itself vibrated and the swaying mast nearly fell.

Once upon a time our bellies were already empty, yet a yellowish, bloodstained fluid kept running out of us.

Once upon a time the bodies of our friends began to stink as soon as they died, so we threw them overboard where sharks immediately ate them.

Once upon a time there were insect bites that sent us mad with the itching.

Once upon a time worms got under our skin, no one knew how, and suddenly emerged again from the middle of a leg, from the belly, even from the eyes.

Once upon a time our legs turned into tree trunks, as wide and rough as elephant's feet.

Once upon a time our gums turned black; once upon a time our teeth fell out and into the water one by one; once upon a time birds caught our teeth in flight before the fish could get at them.

These were the stories that the sailors told Ursula's left ear.

And so, thanks to her ear, I learned about the other side of the discoveries.

None of these stories ever came in useful to me for our maps. Worse, with all the horrors they described they almost made me ashamed of my trade. What monsters are we, I asked myself every time I left Ursula, making documents that help seamen to venture into such infernal places?

Sooner or later, the seamen went back to her.

"What's happened to you?" asked Ursula of the attentive left ear. "Didn't I give you enough relief? Do you want me to drain your balls as well? I always knew they communicated with memory."

"The fact is, I'm going back to sea."

"I thought you'd seen only too much of it."

Then the sailors told her the other story, the opposite of all they had said before.

Once upon a time, in the far north near Thule, there was the brief blue dusk that is the northern night; once upon a time there was the joyful yellow of the sky before the sun wakes and raises his round head above the waters; once upon a time there were a hundred shades of grey; once upon a time the blue sky came back fast next day, as if fearing to have been forgotten; once upon a time there was the long gliding of the ship before a favouring wind, followed by astonished birds; once upon a time there was our miraculous descent down a horizontal mountain; once upon a time there was a friendly wave that took the ship on its back, relieved it of all its cares and carried it beyond the horizon; once upon a time there were warm nights when the fish began to fly; once upon a time we had the ironic company of squawking birds; once upon a time the nose had its revenge on the eyes – ah, the scent of the shore long before you see it.

Once upon a time there was the magic of the sea.

"You ought to know what you really want," said Ursula of the left ear to her client, even if time had taught her the reply, which was always the same. "Why do you all want to go to sea again?"

"It's too dull on land."

My two Dominicans are smiling. We've never been better friends. Accompanying them to the door of my Alcazar, I announced to them just now that at our next meeting, which is tomorrow, I shall tell them at long last about the entrance on stage of my brother Christopher.

Las Casas looks me up and down.

"So far your account has been well and good. But how does it help to explain the madness of humanity? I have heard nothing about cruelty. Have you really reported events exactly as they took place? Or does your love for Lisbon blind you?"

86

I was waiting for this moment, with my reply ready and prepared.

"Some conquests were violent, I don't deny it. And getting hold of slaves, as well as bringing them home, calls for rough treatment. But Africa is so vast. And Asia is even larger. Portugal is so small, so sparsely populated, it could do nothing but graze the crop on offer without doing too much harm. The Spanish, far stronger and more numerous than us, have concentrated their voyages and their greed on far smaller territories."

Hypocrisy, duplicity, bad faith, a strong desire to influence others, hatred of human freedom, contempt for those less intelligent than themselves (meaning almost everyone else on earth) ... yes, the Dominicans have all possible failings. But one has to recognize their passion for understanding.

Las Casas and Jerome look at me with such keen and total attention that it seems to me like desire. I blush, and continue.

"No doubt it is just an illusion of old age to see things in a better light than we did in our youth, but it seems to me that a wish to make quick profits was not the prime cause sending the Portuguese navigators south. First and foremost, a strong wind of curiosity was blowing over Lisbon."

"What do you mean by curiosity?"

"Ah, Dominicans! Get back to your beloved dictionaries. It is not for me to teach you that the word comes from Latin *cura*, meaning care, concern. The curious man is a doctor; he takes care of the whole world."

II

—

Fever

I have found the precise date of the naval battle: 13 August 1476. Five ships had put out from Genoa with cargoes of Greek mastic. They were on their way to Flanders and England when they were attacked off Cape St Vincent by a Franco-Portuguese fleet of at least thirteen vessels. All night long, dozens of drowned or mutilated bodies had been washed up on shore.

That was the latest news and it arrived just in time to spice up conversation over our evening meal.

"What a feast for the crabs!"

"Long live cartographers! Our mistakes may cause shipwrecks – ha, ha, ha! – but we're never sunk ourselves!"

Over the following days, men who had escaped the shipwreck arrived to tell their tales of the fierce fighting.

There was no reason for me to pay them more attention than if they were any other horror story. People were cutting each other's throats all over Europe.

One evening I was told, by one of my comrades, that an old man was asking to see me. "He's waiting at the door of the studio, looks like he might die himself any moment. He speaks Genoese dialect."

Reluctantly, I left my work, which as I remember was the addition of three treacherous reefs to the sea off Brittany.

I didn't recognize him at once.

The man had his back to me and he seemed to be looking for something. He caught sight of the bucket of water that we kept ready to hand in case a fire began in the workshop. Picking it up, he turned it upside down over his head. The newcomer's old age was nothing but the salt encrusting his hair. Water washed it away.

It was like a fairy tale. A young man appeared instead of the old one. A young man with a head of flaming red hair the colour of the setting sun.

My brother Christopher.

I flung myself into his arms.

He said just three words, "I swam ashore."

Then, overcome by exhaustion, he fell full length on the floor and the debris of our work, which was scattered all over it: blunt pens, spoilt maps, chipped beakers.

Las Casas would like to know more. He thinks I am skimming rather fast over this important reunion. Does my haste perhaps conceal something to which I would rather not admit? Come along, Bartholomew, how do you hope to prepare for a peaceful death if you don't unburden your conscience?

Bartholomew agrees. What would you expect? Secretly he consigns the Dominicans to all the demons of hell, but he is wise enough to comply with their wishes.

At the moment when I saw him appear, my first reaction revealed the better part of my nature. Affection, emotion, relief, admiration. And a sudden rush of anxiety, now unnecessary, since while I hadn't even known that my brother was in danger, but anyway here he was in front of me, safe and sound.

Impelled by these noble sentiments, I ran to meet him.

But once I had reached him, to be crushed in his muscular arms and assailed by the smell of salt and sweat about him, I hated him. He had caught up with me in the studio where I was so happily occupied with small things, and I knew he was going to eat me alive.

I felt sorry – terribly, shamefully sorry – that he had managed to reach the shore instead of drowning out there in the sea off Cape St Vincent.

Then he would not have taken me over again.

And my life would have been my own, not a pendant to his: too glorious a life and even more pitiable.

As you can imagine, the whole studio gathered around this man who had collapsed and looked like a kind of corpse. Andrea came along. "So this is the brother you keep talking about?"

I nodded and he smiled.

"Take him to the shed where we keep the paints. He'll be in good, quiet company there."

The shed was the place where we stored paper, vellum, inks, glues, and all kinds of mixtures for priming our work.

My brother slept for three days and two nights. I brought him meals at regular intervals, but he didn't touch them. One morning he reappeared, asking who were the best people to meet if he wanted to find a berth on board a ship.

Andrea offered to employ him in the studio instead. To my surprise, Christopher accepted at once.

That evening, when I asked him why, he said, "You cartographers must know things about the sea that I don't."

The arrogance he has shown on his earlier visit had gone. I can't believe that being shipwrecked had taught him modesty. I am more inclined to think that he had moved on from dreaming to planning. To put a plan into practice you have to learn things first, and learning means respecting those who know more than you, even if it is in a lesser field than your own, but one that is useful to your plan.

From the end of that first day he was regarded with general respect, and I reaped some of the benefit myself. As the others often told me, "Your brother has the whole ocean in his head."

His invaluable advantage over the rest of us was his practical knowledge of the places we drew. He had sailed along most of the coasts whose outlines we traced on paper, had put in at all the ports, passed through all the straits. He had scraped past – and sometimes collided with – many rocks which he still remembered perfectly and painfully. So he could look over our shoulders and correct our mistakes.

None of my companions disputed his authority. On the contrary, anyone in the slightest doubt appealed to him, calling him over from one end of the studio to the other.

"Christopher, is that long shape really right for the shore south of Tangiers?"

"Is there a little island I've left out there, between Lampedusa and Tunisia?"

Although I didn't really believe it, I began to think that my brother had sobered a little. Perhaps he'd had enough of his constant roving and dangerous life. But one day he began to move restlessly. He walked backwards; at other times he leaned first to one side and then to the other. And his habit of constantly narrowing his eyes had come back. These were small signs; and I wouldn't have noticed them in anyone other than my brother, but they were only too familiar to me. They meant he would be off again in the near future. In his head he was already at sea and the movements of his body compensated for the rolling and pitching of the waves to come.

A little later, when he announced that he was off to Thule, the seabirds all the way to the river mouth and beyond must have been able to hear Andrea's fury. His imprecations mingled praise with insults. "You know that you're the best, you're irreplaceable, do you want more money, is that it, you swindler, do you want to be the death of my studio? The sea, oh yes, your sort are always off to sea again! What makes the sea any better than Lisbon?"

You'd have thought him a wife holding up her husband to public ridicule for being a sea captain.

Christopher let the storm blow itself out and then promised to be back.

"If you're coming back, why bother to leave at all?"

"I still have to find out about certain routes."

I went down to the harbour with him. The heavy woollen garments piled on deck told me that once out of the harbour mouth the ship would be turning north.

I asked, as Andrea already had, "What's so interesting about going to the icy countries?"

"The earth is smaller up there." He looked deep into my eyes, as if to make sure that I understood what he was saying. "I've been told that there in the north they say there is land to the west, very close to them."

He was the last to go aboard. The moorings had been cast off. The sea was a dead calm, and the ebb tide had taken over from the wind. The Tagus carried the ship to the last light showing in the city and then the night swallowed it up.

My lords, emperors and kings, dukes and marquises …

The Description of the World is there on the table in my room in the Alcazar, in front of the prie-dieu. When I was asked what I would wish to take with me into my exile on Hispaniola, I named it first, by its title, *The Description of the World*.

I realize that it has never left me. It has undoubtedly been my most faithful companion all my life. Hence its well-worn binding and the decrepitude of the book inside.

> Lords, emperors and kings, dukes and marquises, knights and citizens, and all who wish to know about the different races of mankind and the diversity of the various parts of the world, and about the usages and customs there …

No other book so immediately places the reader in the midst of the action. As soon as my eyes see those first lines, as soon as my lips, even so long afterwards, form the words, the same rhythm takes hold of me, and I set off yet again, with double enthusiasm, on a journey to the court of the Grand Khan, and also to that day in Lisbon when Christopher turned up after his return from Thule. He would not say anything about his voyage north, but he was brandishing a large book.

"To work, Bartholomew. I need you to do a calculation."

"What calculation?"

"You'll soon see. Go on, start reading!"

> There you will find the great marvels and diversities of Greater and Lesser Armenia, of Persia, of Turkey, of the Tartars and India, and many other provinces of Central Asia and a part of Europe to which you come when you travel towards the Greek, the Levant and the Tramontane winds.

I remember the crazy month that followed, with no respite for rest or sleep. I remember the deranged way in which we did not so much read *The Description*, we galloped headlong through it.

> Within the borders of Tauris there is a very religious monastery dedicated to St Balsamo.

"Faster, faster," Christopher urged me.

> In Persia is the city called Sava from which the three Magi set out.

"How many days did it take?"

Page after page, that was the only question that Christopher asked. He was not interested in the marvels of the landscapes, the people and the customs described by Marco Polo of Venice. I did what my elder brother wanted, just as I had since childhood, and concentrated on reading aloud in a monotonous tone, going faster and faster. I raised my voice and slowed down only occasionally, when my eyes fell on indications of the distances that the Venetian had travelled.

> A man leaving that city of which I told you above rides for *a good twelve days* between the Levant and Greek winds …
>
> Let us leave this subject and speak of another province which is *seven days' journey away* in the direction of the sirocco, and is called Kashmir …
>
> A man leaving Carcassonne and the Altai mountains will pass through a country towards the Tramontane which is called the plain of Barger, and it will take him *forty days*.

In his notebook, Christopher scrupulously wrote down twelve, then seven, then forty.

❧

It is known that on his return after twenty-three years of travelling and living in distant places, after escaping the widest imaginable range of dangers, Marco Polo was imprisoned by the Genoese.

I am well acquainted with my compatriots and their passion for stories, all stories whether true or false, with a preference for the latter because they know that one true story will provide material for ten false ones. They couldn't let a man go if he had seen so much, so many sights, so many creatures! In prison, he dictated his memoirs. Now that old age, that other prison, has taken me captive in my turn, now that Christopher has run his race through life, I have leisure to plunge into *The Description of the World* again, this time slowly, very slowly. All its pages call me to the enchantment of the story. I open the book at random.

Listen to this:

The great and noble ladies of that country wear trousers down to their feet, like the men, as I will recount, and they make them of cotton and fine silk, perfumed with musk. And they conceal many items inside the trousers. There are ladies who will place a good hundred lengths of very fine linen and cotton, each measuring a yard, wrapped around their persons like swaddling clothes. Some put on eighty lengths and some sixty, according to their means, and the wrappings make them appear very bulky. They do this to show that they have large buttocks and so be thought beautiful, for the men love stout women, and those who look largest below the waist appear lovelier than the others. That is all there is to say about the affairs of this kingdom, so now let us leave it, and I will speak of another people living to the south, ten days' journey away from this province ...

Or this:

And I will tell you about another strange custom that they have, and that I forgot to write down earlier. You must know, and it is very true, that when there are two men one of whom has had a son who is dead – the child may have died at the age of four, or any other time after that before he was of marriageable age – while the other man has had a daughter, who also died before the age of marriage, the two fathers marry the dead children to each other when the boy would have been of the age to take a wife. They give the dead girl to the dead boy as his wife, drawing up a contract of marriage, and then a necromancer throws the contract on the fire and burns it. Seeing the smoke rise, they say that it is going to their children in the other world and telling them of their marriage, and thenceforward the dead boy and the dead girl in the other world will consider themselves man and wife. Then a great wedding feast is held with much food, and the fathers say that it is spread before their children in the other world and that the young wife and the young husband share in the feasting. And having set up two images, one in the form of a girl and the other in the form of a boy, they place them on a vehicle as handsomely adorned as possible. Drawn by horses, the vehicle carries the two images all through the vicinity, with great rejoicing and merry-making; then they take it to the fire and burn the two images, praying to their gods to ensure that the marriage is known to be a happy one in the other world. They also do another thing: they make paintings and portraits on paper in the likeness of stags and horses and other animals, clothes of all kinds, bezants, furniture and utensils, and all that families usually give as a dowry, but without really doing so. They then burn these depictions, and say that their children will have all those things in the other world. That being done, all the relatives of each of the two dead spouses consider themselves related by marriage, and maintain their relationship as long as they live, just as if their dead children were alive.

❧

I remember ... I have only to call on my memory for my body to be back at once in the state of extreme exhaustion that it felt at the time. I don't think I slept for weeks on end. Our days were spent in cartography, our nights in following the trail of the Venetian. I swayed back and forth, like the Jews when they pray. My mouth was dry as sand from having to read so much aloud in a low voice. Then I suddenly stopped. I cut my frenzied mumbling short. And I rubbed my eyes – eyes that someone who wished me ill had surely replaced with two burning coals, they hurt so much.

Was it possible that their torture ended here? I checked, with a small movement of my forefinger: no, the page before me now had no more text after it. This really was the last paragraph, so it deserved solemnity. I raised my voice.

For as we said in the first chapter of this book, there was never a man, whether Christian, Saracen, Tartar or pagan who travelled to such vast parts of the world as Messer Marco, son of Messer Niccolo Polo, that great and noble citizen of the city of Venice."

I closed the book and raised my head. "That's the end."
"The end of what?" asked Christopher.
"The end of *The Description*. Messer Polo went home."
"His pride is ridiculous. All he did was follow known routes. I'm going to find a new one."

※

There was no rest yet for the Columbus brothers. What pact do sailors sign with the Devil, enabling them to fend off sleep; what part of their souls have they sold in exchange for the ability to keep awake when ordinary mortals have been staggering with exhaustion for days? For three nights, three whole nights I had to apply myself, under Christopher's implacable gaze, to going over the entire huge book again to make sure I had not missed out a single day. The exact number of days spent by the Venetian on his voyage obsessed my brother to the point of madness. And I still had not understood the point of that gigantic addition sum.

But in any event, the result delighted him. 2015! 2015 days spent travelling from Venice to eastern China. Christopher had half risen from the stool where he was sitting as he repeated the number: 2015! He was waving his hands about. All at once sleep struck him down in the midst of his joy. His nose hit the table as if he were kissing it and he fell asleep bent double where he sat.

I wanted to understand. I shook him. "So what? What's the importance of that huge number?"

"What?" His eyes rested on me in astonishment. You'd have thought he didn't recognize me. Perhaps he was surprised to find that anyone so stupid could exist.

"What's the importance of it? The wider Asia is, the less is the distance by sea between Europe and Asia."

And when his eyes closed this time they stayed closed. I was not good for much more, even if, very far away in my head, a small, mocking voice was telling me that a day is not and never would be a unit of measurement. I fell asleep in my turn. The eyes of the brothers Columbus did not open until three days later, when an apprentice from the studio came to hammer on the door of our attic. Andrea thought we must have been murdered.

I did not hear the mocking little voice again until much later, at a crucial moment for our Enterprise. That time it came not from inside my own head, clouded that first time by weariness, but from the keen intelligence of José Vizinho, a member of the Committee of Mathematicians.

And Christopher had a good deal of difficulty in replying to him.

"Do you mean to say that you are measuring the sea by the number of days spent in a journey on land? Do you know what difficulty the great scholar Eratosthenes had in assessing the distance between Alexandria and Syene in terms of the footsteps of camels?"

"You can have the islands!"

As soon as we had finished assessing the measurements of Asia, Christopher began to organize his voyage, which from now on he called the Indies Enterprise. He was already apportioning tasks to his army of two (himself and me).

And he was already handing out the elements themselves.

He himself would have the sea and its currents, the winds and the sky, the courses of the stars showing us the way. He would be in charge of navigation, the choice of ships, the recruitment of crews.

I was to be responsible for maps, for contact with certain authorities, and above all I was to have the islands.

The matter of the islands had separated us ever since our Genoese childhood.

One day when we could hardly walk yet, we made our escape from home to go and look around the harbour. It was difficult. We could scarcely talk either, but we asked where we could board a ship.

As no one paid any attention to our requests, we took advantage of the siesta hour to smuggle ourselves on board a vessel. Christopher must have been eight at the time and I would have been six.

That was the first time we went to sea, snuggling close to one another between two sacks of mouldering wheat.

We also had our first experience of sea-sickness, and felt sure, as I still do today, sixty years later, that it is worse than death.

And so we came ingloriously ashore on Elba, our first island; as soon as we were approaching its shore the skipper of the boat threw us into the water. No great ceremony, apart from hearty laughter, welcomed two dripping wet little boys on land.

We began our exploration without delay, followed by several dogs. Christopher was grumbling, "It's too small! It's too small!"

But I was enchanted. The earth and the sea, the mountain and the countryside, the fields of olive trees, the vines, the beaches and woods, there was even an iron mine … all of that in a space that we could almost have covered in a day if our little legs had been stronger.

I discovered that huge expanses were no real use. You could live in modest areas that none the less had everything necessary. It was a discovery that delighted the child I was at the time, always humiliated by grown-ups because I was small and didn't take up much room. Islands were not arrogant like continents. Islands occupied the right kind of space. Islands had a human dimension.

Another discovery was that Monte Capanne seemed to have been placed where it was so that from its peak you could see and greet the little islands that kept their big sister Elba company. I had forgotten their names later, but they come back to me today, like so many other things from my youth, now that the rest is gone: Gorgona, Capraia, Pianosa, Giglio, Montecristo and Giannutri.

I was only six, not an age for philosophizing. Only much later did I find the explanation for the happiness that overcame me that day. I had felt, for the first time, two sentiments that were to grow throughout my life, and they explain my return to Hispaniola and my wish to finish my days there: I like what is small but complete in itself, and a strange sense of fraternity links me with archipelagos. Put together, those preferences have always given me a permanent need for islands.

We did not get back to Genoa for two days and two nights. Given notice of our return by I don't know what bird that must watch over children, our father Domenico was waiting for us on the quayside.

Just before the thrashing that concluded our adventure, Christopher had time to decide, even then, on our respective roles.

"You can have the islands. I'm going further."

⚓

Proud of that mission, as I was to be proud, unfortunately, of all that he would subsequently entrust to me, I set to work without delay.

How was I to deal with such a great task, even within the space of a whole lifetime, when my brother wanted quick results?

The first restriction of the field was to exclude the *islands of the Inner Sea*, those sprinkled by the Creator over the Mediterranean.

Christopher's voyage did not follow the travels of Odysseus. In going west, he would be turning his back on the islands of that hero's world; he was not concerned with them.

There remained the others. Marco Polo counted 12,700 of them in the vicinity of the Indies alone, while the Catalan Atlas calculated the more modest figure of 7,648 for the same region.

Who was I to try discovering the exact yet variable quantity of islands? Some numbers, for instance the number of the stars, are known only to the Creator, who will always keep the secret to Himself.

Amidst all this diversity, I had to concentrate on the islands necessary to the Enterprise. Christopher had confirmed that he did not want to confront headwinds, so he would not be taking the northern route. Consequently neither the islands off Thule nor the island that is the land of the Angles, by which I mean Albion or England, called for my attention.

Only the southern route mattered.

I knew my brother hoped that island would follow island all the way from Portugal to the Indies, like a ford allowing him to cross the ocean as easily as if it were a river. We would be moving from one stepping stone to the next.

He had heard tell of Madeira and its little sister Porto Santo. Beyond them came the Fortunate Isles.

But after that, what islands lay to the west? It was my task to find him the rest of the chain. I immersed myself in stories that amounted only to legends.

A week was enough to show me that my task was impossible, and I warned Christopher, "There are more islands in the sea than birds in the air, and they're as hard to get hold of."

He replied that so far as the number went, I was only saying the same as Ptolemy and Marco Polo, and this great number was good news; the more havens we had, the less dangerous the passage between them would be. As for the difficulty of getting hold of islands, how did I come by that far-fetched idea? No doubt it just showed my famous laziness when I was asked to do work of any difficulty.

The rest of our discussion casts light on both my brother's madness and the beauty of his character, the main reason why he carried out projects on a scale impossible for other mortals to realize or even to envisage.

As I was patiently explaining to him that no cartographer with any regard for the truth could draw up a reliable, exact inventory of the islands in the ocean, since most of them were imaginary, he looked at me uncomprehendingly before uttering the following words, which I consider his motto.

"Well, what about it? Where does what's imaginary come from, if not those countries still unknown to us?"

I went to work again without bothering any more about the factual nature of the ideas I put forward. I felt that I was following in my father's footsteps. On Saturday evenings, to send us to sleep, he used to tell us improbable stories that passed into our dreams and made Mass next morning a very dull and dismal affair.

I copied his method.

My brother and I shared a room rented to us by Master Andrea. I would wait until we were lying in bed with the candles blown out.

"Christopher, did you know that Roderick was the last Visigoth king of Spain? He held out for a long time, but in the end he was defeated by the Arab leader Tarik ibn Ziyad. After that the whole of the peninsula, including Portugal, was occupied by the Muslims. Many Christians, feeling that they could not live under Muslim rule, tried to flee, and that was why the Bishop of Porto put to sea, accompanied by six other prelates and a large company of faithful believers. For a long time, Christopher, they followed your future route, sailing west. It's said that they went far beyond the Azores. When at last they saw land on the horizon, some of them called it *Ante ilia*, the island ahead, which soon became Antilla. Others called it the Island of Seven Cities, because each of the bishops built his own city there.

Christopher never tired of hearing this legend, and was never satisfied with that outline of it but kept asking me for further and more precise details. As I didn't know any, I made them up. I drew a map to help me with my idyllic descriptions and I have always kept it like a talisman. Why am I so fond of this parchment island, the creation only of my own brain and thus without any reality at all? Today it is dirty, torn and almost illegible. But every time I look at it, which is daily, I feel the same astonishment to see how much the Antilla that I dreamed up is to the real Hispaniola.

I could almost believe that my brother was right: God has installed a miniature version of his entire Creation in our heads. It is up to us to explore that part of it in which we are interested.

Christopher's other favourite story was the tale of St Brendan.

This story gave me a rest, because I didn't have to tell it myself. A man by the name of Benedeit wrote it down in the twelfth century, so I had only to read aloud in a voice suitable for legends – adopting a monotonous and distant tone as if it came from very far away.

Brendan, God's saint, was born of the royal line in the country of Ireland. As he was of high descent, he well knew that Scripture says: "He who flees the joys of this world will have all the joy he could ever desire with God hereafter." This son of kings therefore forsook false honours for those that are true; he took monastic vows in order to be humble and, as it were, an exile from his own time. He was soon chosen abbot of his monastery, acquitting himself so well in that office that many joined him and remained faithful to his rule. The pious Brendan had three thousand monks under him, living in many places, and they all took his great virtue as their example.

Now he had one great wish: he often prayed to God to show him Paradise, the place where Adam first lived, the inheritance from which we were cast out …

He chose, first, to make confession to a servant of God, a hermit called Barin, a man of virtuous customs and a holy life. This devout believer in the Lord lived in a wood with three hundred monks. It was his advice that Brendan asked, wishing for his opinion. And Barin told him in fair words, with many examples and maxims, all that he had seen on land and sea when he went in search of his godson Mernoc.

On hearing this tale, Brendan took fresh heart. The good abbot made his preparations; he chose fourteen of his monks, all of them excellent men, and told them what he meant to do to find out whether they approved. The brothers talked it over two by two, and they all with one accord told their holy father that he should undertake the venture boldly and begged him to take them with him as his true and faithful sons.

"If I speak to you of this," said Brendan, "it is so that I may have confidence in those whom I take, and so that I will not be sorry for it later."

They all assured him that nothing would hinder him by their fault. So having heard their reply, the abbot took his chosen companions with him to the chapterhouse, and as a man of good sense, he said to them:

"Brothers, we do not know the dangers of the venture upon which we set out. Let us pray to God to teach us and, by His good will, to guide us by His hand; and let us pray for forty days, fasting every three days."

None of them hesitated to do as he required them. The abbot did not desist from his prayers until God sent an angel from heaven, who instructed him in the subject of the voyage. The angel revealed to him in his heart that God would willingly consent to his putting out to sea.

So Brendan went out towards the high seas, where he knew from God that he must sail. He did not turn aside to visit his family, he was bound for a place dearer to him. He walked as long as there was firm land underfoot, never stopping to rest, until he reached the rock called by the common folk Brendan's Leap. This rock goes far out into the ocean like a promontory, and has a harbour in the cliff where the sea makes a very narrow little gulf; I do not think that anyone before Brendan ever reached the far end of it. It was here that he had timber of the kind used by coopers brought to build his ship. He made all the inside of it from pine wood, and covered it on the outside with ox skins; the hull was well tarred with pitch, so that the ship would glide smoothly over the waves. Then Brendan placed in it all the necessary tools that the new ship could hold and the provisions that they had brought: victuals to last forty days at the most.

Then he said to the brothers: "Go on board the ship and give thanks to God; we have a favouring wind!"

They all went aboard, and Brendan followed them.

The monks raised the mast and hoisted the sail. Those devout men went on at a good speed. The wind blowing from the east carried them westward. They also rowed with all their might, never fearing to exert their bodies in order to reach the end of their voyage.

Always going west, the monks kept coming upon islands, each separated from the next by a dangerous and interminable distance for them to navigate.

They included the Devil's Island, where the Evil One has a palace made of marble and crystal set in gold. This is where he devises temptations to corrupt human beings.

The Island of Sheep, which are the size of stags there.

The Moving Island, which turned out to be the back of a vast whale.

The Island of Talking Birds, who said that they were fallen angels, cast down from heaven for following the Evil One in his rebellion against the Most High.

The Island of the Monastery of St Albinus, where no one lives except for the monks of an abbey whose needs are miraculously provided for by the grace of God.

The Island of the Fountain of Sleep, where those who drink too freely from that fountain risk never waking again.

The Island of the Golden Pavilion, dominated by a huge pillar the colour of sapphire.

The Island of Hell, where fire rises from incandescent rocks, and a demon blacksmith appeared to them. He was brandishing a gigantic hammer, pincers, and a red-hot sword blade.

The Island of Judas, where Judas was chained alone to undergo a thousand fascinating torments, which he describes:

Near this place is the land of devils, and I am within earshot of it; near this place there are two hells; to suffer there is to pay a heavy price. Near to this place are two hells which last both winter and summer. Even the less painful is terrible for those who are in it: they think that it is impossible to suffer more than they do anywhere. Except for me, no one knows which of the two is the more painful, for no one else suffers in both; but I, wretched creature that I am, undergo both those hells. The first is above, the second below and a sea of salt separates them. It is a marvel that the sea itself does not burn. The hell up above is the more painful, the hell down below the more horrible; the hell close to the air is stifling and burning, the hell close to the sea is icy and stinks. I spend a day and a night up above and then the same time down below. One day I go up, the next I come down; there is no other end to my torment. I do not change from one hell to the other for relief, but to undergo yet more torment.

On Monday, night and day, I am tied to a wheel and turn in the wind, which carries the wheel furiously through the sky. I come and go unceasingly all the time.

On Tuesday, crossing the sea, I am flung into the other hell where I suffer just as much. I am strongly bound and the devils howl imprecations at me; I am placed on a bed of thorns and I am crushed down on it with stones and lead; I am pierced by swords so often that you can see my body full of holes.

On Wednesday I am taken up again and now the tortures are changed. I spend part of the day boiling in pitch, which has made me the colour you see me today. Then I am taken out and put to roast between two braziers, tied to a stake placed there especially for me. It is red, as if it had been held for ten years in a roaring furnace. Then I am thrown back into the pitch so that I will burn better. There is no marble so hard that it will not melt in that fire, but its blazing heat has made me such that my body cannot perish. And although that pain overwhelms me, I suffer it for a whole day and a night.

On Thursday I am taken down to suffer the opposite torment; I am shut up in a frozen, dark and shadowy place. I am so cold that I long to return to the fire that burns so fiercely. At the time I think there can be no worse torment than the cold, and every torture seems to me the most cruel as I endure it.

On Friday I go back up above, where I have died so many painful deaths. The devils flay me alive until I have no skin left and then they bury me, impaled on a red-hot stake, in salt and sweat. As I suffer this torment I grow a new skin. The devils flay me like this and force me into the salt ten times a day, and then they make me drink molten lead and copper.

On Saturday they throw me down to undergo new pains. I am put in a prison; there is none more terrible and repugnant in all of hell. I am cast down into it without a cord, and there I lie in the dark, with no light, and in such a stench that I fear my heart will burst, but I cannot vomit because of the copper I have been made to drink. I swell, my skin stretches, I fear that it will crack. Cold, heat, that stench, those are the torments suffered by Judas. Yesterday was Saturday; I come here between nones and noon; today I rest. Soon I shall have a cruel hour when a thousand devils come and will leave me no peace.

At last, after visiting a hermitage to see a hermit called Paul, who was one hundred and forty years old, and who explained his amazingly good health and unusual longevity by the nature of his diet – he had spent thirty years living on nothing but fish and the following fifty years on nothing but pure water – Brendan and his sailor monks approached their destination, Paradise.

Then the brothers saw a handsome young man, a messenger from God, coming to meet them. He called to them to land on the shore, welcomed them, calling each by his real name and then kissed them with kindness. He calmed the dragons, who were lying docile on the ground and offered no resistance. At his command an angel removed the flaming sword, the gate to Paradise was opened and the pilgrims all entered into its glory.

The young man led them into Paradise. That land was well provided with very fine trees and rivers, the countryside was a garden always in flower and the fragrance of those flowers scented the place fittingly all the time the pious monks stayed there. In every season Paradise had excellent fruits and wonderful scents; you found no brambles or thistles or stinging nettles there; every tree and herb provided delicious things; flowers lasted in bloom and trees in leaf all the year round. It was always summer in Paradise, with the trees covered with fruits and flowers, the woods full of game. Rivers of milk teemed with good fish; there was abundance everywhere. The dew that fell from the sky turned to honey, the mountains were made of gold, the rocks themselves were worth a fortune. The clear sun always shone, not a breath of wind stirred a single hair, no cloud tarnished the clarity of the sky. Anyone living there was protected from all harm and knew that none could come to him; he knew nothing of heat, cold, sickness, hunger, thirst and pain. He had all he could desire in great abundance and would not lose heaven, for he was sure of living in Paradise for ever.

On seeing such felicity, Brendan found the time passed quickly. He would have liked to stay a long time in that place … The handsome young man went ahead of him and told him many things. He described, in fair words, the rewards destined for everyone. Brendan followed him up a hill as high as a cypress tree, and from the summit they saw marvels that can hardly be understood. They contemplated the angels and heard them rejoice at their coming. They heard the great melody they made, but they could bear no more of it. Their human nature could not stand up to the spectacle of that glory.

So then their guide said, "Let us go back; I will take you no further, for you are not capable of it. Brendan, here is Paradise that you prayed to God to show you. Before you, down below, there is a hundred thousand times more glory than you have yet seen. But you cannot know more about it until you return, for you have come to this place in flesh and blood, but you will soon return to it in spirit. Go now, turn home and you will be back to await Judgement Day. And as a memento take these golden stones to give you courage!"

❧

Christopher, usually so reserved, clapped his hands.

"There, you see, Bartholomew, the accounts all agree. When will you stop being so sceptical? There are islands to the west, and they will be scattered along my route all the way to India!"

At the end of every story he hugged me. I had never seen him so happy before, and I provided him with other legends, linking them to his future voyage.

"There are some islands that no one can see, Christopher. Do you remember the seven bishops who would not submit to Arab rule? God gave those brave prelates magic powers. They could make the island where they had found shelter disappear whenever they liked. What better protection could there be against the Muslims who would have wished to pursue them? There's nothing to suggest that those islands are real – apart from a flock of birds circling endlessly over a part of the ocean that looks deserted. Watch the birds, Christopher, there's an island under them, I assure you, so don't worry if your eyes do not see any land, trust the birds! The writers state categorically that from time immemorial there has been profound complicity between birds and islands. And what's more, Christopher, now that I come to think of it, are not birds, which last longer than clouds, islands in the sky?"

110

He listened to me, open-mouthed. Those who did not know Christopher are unaware that in some ways he never ceased to be a child, loving distances, brilliance and showy costumes, as children do. And as a child does, he sought first for the love of his father and mother, only this time not of Domenico and Susanna but of the king and queen, Ferdinand and Isabella.

It is in the long childhood of the little Genoese boy that the wellsprings of his soul are to be found.

∗⁂

Those few people who still take an interest in me, and come to my retreat to ask my news, always ask me why I chose an island for my last home.

Las Casas is no exception. I look at him, I smile, and by way of thanking him for his attention to my story, I carefully explain my way of approaching death.

Everyone is an island, wouldn't you agree? An island surrounded by other islands, separated from them by currents that are sometimes easy to cross and sometimes difficult. It varies from day to day.

What is old age?

The island that I am is beginning to shrink, eroded further every year by the pitiless sea of time. One by one, whole parts of my life have fallen into the water: laughter, love, a taste for wine. I move less and less far as time goes by. I meet people less often, I eat and sleep and dream and remember less and less. I hear more faintly and see more dimly all the time. The shadows are laying siege to me. Soon they will swallow me up.

Now you understand why I chose an island for my last home: the island reminds me that I resemble it. Like the island, I am fragile; like the island, I am under threat. The sight of the island teaches me how to die.

Las Casas will go back, delighted, and tell everyone that the former governor, Bartholomew, has achieved wisdom and is awaiting his last hour in peace.

Absolute nonsense!

I don't talk to anyone about the real war I am waging.

The more we shrink with age, the more room in us is taken up by our ghosts. I know them. They take their time. They are preparing for the last assault. Listen: the dogs are barking.

Suddenly, and there was no advance notice of this whim, my brother decided that it was time for him to take a wife.

Was it the daily work on our parchments that had aroused such a wish in him? They used to say that our inks gave off vapours making cartographers indulge in the unhealthy practice of solitary pleasure. They also used to say that the constant scratching of our pens on the maps irritated the nerves to the point of madness. And that narrowing our eyes so much to write out, in fine calligraphy, tiny names of ports and capes all along the coastlines gave cartographers hallucinations that usually involved naked women …

Or should the spices of Lisbon and the *vinho verde* of Porto be held solely responsible?

I am inclined to think that the reason for Christopher's conduct is to be sought elsewhere, not in any physical disorder but in common sense. My brother knew that an insignificant Genoese like him could never carry out his wide-ranging projects without money or patronage.

"We'll start by learning Latin." For once, he condescended to explain his logic to me without any sarcastic remarks. "First, then we'll be better informed when we take part in divine service, and we'll be able to praise God better. Next, it will help us to read the works we need to know for the Enterprise more easily, without calling on anyone else for help. Finally, a good reputation as a Latin scholar can only be useful in my plan to marry: seamen, and more particularly Genoese seamen, often appear very uncouth to the nobility."

"You want to marry an aristocratic lady?"

"Yes, or what's the point?"

"And why do you want me to study Latin with you?"

"For your personal education. And to make it more difficult for people to work out my game."

Vere dignum et justum est, aequum et salutare, nos tibi semper, et ubiques gratias agere.

Latin lessons were held on certain evenings of the week by a priest of St Julian's Church. The other students in our little class were five black men. The episcopate had chosen them for their intelligence. They had been taught the true faith, and now they were being prepared for ordination before they were sent back to Africa to convert their savage brothers.

To accustom us to the order of words, our teacher began by making us repeat that easy phrase: *Vere dignum et justum est [...] gratias agere.*

"It is very meet, right, and our bounden duty that we should at all times and in all places give thanks unto thee, O God ..."

I don't know the reason – it must be buried deep in the mysteries of their race –but this manner of speech set off great hilarity in our African companions.

At first the priest was taken aback. Then he went on.

In qua nobis spes beatae resurrectionis effulsit, sit quos contristat certa moriendi conditio, eosdem consoletur futurae immortalitatis promissio.

This reference to certain death and the promise of eternal life redoubled the mirth of the future black missionaries. Their roars of laughter echoed through the vault of the church, much to the alarm and indignation of a group of old women who used to pray there in the evenings. Then they began clucking like turkeys and their bodies were racked by unseemly undulations.

The priest, a small man with a big belly, expressed his displeasure to his superiors. He called on my brother and me, the only two white men in the group, as his witnesses when he wondered what deranged mind could have conceived the idea of believing in the intelligence of the negroes. And it was to these savages that preaching the Gospel was to be entrusted! Meanwhile, he said, he saw it was up to him to tame these wild creatures. They would find out who they were dealing with! He wagged a menacing finger and cried, in rather too shrill a voice, "If you are possessed by the Devil, then leave the house of God!"

Two deacons had already been summoned and were on their way towards the demonic figures, who gradually calmed down, although they were still shaken by violent hiccups.

One of the blacks, not in the least abashed, gave us the explanation. For some time God had been lavishing good things upon them. First they were freed, then came an end to whipping and much better food, followed by recruitment to train as priests and instruction in the catechism. How could they not rejoice in the Most High? And was not the joy of his creatures a way of praising the Creator? Should he have spurned the new and immense privilege of learning Latin, the language of the servants of God? And the prospect of resurrection had delighted them so much that they were unable to restrain their joy. Should the improbable gift of escaping the common threat of death be considered a small and worthless thing? Why did the Portuguese, although according to themselves they were devout believers, always look so glum when eternal life awaited them?

There was no stopping him. The overflowing emotion that had made him burst out laughing now set off this flood of words.

The argument went on for a long time. The priest had a hard time of it trying to get his class back to learning Latin. The church closed, and the lesson had to come to an end.

However, our teacher was beaming. "We didn't get very far with Latin today, but the lesson that this primitive man has given us is worth all the grammar lessons in the world!" He cast an indulgent eye on the excited movements of our five new friends. "And now they're dancing! How very discerning our bishop was! Whatever other people's opinion may be, I always supported him. Go in peace, I'll see you tomorrow evening, and don't forget the first declension!"

And so we learnt Latin in the cheerful company of those remarkable African dialecticians. I took advantage of it to learn their native tongues.

I did so against Christopher's will. In his usual way, my brother allowed himself no rest nor any deviation from the path that he saw ahead. He had decided that Latin was necessary for him, so he put his mind to it day and night. He couldn't understand why I didn't concentrate my energies.

"Spreading your interests so widely is leprosy of the spirit, Bartholomew, and you're the worst leper of all! If you really want to acquire knowledge that will be useful to our Enterprise, learn Chinese or the language of Cipango! Pull yourself together. What use will the dialects of the south be when we're going to sail west?"

Much to Christopher's annoyance, I remained faithful to my own nature, which was so different from his. I let myself take long excursions into the language of our black friends.

In that way I learned that on the Gold Coast, water is called *enchou*. "Welcome" is *berre berre*, the term for a chicken is *couque roucouque*, and gold is *choqua*.

If I remember all those words today, when I have forgotten so much else, it is because they must have lodged in the last nooks and crannies of my brain that are still alive and well. One of them has never left me. I have only to speak it for a wave of merriment to pass through me, even at moments of my deepest despair: *choque*.

I had to go to some trouble to learn it. When I asked the future priests what words were used in their African home for the game of love, they wouldn't tell me. They claimed that God himself would blush to hear them spoken.

Thanks to the wine of Porto, however, I loosened those pious tongues. *Choque choque* was the term they used at home for such shameful practices.

Now that the time for confession has come, I can answer my brother in the matter of useful knowledge. Unfortunately for the salvation of my soul, I must admit that I used few other words so often. I had a great liking for black flesh and it has never left me all my life. *Choque choque.* I had only to repeat those words to have the most strongly barred doors opened to me, so homesick were black women for their lost and distant land. I note that with the exception of a single letter that word is the same as the word for gold in those parts, *choqua*.

At last Christopher thought that he had made enough progress with Latin and had a reputation in the city as an assiduous student. He could now move on to the second phase of his campaign.

One fine morning he asked Master Andrea for a private word with him. Our master made a face. He was expecting what, thrifty man that he was, he feared most: a request for higher pay, along with a threat to go and work for one of his many competitors if it was not forthcoming.

Imagine his surprise – and relief – when Christopher told him of a less harmful plan: he wanted to get married. But whom should he choose for a wife and where could he find her? As a good geographer, Andrea certainly knew those parts of the city where he would have some chance of meeting the eye of a young girl of good birth.

"All Saints' Convent," he promptly replied.

Before the more prudent of the crusaders who set off from Lisbon to fight the infidel left, they had taken the precaution of immuring their wives in a convent where their chastity was sure to be preserved. They were soon joined by young ladies whose virginity was medically proven and who were kept under strict supervision.

What prayers, threats, supervision and dietary regime did the nuns of the Order of St James use, over the centuries, to keep the Devil away from a hundred or so female bodies deprived of pleasure? It is a mystery and a miracle. But whatever the facts of the matter, the Convent of All Saints enjoyed the very highest reputation.

On the recommendation of our master Christopher, as "the scion of a noble Genoese family, having escaped from a terrible ship-wreck and thus obviously marked out by God for a brilliant future," described also as "a young man of exquisite modesty who is known, despite his youth, as a great navigator," was allowed to gain entrance to the well-guarded precincts of the convent.

Attendance at Mass there three times was enough for him to bring his plan to a successful conclusion. On the first occasion, his height and the fiery colour of his hair attracted all eyes. Over the following six days, the young ladies of the convent were busily discussing him, asking naïve questions, for few of them had ever met a redhead before: wasn't hair of that colour a sign that he was possessed by a demon? Did the freckles on his face, they wondered, keeping their voices down, go on under his shirt and even lower? It was a pleasantly intriguing idea. Anyway, they hoped he would come back. There wasn't much fun to be had in the Convent of All Saints.

At the second Mass, the nature of the young ladies' curiosity had changed. Andrea had circulated the information that this man, who was the colour of the setting sun, had decided to start a family and had chosen this convent, with its high reputation, as a place where he might meet the future mother of his many children. The information worked so well that calculating glances were cast at Christopher, even by the married women: supposing, they thought – and God forbid! – that my husband never comes back, but is lying in some infidel graveyard, might not this energetic Genoese offer me the unhoped-for chance of a second marriage? As for the girls who still had their virginity and were beginning to find time hanging heavy on their hands until they lost it, while the Portuguese suitors who came to the convent Sunday after Sunday were too dull and too small, they decided to try their luck.

At the end of the third Mass, after a certain amount of jostling, one bold young lady came closer to Christopher than the others and dropped her missal, whereupon he picked it up.

He returned to the studio in high delight.

"If I heard it properly through all the noise, her name is Filipa Moniz Perestrello. What do we know about that family?"

Andrea made some inquiries. You may wonder why our master was helping Christopher with so much enthusiasm; it was because he didn't want to lose him. Cartographers are seldom able to employ someone who knows as much about the sea as Christopher did, and if Andrea could get him married off in Lisbon, he had a good chance of keeping him. He soon reported back to us.

There was nothing very striking about the maternal, Moniz side of the beautiful Filipa's family, but it was of a good and old noble line that had provided many blameless servants of the Crown. Fortunately Filipa's paternal family, the Perestrellos, were of a very different kind. A gentleman of that name had left Piacenza in Italy to settle in Lisbon around 1390. The climate agreed with him, and he had four children there. Richarte, the eldest, took holy orders, and in spite of his strikingly dissolute way of life became Prior of Santa Marina; he had two sons. A close alliance of debauchery with religion seems to have been the speciality of the Perestrello family. Richarte's two sisters, Isabel and Branca, succumbed at one and the same time to the charms of the Archbishop of Lisbon, Dom Pedro de Noronha. These doubly illicit relationships produced three children, all of them recognized as his by that holy man the archbishop, who proved as good a father as he was an ardent lover.

This was the first part of Master Andrea's report, and he thought it a good moment to stop and get his breath back, feeling exhausted by telling a tale of such depravity. But Christopher was not allowing him any respite.

"You said there were four children. There's still one missing, if I counted them correctly."

"Ah, the fourth was your future father-in-law, first name Bartolomeu – another Bartholomew, like your brother. Before I draw you his portrait, which is not very edifying, I should point out that if you decide to enter the Perestrello family by marrying this girl, it makes you something like a brother-in-law to the archbishop."

"Go on."

Apparently that sorry character Bartolomeu, my namesake, did nothing with his life but roam around down by the harbour. Christopher gave a start.

"So what was he doing there?"

"How should I know? Whatever it is that men commonly do when they are down by the harbour. I suppose they run after women of ill repute and pick up stories. That's what I've heard about him; he had a liking for the secrets of the sea."

One fine day, Andrea went on, two sailors told him that they had discovered an island to the north of Madeira with a very good climate as well as a wealth of luxuriant flora. Bartolomeu went straight off to the king and had himself appointed hereditary captain of this new land, which he immediately called Porto Santo.

The following week, guided by the two sailors from whom he had heard of the discovery, he set off at once to take possession of his domain.

Unfortunately Bartolomeu Perestrello, alarmed by the terrible prospect of living on a vegetable diet alone, in other words dying of starvation, had tried to bring his own meat supply in the form of a rabbit – to be precise, a pregnant female rabbit. It was a bad mistake. As soon as the rabbit's paws touched the ground she gave birth. The litter quickly grew. By next Easter, brother rabbits were copulating with sister rabbits. By Pentecost there were yet more young. And so on – and on, and on.

In September the first rabbit had dozens of descendants, and they had eaten every plant on the island. The furious Bartolomeu gave orders for a huge fire to be kindled. It destroyed all the rabbits, but also the huts that had been built with such pains. All that the hereditary captain of the island could do with his inheritance of ashes was to return to Lisbon, crestfallen, to be met by laughter even louder than the chronic hilarity of the seagulls. Portugal, normally a solemn nation, had never laughed so much. "It's said," Andrea concluded this tale, "that the poor man died of such a gale of mirth. That was some twenty years ago."

But my brother was no longer interested in this story and its comic side. I am sure that some time before it ended he had gone aboard his favourite ship, the ship of dreams. Slowly, like someone going to see a house once more before deciding to buy it, he nodded his head. Yes, he would accept a marriage into the Perestrello family. It suited his purpose.

When Andrea said he could go on looking into the Perestrello family (there were still many shady aspects to it), Christopher was almost angry. He already felt linked to these people. "No, that will do," he said, clapping the cartographer on the shoulder. Once again my brother's self-confidence amazed me. That is the way those in command treat their subordinates, whereas Christopher was only twenty-five and it was our master who had been working on his behalf. That very evening he went to ask for the young lady's hand and the next day preparations for his marriage to Filipa began.

My brother's will was at work in an almost godlike manner. He made the decisions. And what he had decided, whether it concerned events or people, became reality. He had decided that it was time for him to marry. And a wife had duly presented herself. A wife who, miraculously, already loved him, and whom he, no less miraculously, would also love. His will had the power to create amorous sentiments.

*

I was my brother's keeper. It was for me to make sure whether this marriage, like so many other marriages, might not become the enemy of a man's dreams and triumph over them.

I took advantage of a visit that Filipa was paying to some cousins to invite them to the wedding in person. They lived on the road to Santarém. I offered to escort her and she accepted. She was no fool. She knew that she would not escape my questioning.

As we went along I asked her, without beating about the bush, what kind of love she felt for her future husband? She told me that she was not one of those knowledgeable persons who can distinguish between different kinds of love, but that a wave of heat had overwhelmed her a moment after they first met, and now it filled her from the top of her head to the tips of her toes, and that according to what her mother had rather ambiguously told her, this wave was the extreme form of love: "You should be glad of it, daughter. Your poor father, may he rest in peace, never swept me off my feet with such warm and whole-hearted sensations, far from it!"

I blushed, and went on with my interrogation. "Do you think you'll be able to accept him exactly as he is?"

"You'll hear me say it in church. I shall tell the priest so, loud and clear!"

"Are you ready to sustain the dream that he carries about with him?"

"With all the power in me."

"Even if he devours you alive, as he has devoured me and is devouring himself? And what power do you think you have, with your pale complexion and a constitution that seems so frail?"

"My pallor and fragility are only a memory of the time when I was still cold, and waiting for a flame to give me life. Do you hear how I am speaking to you? That's the proof that warm blood is returning to my veins already."

"Didn't your mother warn you to be on your guard?"

"My mother says that his dream, and the future glory it will bring, will save our family from the ridicule we have suffered ever since that matter of the rabbits."

We were walking along the banks of the ever-tranquil Tagus. I thought of certain considerably more turbulent geographical areas. I thought of that notorious island Porto Santo, which I did not yet know, where Filipa had spent her childhood. How do islands stand up to the constant battering of the sea? When you live on an island, even an island plagued by rabbits, its courage inspires you. It must certainly have been there that Filipa forged so indomitable a spirit, and her body could only obey that spirit willy-nilly. Out of the corner of my eye I watched her walking along beside me. When she slipped on the pebbles she caught at the branch of an olive tree to save herself from falling, and then she went on again without complaining of the fast pace I set. Beads of sweat broke out on her temples. And a wind arose inside me, a wind that I know more intimately than any other, the keen wind of jealousy. Listen to me, Las Casas: I never, not once, desired this woman; she was much too thin for me. I like real flesh, ample and sturdy, all-enveloping bodies that carry you away, bodies in which you can lose yourself. No, I was jealous of the fine flame of love that my brother had lit. What fire did he have in him that set everyone he met alight?

A little later I went on with my inquisition, but I had already made up my own mind.

"And where are you thinking of living?"

"Wherever he wants to."

"What's your opinion of his Enterprise?"

She was finding it difficult to talk because she was so short of breath. Taking pity on her, I suggested a rest and we sat down on a little rise in the ground. While Filipa got her breath back I told her how well I thought of her.

She turned to me. "I didn't need your opinion, but I'm happy to hear it."

I told myself that the crew of the Columbus Enterprise had just acquired a valuable new member.

A man who loves his brother and, on hearing of his imminent marriage, sings and dances, proclaiming to all quarters of the compass his delight in the good news, the best thing to have happened since the creation of the world, is a liar.

It is obvious that a part of him is happy; how could he fail to welcome the coming happiness of a beloved brother?

But another part of him is making a wry face or weeping. Someone hitherto unknown is taking away his elder brother, and soon all he will have of that brother, at the best, will be scraps and morsels.

Coming out of the church where Christopher had just been married, I staggered and stopped dead on the forecourt outside the building, at the top of a flight of steps, while the church bells ringing a peal did their best to brighten the sky. I felt as if one more step would take me plunging into a great gulf, the gulf of a life without him.

I can hear you laughing at me. What a delicate nature our friend Bartholomew has! What feminine sensitivity! Hadn't Christopher, whom he claims to have loved so much, already accustomed his brother to parting from him since childhood, parting from him again and again?

When you come to think of it, marriage is a route to be navigated like any other. That idea gave me fresh courage.

Next day, when I thought he would be busy with entirely different and very intimate matters, whom should I see arrive, with open arms and a smile on his lips, but my brother the newly married man.

Knowing that his presence was the rarest and most unlikely of gifts, he used it with consummate art: he would arrive when he was least expected, sure that his appearance would leave its mark on the souls of others forever. Sure, too, that by this means he was binding those souls to him for life … and could ask them to do anything.

Christopher did not change his method that day. No sooner had he embraced me and said a few cajoling words about his happiness in seeing me, Bartholomew, at his wedding, the only representative of his family in Genoa and thus incomparably precious (etc.), no sooner had he sworn that his marriage would not change in any way the indescribable, inalienable, indestructible (etc.) fraternal bond between us, than he lowered his voice and made his request.

"I need you, Bartholomew. I have something to ask you."

"Ask away."

Christopher had such charismatic force that serving its purposes, whatever they might be, always appeared to you at the time the sole reason for your existence. Whether you were man, woman, plant or animal, you had come here on earth only to contribute to the dreams of this tall, red-headed seaman.

"It's about a book, Bartholomew."

We had fallen easily into our old habits dating from before his marriage, and here we were again, just as if Filipa had never existed, sitting in front of a glass of *vinho verde* at our favourite tavern, the Silent Parrot.

"My in-laws have put me on its trail. Apparently this book tells you everything."

"Everything about what?"

"Everything about the shape and size of the earth. Everything about the dimensions of the oceans and thus the distance of the continents from each other. Everything about the possibility of living on the equator and on the other side of the globe."

He was constantly interrupted by friends, cartographers or sailors, startled to see this very new husband so early in the day. What are you doing here? Finished already? You don't waste much time, do you? Quicker off the mark than a rabbit! ... As Filipa was of noble family, the wedding had been celebrated with great splendour and no one in Lisbon could have failed to know about it.

Christopher sent these nuisances unceremoniously packing, waving them away with the back of his hand as if swatting insects unworthy of any explanation.

He leaned forward, his mouth brushing my ear.

"*Ymago mundi*, the *Image of the World,* That's the title. The author is a certain Pierre d'Ailly, for a long time the Bishop of Cambrai, a town in the north of France. I need that book."

And off he went, back to his marriage, without so much as another glance for me. He was well aware of the hold he had on me. He knew that I was already fully occupied by my mission, and thus reassured of my place in his life I would be happy to devote myself to him. If he gives me the task of this research, I told myself, confidential and important to his Enterprise as it is, it is first because he trusts me more than anyone else; second, and mainly, because in spite of the arrival of Filipa in his life, his brother Bartholomew (me) still has a special place in it.

With these ideas in my head, and my jealousy dispelled, I told Master Andrea that I had made a vow to go on pilgrimage. It was my pretext for setting off north next morning. I did so with some trepidation. I had always lived close to water, and in going from Genoa to Lisbon I had either skirted the coast of the Mediterranean or crossed parts of Spain making for the shores of the ocean.

This time, moving a little further from the shore of any sea or ocean with every step I took, I felt as if I were tearing myself away from life. I did not expect to encounter anything but sorrow and difficulty.

How can anyone feel free, I wondered, living far from the sea? How can anyone keep from stifling, surrounded by land and nothing but land? It's not surprising that those unfortunate prisoners who live in the middle of fields and forests never stop making books. When you have no ship – or rather, no water where ships can sail – your only means of escape is reading.

I had decided to start my research in Strasbourg, the source of that recently invented industry known as printing.

I had seen very few of the books produced by that method myself, and I had not been impressed by the quality of those few. On the other hand, I did know that printing had made life very much easier for the priests.

Perhaps, Brother Jerome, you have forgotten the principle behind *confessionalia*, the confessional letters also known as indulgences? I have noticed the cheerful cast of your character: you can brush aside any distressing subject without much effort. So I had better refresh your memory. Christ and the saints, having never committed any sin, accumulated an abundant store of merit. So why not allow Christians of good will who, none the less, are miserable sinners like all men, to benefit by it? Mother Church, blessed be her name, therefore had the idea of selling such letters to the faithful. In exchange, their sins were forgiven.

And the Church could have made even more out of these transactions if it had not taken so long to write out indulgences. Priests had to copy out the form in detail every time. If they did not take such care, buyers didn't trust their purchases. You can understand why they were so demanding, when their entry into Paradise depended on it.

Any method of reproducing letters of indulgence easily was therefore welcome. If the invention of printing meant that plenty of them could be manufactured, the wealth of Mother Church would grow, and consequently would allow her to raise armies and navies to fight the Turk better, that was all to the good!

But it remained to be seen whether this clever manipulation of leaden characters could produce masterpieces to compare with those of our illuminators, and my expectations were not high.

I will not tell you the detailed story of my journey. I have too much else to say in what time remains to me. You should know, however, that I developed a taste for crossing those landscapes. My longing for the great, ever-moving presence of the sea was assuaged by the sight of the plains. How could I not see them as long waves frozen in place, as a result of God's decision to put a stop to any horizontal movement in this part of his Creation?

At last I saw a tall spire of red stone appear, and the pedlars who were on the road with me said it was Strasbourg Cathedral.

So I had reached another kind of port, a haven from which books rather than ships set out. And when you come to think of it, ships and books are like each other in that both make discoveries. I asked a passing cleric to direct me to the printers' quarter of the city.

In the rue aux Ours, workshops stood side by side and work seemed to be in progress night and day. The new industry was not short of commissions.

I opened the first door I came to and met with a friendly reception. At the inn where I was lodging, I had taken trouble to spruce myself up so that my youth and foreign accent would only add to the good impression I made. I introduced myself as a Portuguese envoy from the Royal Committee of Mathematicians.

"Is the book *Ymago mundi*, written by Bishop d'Ailly, by any chance among those that you print?"

They said they had heard tell of the book as an unparalleled collection of knowledge, but had never seen it.

As if by way of apology, they insisted on showing me the latest products of their workshop and I was obliged to reconsider the disdain that I had brought with me: some of the printed books stood comparison with our illuminated volumes.

As soon as I had mentioned the magnificent Bible in the possession of my Portuguese king, I was almost submerged. The two men employed in the printing works ran to their shelves and came back with their arms full.

"What do you think of this one?"

"No, I think this is the Bible the young gentleman would rather see."

They jostled each other for the chance to show off their work, arguing all the time.

Some of the Bibles were plain and simple, slightly smudged black characters on grey paper of poor quality. Others were genuine masterpieces, with illuminations in three colours set on the page like the pediment of a church.

How can anyone escape Bibles?

Just as in Holy Scripture of blessed repute, stories give rise to other stories, more and more new stories, these Bibles seemed to be giving birth to other Bibles, more and more of them. Would Bibles one day, perhaps, endlessly multiplied by these magic printing presses, invade the earth and stifle humanity? I took care not to put my iconoclastic thoughts into words.

Prudently, and not without expressing my respect for the sacred texts, blessings on them, I asked if the printers had other publications available.

"In what field? Our catalogue is getting larger every month."

"Science," I stammered.

The two young men were visibly disappointed. They had thought my mind was on more elevated matters. They went to search in the store behind the shop and came back with publications which they thought might suit my interests, holding them at arm's length as if they stank. I should say that they concerned the workings of the human body.

I remember that there were two calendars: one setting out the most suitable times at which to bleed a patient, the other offering the same kind of advice on purging, calling on the authority of the stars in their courses. The German titles stick in my memory: *Aderlasskalender* and *Laxierkalender*.

I praised them as interesting, said how grateful I was very politely and went on to the next shop, where the same thing happened.

I was beginning to despair of bringing back the book that Christopher wanted when a man selling simples, who happened to be in one of the shops and heard my request, told me that he had once had the *Ymago* in his hands, and he remembered seeing the name of the city of Louvain on the cover.

I cursed my brother. Now I would have to go even further north.

And I set off again, not happy with my fate but resigned to it. Christopher was my elder brother. God himself had wanted me to be the younger and therefore under my brother's sway. No doubt our roles would be shared out in the same way in future: the sea for him, the roads on land for me. Navigation for him, the wind, the sea air and the wide horizons. The dust of the roads for me, along with the dust of books and the asphyxiation of those who shut themselves up – or let themselves be shut up – in pages or on missions that are subordinate but necessary.

Although our main business at Master Andrea's studio in Lisbon was cartography, we also sold books, like all our competitors. The finest of the printed works to have passed through our hands was one from that mysterious city of Louvain. Merchants are usually glad to find a buyer quickly. In this case, we were very sorry to sell it. We had hardly received the little volume when a book-lover turned up, having got wind of it I don't know how. Others followed him, and went sadly away, for we had already sold it. No doubt the enticing title, *De duobus amantibus*, played a certain part. It contained licentious pages that I enjoyed very much. The two protagonists, Euryale, a young prince in the Emperor's retinue, and the beautiful Lucretia, unhappily married to an old Siennese count, had an illicit but strong and frankly described passion for each other. Andrea's regret at parting too soon with this delightful work changed to fury when he heard its author's story. Enea Silvio Piccolomini had been elected pope in 1458 under the name of Pius II. Imagine the price we could have asked for a work of that kind if, poor innocents that we were, we had known that its author's charming name concealed a sovereign pontiff.

Admiring the quality of the printing and the elegant typography, I had been careful to make a note of the names of the two publishers: Thierry Martens and John of Westphalia.

I asked for them as soon as I arrived. I was told that the two masters were no longer in partnership, and Martens had gone to pursue his profession in the port of Antwerp. So I went and introduced myself to the publisher still in Louvain.

John of Westphalia received me at first with ordinary civility, but very soon his courtesy changed to lively interest. He had never seen any oceans. He wanted to ask me about them. By that evening we were friends.

☙

Throughout my visit to Louvain, I met men every day who, to my astonishment, took not the faintest interest in the sea. They had other preoccupations, which seemed to fill their days and a good part of their nights, judging by the number of candle ends that a cart took away every morning.

I was both staggered and, to be honest, slightly relieved to discover that it was possible for a man to devote himself body and soul to tasks other than finding the western passage to the Indies.

⁂

Here is a scene to give you some idea of the climate that reigned in that city. My memory contains ten or so others of the same kind.

There's a sudden knock at the door. The new arrival comes in without waiting for a reply; he is a very young man with curly hair. Both his hands are raised in the air, and he is jumping up and down like a puppeteer.

"It's coming, it's coming!"

The librarian leaps to his feet, and despite his frailty, for he is skeletally thin, rushes outside. A group is approaching: a man whose dusty garments show that he has come a long way, surrounded by students joyfully escorting him.

The librarian stops on the threshold of his house, in the manner of a man receiving illustrious guests. The dusty man suddenly dances a jig as if a flea had bitten him. But he simply wants to get at something in a pocket – what kind of thing? It is wrapped in cloth, and at last, to applause, he succeeds in extricating it from the depths of his pocket. Then he places it in the hands held out to him. While good souls lead the dusty man away to his well-earned reward of enough beer to quench his thirst, we return to the peace and quiet of the library. The longest table is chosen to receive the wrapped object.

Two candlesticks are brought in. Slowly, the packet is opened. A cover comes into view. I bend over it: Roger Bacon, *Summa de sophismatibus et distinctionibus*.

"This is it," murmurs the librarian. "This is what we've been waiting for so long. Thank you, God, for allowing it to reach our university intact!"

"Amen," my neighbours reply.

A lay brother brings a basin. Everyone has to wash his hands before he is allowed to touch the book lovingly.

Then the librarian picks it up, raises it, and says, indicating the shelves where the most valuable books are lined up, "You are welcome among your own kind!"

Up to this point I had kept quiet as if I were attending a religious ceremony, fascinated by this ritual and the fervour surrounding it. I was burning to ask a question and couldn't resist it any longer.

"Do you welcome all books like that?"

"Why, yes, when they come from so far away and bring so much knowledge with them."

I turned and went thoughtfully back to my inn.

If Louvain was a land-locked harbour, its ships were books, ships with invisible crews since only their captains, the authors, were on view. However, they too came into harbour carrying treasures to be deposited not in warehouses but in the pages of the books.

There were two differences: these ships, ships on dry land, made only a single journey. And once they had revealed their secrets, they did not clutter up the quays but rested quietly on shelves, like pigeons asleep on their perches.

My contact with these scholars who were just as feverishly anxious for knowledge as my brother made me wonder: was it not vitally important to the human mind to be possessed by this kind of fever, whatever the reason for it?

Another question, even more threatening than the first to the fraternal bond between Christopher and me, was: well, why not?

Why not medicine?

A cheerful trio of medical students, my drinking companions, were trying to persuade me. Beer after beer, I imagined myself immersed in the secrets of the body, the dazzled observer of women who would have to be undressed because they needed medical care. Then, with the aid of more beer, and to the applause of my friends, I became the knight chosen by God to push back the borders of sin.

Twice, the trio took me off with them to the undertaker who, it seemed, was popular with these young men. For the price of a coin, the good fellow would open up corpses for us. Thanks to those corpses, I learned how to cut open a stomach; how to saw through ribs to take out the heart; how, in an attempt to approach the mystery of virility, to dissect the male organ. We had brought beer with us, plenty of beer. We drank all night to celebrate our skill as surgeons of the future. What could be better, afterwards, than vomiting the beer among friends? Too bad for the dissected corpse if no one was still in a fit state to close it up.

⁂

Why not botany?

It was the day after a drinking session. As I took small and cautious steps through the countryside, I was trying to recover my sense of equilibrium after the dissipation of the night before. A pale, tall young man was coming towards me over the field, bent double.

I asked if he wanted help and what was the nature of his terrible malady. Was it congenital or accidental?

Miraculously, he straightened up, brandishing a basket brimming over with stems and leaves. "I'm botanizing."

"You seem very calm on this earth where everyone else is in a state of agitation."

"It's the sight of plants, and even more their company. They are born, they love, they die just like us, but they do it in silence."

"Yes, but how boring to be a plant! Forced to spend your whole life with your feet in the same plot of soil!"

"Oh, make no mistake about it, plants wander around."

I was beginning to understand. I recalled the strange cages full of plants that the navigators brought back.

We talked until nightfall, bending over most of the time to pick this or that remarkable individual member of the vast plant kingdom.

I still regret having gone no further in my acquaintance with those beings, just as alive as we are, but far more dignified in their silence.

※

I could go on with my almost infinite list. Why not this, that or the other? Louvain was full of knowledge and cheerful young men exploring it, all of them lovers of good beer. How could anyone choose between all those fields of science, all those possible ways of life? Why not chemistry, which studies the secret attractions of matter? Why not physiology, which studies the workings of the body? Why not astronomy, which finds logic in imagining the stars?

※

John of Westphalia had immediately found me the book for which I had come, on my brother's orders: the *Ymago mundi*, which was to be so important in the history of the enlargement of the world. Once my mission was accomplished I could have gone back to Lisbon at any time. So why did I keep putting off my departure day after day?

There are times when your life hesitates: another road comes into view beside the way you have foreseen. Friendship, like love, can change the course of a man's existence. John of Westphalia suggested that I could settle down close to him, and we would open a printing works together. He argued that I already knew part of his trade and that I had the patience to excel in it, along with meticulous attention and a taste for learning and passing on what I had learnt. Moreover, he said, the great advantage of that trade, inestimable for natures like mine, curious about everything, was that it approached all knowledge without limiting itself to any one field. Once a book is finished, you see, he told me, you immediately become just as enthusiastic for another field of knowledge. Books, he added, were as good as ships at increasing human understanding and reading was a voyage. Above all, a great intellectual movement was developing here in the south of the Low Countries, and if I agreed to stay for a few weeks he could introduce me to certain philosophers whom he knew well. They spoke of liberty and offered exciting prospects to mankind.

133

I spent a whole week trying to make up my mind.

Christopher never knew anything about this indecision. If I had told him, he wouldn't have listened, still less would he have understood. He thought only of the west.

Why did I finally decide not to change course?

Regrets are no use. We are made of water, and like water, we follow the main slope of our lives.

No living person has ever kept me such close and intimate company as the *Image of the World* all through my journey home. We were like a married couple besotted with one another, we were never apart, we slept, ate and went on our way together, the skin of one next to the skin of the other, in my case human skin, in the case of the book calfskin, vellum, with gold lettering sunk into its pale cover.

At first the cold weather had protected me. No one is surprised to see a traveller wearing a heavy cloak, and who could guess that this particular heavy cloak concealed a treasure?

Further south, approaching the city of Poitiers, mendacity came to my aid. I mingled with a group of pilgrims, saying that I was on my way to the shrine of St James myself.

"What's that book you carry close to your heart?" asked one of them. "It seems to be very precious."

"Take a look. It's a work by a cardinal, Pierre d'Ailly."

"What does he write about?"

"Schisms in the Church. Debates between theologians."

"There's only one God, surely? So why make life more complicated?"

And he struck up a *Veni creator* in a voice loud enough to scare all the vipers for miles around.

As so often in my life, it was the sin of curiosity that nearly caused my downfall. My pilgrim companions had left me for a day, going off at a tangent to pay their respects to the relics of a saint, I don't remember which. On the pretext of having a sore foot, I said I would wait for their return.

But as soon as the back of the last pilgrim had disappeared behind a hedge of hazels, I threw myself upon the *Ymago*. I had never before had the time to look through it at any length without being disturbed.

After ascertaining, with a swift glance around the horizon, that there was no living creature in sight capable of taking any interest in cosmography – neither the two larks singing just above my head on the juniper bush, nor the cows at the far end of the field, still less the earthworms at work beneath the grass or the crayfish lazily lying in the stream – I began to turn the pages.

> To the right of Mount Imaus, where the Caucasus ends, lies the promontory of Samara … The magic arts were born in Persia, where the giant Nembroth went after languages were confused, and he taught the Persians how to use fire …

You could certainly travel through the pages of a book as well as you could sail on a ship, and with no risk of sea-sickness or scurvy.

I had immersed myself in Chapter Two, "Of the spheres and other divisions as they are set out in the Heavens", when I found that there was not enough light. A cloud must have hidden the sun. I raised my head. A troop of men of sinister appearance surrounded me. I had never heard them coming. I knew my own physical weakness: when I read my ears are closed; I am deaf. I am only a pair of eyes following the letters along the line, fascinated.

The fiercest of the men spoke to me in a language that I did not know. Guessing what he wanted, I emptied my pockets and my pouch. But not fast enough. Blows were beginning to rain down on me and fell even harder when they saw what poor pickings I had provided. So far I had clung to the *Ymago*, but now it too was snatched away from me. No doubt these bandits thought there was wealth hidden inside it (and they were correct). The book was quickly torn apart and its pages ripped out one by one, inspected and then thrown away in growing fury.

After another hail of blows, I must have lost consciousness. I remember the relief that I felt as I fell into the void; evidently these men, who did not respect books, could not be rival cartographers. When I came round again, calm reigned once more.

Luckily it was not raining. A second stroke of luck was that there was no wind. You might have thought that the countryside was holding its breath now that the bandits had gone. The air waited to see what would happen next. Even the birds seemed to be fixed motionless in the sky.

A third piece of luck was that the herd of cows was at the other end of the field. They had come closer to watch the scene of violence. What could be more of a pleasant change, when you spend your life ruminating, than watching a fight between human beings, even if it ends abruptly?

Luckily a stream had prevented them from coming closer. I felt sure that inside their large, slobbering heads they were regretting their inability to add these white leaves to their diet of grass; they looked so good to chew. How did I know? The cow is such a placid animal that it seldom shows its emotions. I told myself that at least cattle have that in common with the people of the British Isles, and this powerful political idea gave me the courage to begin my task.

How many hours did it take me to collect all the pages scattered around the meadow one by one? I reached the last when it was dark night. I put them together again as best I could, tucked them inside my garments against my skin, did up my clothing, lay down beside a bank and, lulled by the gratitude that the *Ymago* seemed to be expressing to me, fell asleep at once.

God sent me no other misadventures before I reached Lisbon. In His infinite kindness, He had only wanted to test me, and warn me of the dangers lying in wait for those who are in possession of that authoritative book.

And here was new proof that it was the will of God for the *Ymago* to reach my brother, the man to whom He had clearly given the task of enlarging the visible world.

On one of the scattered pages I had just had time to notice the name of Piccolomini, the author whose work *De duobus amantibus* we had sold at too cheap a price. Not content with venturing into the heated passions of illicit love, the future pope had brought together his geographical and cosmological knowledge in a treatise highly regarded by experts: *Historia rerum ubique gestarum.*

Pierre d'Ailly quoted this work by its title and commented on it with respect.

Today I dream again of the full life of Piccolomini, and I thank God who let us live at a time so rich in people of his elevated kind, men of rich and diverse talents.

Such close bonds were forged between the *Ymago* and me that it seemed less like a book than a member of my family, an ancestor too frail to move about without help, but full of authoritative information from the times when he had lived long ago.

Besides, I had formed the habit of speaking to the book as if it were a travelling companion for whom I was responsible. Are you cold, Ymago? What idiots these soldiers are! I know you can't see the countryside, Ymago, but never mind, it's not interesting.

I felt it was almost a human presence and missed it badly when I gave it to my brother. It had become a friend. For a long time I had to guard my tongue to keep it from talking to the book.

Navigation, perhaps because of the constant movement of the ship, perhaps because of the void all around it, helps you to think or at least to daydream.

As I made for the island of Porto Santo where my brother now lived, I thought of the man who first put it on a map, the Jew Abraham Cresques, author of the *Catalan Atlas*. I thought of the navigator who had told him about it: after what adventures, carried over the sea by what currents and winds as well as by his soul, had he sailed so far west? I thought of those peoples, Phoenicians, Jews, Bedouin, who carry an awareness of routes in their heads. I thought of the island of Majorca which, thanks to the Jews, had been an Alexandria of geography for a while, a temple to the knowledge of maps. I thought again, as I always think, of islands and how they appear and disappear.

The wind was steady and fair, the crew had few manoeuvres to carry out. To pass the time, and perhaps also to avert bad luck, they began discussing storms.

Every man told the usual horror stories of storms at sea and his own luck in surviving them.

I had kept silent so far, but they knew how much experience I had of the sea and wanted to hear my opinion. I hesitated to tell them, since it is not a popular one among seamen and could bring me real trouble. They insisted. So I told them that storms were necessary and furthermore were evidence that God wanted to make the human race pay more attention to His creation.

Ignoring the protests that my remarks aroused, I went on.

"How did Captain Gil Eanes round Cape Bojador, known as Cape Fear, the northernmost limit of Africa, a headland that no one dared to pass? Thanks to a storm. It had carried him far to the west, and once the weather was calm again, he saw that he had rounded that much-feared frontier and his ship had not fallen into an abyss, nor was it burning in Hell.

"Or take another example: how did Captain Zarco, sailing back from the Gold Coast at his leisure in 1419, discover the island of Porto Santo to which we are bound? Again, it was a storm that blew him away from his coastal route skirting the kingdom of Morocco.

"I conclude that storms are useful enemies of our laziness, in league with the noble fever that we call by the name of curiosity. In leading us away from the routes we usually take they force us out of ourselves." And giving way to my taste for philosophizing, I added that our lives on land also had to face storms in the form of bereavement, double-dealing, illness. Either we perish in those storms or we emerge from them greater in stature than before.

As I had expected, I almost ended up with my throat cut or simply thrown overboard. I owed my escape only to the clever diversion of Captain Esun, who offered a double ration of rum to whoever was the first to sight Porto Santo.

But days passed by, and still we did not see our destination. I began to suspect more magic on my brother's part. Don't forget that when he arrived in Lisbon, he had placed me in charge of the islands as he prepared for his voyage. I ended up by acquiring a great store of knowledge about those curious geographical features. Some are fixed, some wander. According to Dionysius of Alexandria, the phenomenon of movement is common among islands. They are surfaces with nothing to link them to the plinth of the earth, so they drift, carried along by the wind or by other forces.

Christopher was sure to have chosen a drifting island for his family home and obviously one that drifted westward. The length it travelled would cut short his great voyage by the same amount.

At last heights rose above the horizon and the captain pointed out to me, rather ironically, that Porto Santo had not shifted at all since he last saw it. Privately, I was cursing myself; I ought to keep a cool head and make sure I didn't credit my brother with greater powers than he really possessed.

Navigators know that sailing the seas is always a matter of guesswork. You understand the real nature of the shore only gradually and you must keep making corrections. What were those shapes emerging from the water after days of empty ocean? I narrowed my eyes and tried to find resemblances. One might have been a saddle, yes, the immense saddle of a gigantic horse. Nothing abnormal about that; didn't Christopher envisage a swift journey?

As we approached, reality took over again. The saddle was only a wide valley between two groups of peaks.

And what was that long, pale ribbon? What was that interminable, long beach doing in the middle of the Atlantic, if not serving as further proof of the infinite goodness of God to sailors? What better could they hope for, after days at sea, than an island with a beach of fine sand around it? I let my eyes wander. Seeing no bay along the coast, no jetty, no landing stage, I asked where we would find the harbour.

"No use looking for one," the captain told me. "We just have to cast anchor. The mountains protect us from all adverse winds. The whole island is our harbour. That's why, to avoid making anyone jealous, it was decided not to dedicate it to any particular saint. Hence its name of Porto Santo."

๕

My brother was waiting for me, carrying a baby in his arms: his son Diego, later to be governor of Hispaniola and viceroy of the Indies. That same Diego whose steps I can hear in the room just above my head, pacing round and round as he comes to a decision, or when he suddenly goes off with a firm tread to pay a visit to his wife.

As was expected of me, I praised the baby's good looks and lively expression. Then the family dined together. Senhora Moniz-Perestrello presided over the company. Luckily she condescended to pretend to be interested in me and asked me about my activities, for the rest of them were interested only in themselves. Her daughter Filipa was looking at my brother and together they were gazing fondly at his little lordship Diego.

Then Christopher took me to see his realm.

Some islands, small as they may be – and you could go all around this one in less than a day – have firmly made up their minds to dissociate themselves from the sea.

Two dogs were barking apathetically at each other without really seeming to believe in their old quarrel. A cart must be coming home; even without seeing it you could hear the rattle of its wooden wheels over the pebbles of the road. A woman was singing. A child was running after birds, chasing them away like thieves. Countless miniature windmills watched over countless fields no larger than sheets dyed pale yellow. None of the windmills was turning. Their little white wings were spread, waiting for wind and they were all facing the setting sun, like those flowers that always follow the course of that heavenly body.

Soon night would fall.

After the hurry and bustle of Lisbon, such peace and quiet gave me vertigo.

"How do you manage to fill your days here?" I asked Christopher.

"Looking after my family's business."

Ever since our Genoese childhood I had been used to expecting anything of my brother – but not that he would turn into a farmer.

Unperturbed, he went on describing his rustic existence. "I'm learning to grow barley. Horses love it and the generals give us a good price to feed the mounts for their cavalry. And I'm getting better acquainted with the dragon tree every day. Did you know that its sap is the colour of blood, so it is much in demand by the Flemish dyers?"

"How long do you plan to stay on this desert island?"

"My first son has just been born and I want him to belong to the west. Porto Santo will be his first ship."

Three times I tried reminding him why I was here: he had ordered me to get him the *Ymago* and here I was with it, after making a long journey. Far from thanking me, as I had hoped, far from abandoning everything else to immerse himself in reading it, he waved away my allusions.

"Later, Bartholomew! You should rest now. Don't you like this landscape?"

Then he sang the praises of his son again. "What do you think, Bartholomew? Be frank with me. Doesn't he have all the intelligence in the world in his eyes?"

And once again he spoke of his beloved Filipa. "She was so sorry not to come with us, Bartholomew, but since we lost our second

141

child at hardly a month old, she has suffered from sudden attacks of faintness."

Once again he spoke of projects that no longer had anything to do with the Indies Enterprise, or at least not for two or three years to come while Diego grew out of infancy. His first concern was to re-gild the family crest by going in for various business ventures, including the sugar trade, which was thriving on the neighbouring island of Madeira.

Going back to my room, and happening to meet Senhora Moniz-Perestrello on the way, I told her how surprised I was, confessing that I hardly recognized my brother.

She raised her arms in the air. "Oh, you don't have to tell me! I chose a conqueror for my son-in-law, Bartholomew, and I got a merchant instead!"

I asked her the reason for this change. She told me, as upset as I was, that love alone was to blame.

"I understand your distress, Bartholomew, and I myself am greatly put out and even more surprised. My daughter makes your brother too happy."

The rest of my visit only confirmed what she had said.

The next day, I made him sit down and finally gave him the *Ymago*.

Incipit *Ymago mundi*
Ymago mundi seu eius ymaginaria descriptio Ipsum velut in
materiali quodam speculo representans non parum utilis esse
vedetur divinarum elucidationem?
Scripturarum

Here begins the *Image of the World*
*It seems that the image of the world, or at least the account that one
can give of the world in showing it as if in a mirror, is not without
utility for the understanding of Holy Scripture, where its various parts
are often mentioned, above all those of the inhabitable world.
For that reason I have been led to write this treatise, and set down
faithfully in abbreviated form all that I thought worthy to be collected
from the works of those scholars who have written on the subject.*

142

The treatise contains forty chapters.
The first chapter treats of the Earth and its parts in general.
Second chapter – Of the spheres and other divisions as they are set out
in the Heavens.
Third chapter – Of the course of the Sun, of the Year, and of the Days
that it shapes.
Fourth chapter – Of the four elements and the way they are distributed
in the world.
Fifth chapter – Of the volume of the Earth and of its dimensions.
Sixth chapter – Of the division of the entire Earth.
Seventh chapter – Of the various opinions of the inhabitability of the Earth.
Eighth chapter – Of the quantity of the Earth that can be inhabited..
Ninth chapter – Of the various climates of the inhabitable earth,
according to the astronomers.
Tenth chapter – Of the longitude and latitude of climates.
Eleventh chapter – Of the anticlimactic and postclimactic zones.
Twelfth chapter – Of the uninhabitable regions.
Thirteenth chapter – Of the differences between the inhabitable regions.

As he read, a fit of the old fever came over him. "How much Pierre d'Ailly knew!" he exclaimed. "Thank you, Bartholomew. This book will be our beacon!"

But after an hour, a single hour, he was happy to be interrupted by his wife and his son, who had come to show him a baby bird fallen out of its nest.

৵৻

Only once in my life did I see a fine, rich and sweet understanding between a man and a woman.

And as never before or after in my life, I felt jealous in Porto Santo. Jealous as a brother is jealous, which is to say from the depths of his soul, whence the least admirable forces of his character arise.

I saw my brother's face soften every time he spoke to Filipa, I saw his features relax; again and again I saw a miracle as he lost years from his age, childhood returned to him – the confidence of childhood and its delights.

I heard my brother's voice every time he spoke to Filipa, and every time I wondered: who is this speaking? Surely not Christopher, who can only put his case forcibly, go on the attack, lose his temper! Whose was that almost diffident tone of voice, taking its time, choosing words that would inflict no wound?

I was taken aback to see the attention and consideration that he devoted to everything his wife said, however insignificant, and the immediate conclusions he drew from it, while no other human being's opinion so much as penetrated his mind unless it agreed with the convictions that he already held.

I saw him concerned for her – Christopher, utterly indifferent to all that was not part of his project; I saw him fetch her a woollen shawl when day was drawing to a close and the air was turning cool.

And I saw her always concerned for him, for instance when he had spent too much time over his account books.

"What good will it do you to put such a strain on yourself? What use will it be if you go blind? Do you think you can be a sea captain if you've just lost your sight?"

And when he agreed, but still went on with his calculations. I saw him go all over the island in search of camomile, the only plant that can soothe the eyes.

I heard him reassure her on stormy days, putting his hand on her shoulder, promising that the wind would soon die down, and meanwhile the island was firmly fixed in place, swearing by St Augustine, St Peter, St Paul and all the other saints that it would never, never drift away. Then he would tell her stories set on firm land until morning came.

And I heard her reassure him on calm days, when the island seemed to be lying on an infinite mirror and nothing in all Creation moved, not the clouds nor the grass nor the birds. She admitted that yes, without wind no one could navigate, but next moment she was swearing by St Martha, St Mary Magdalene and all the other female saints that never, never since the time of the Book of Genesis and even earlier had anyone known the wind to disappear for good. It was in its nature to come back one day.

I saw them walking in heavy rain and couldn't tell which was clinging to the other; he more solid but she more agile, better at picking her way along a slippery path.

144

Without knowing whether I hoped it or feared it, I told myself that this wonderful, rich love and sweet understanding was going to be the death of the Enterprise.

Why would he want to find a new route to India when he had love within him from dawn to dusk and all night long, which is as good as to say all countries united?

Not that Filipa murdered his dreams. Nor, unlike her mother, did she have her mind on revenge for her family. Her support for the Enterprise sprang from something stronger and more peaceful because it was based entirely on logic.

Fascinated by the energy she showed, despite her frail health, in coming to my brother's aid, I asked why she felt such a commitment to the plan.

She smiled. "Do I really need to tell you? It's so simple! I thought you were more intelligent. I love your brother. Your brother *is* the Enterprise. So I love the Enterprise. Give him time. You can see that just at the moment he is reining in his ambition. He is only waiting for his son to be old enough to go with him."

Almost as soon as Diego was born he had been initiated into the Enterprise. Every day, whatever the weather, and sometimes even at night, Christopher took him walking and gave him lessons: lessons on the movements of the sea, the language of the clouds, the influence of the stars, the way to catch crabs and hoist sails.

Diego, who wasn't even a year old yet, seemed to enjoy these lessons very much and babbled interminably on and on. That was not the kind of response that his teacher expected. Christopher was annoyed. His voice rose and the unsatisfactory pupil was handed back to his mother. "The child's too stupid!"

"The child is still a child," replied Filipa gently.

"Children are too slow."

"Children go their own way."

"Well, we must speed up his!"

Something else that troubled Christopher was the size of our family. "There are not enough of us, Bartholomew!"

"Why do you want there to be more?"

"Only large families influence the world. Look at the Grimaldis and the Spinolas. Why don't you get married and have children?"

"I've never found the right woman for me."

"Or let's say you often find too many of them."

"Your Filipa isn't expecting again, is she?"

"Unfortunately not. She has to recover her strength first."

I had no real place in this peaceful family life nor any part to play on the island. Leaving the *Ymago* behind, I set off without any regrets on the first ship to put in.

On my return I found drama waiting for me or rather a disappearance.

I have told you before: a great wind of freedom was blowing in Lisbon at the time. And that was very true. But that freedom had a master and its master was Secrecy.

⁂

Listen carefully, Las Casas, for you are a man as plagued by curiosity as I am.

Knowledge always wants the whole world to benefit by the light it casts. Knowledge is all generosity, while Secrecy is miserly and jealous. It keeps what it has to itself; it stores and hoards what it has.

The two can never agree and are bound to tear each other apart. And yet it is to the alliance of Knowledge and Secrecy that the successive kings of Portugal had, in their wisdom, given the keys of the kingdom.

That led to permanent and violent disagreement, and the success of the Voyages of Discovery.

In obedience to Knowledge, Lisbon welcomed with open arms all peoples or trades the object of which – sometime of necessity – was to teach and learn: Jews, merchants, cartographers, mathematicians, booksellers, cosmographers, watchmen, translators.

But to satisfy Secrecy these experts were formally forbidden to transmit knowledge of any kind to anyone other than the notaries of the Crown.

Sigila, Secrecy, is also a seal, the sign of ownership and the bolt guaranteeing it.

No power, no malady devoured more human lives than the appetite for Knowledge. Secrecy, at least in the tiny kingdom of Portugal, contented itself with ears.

Why did the indiscreet have their ears cut off rather than having their eyes put out? I have thought about that and I have found two answers.

Either the kings thought that you learned more by hearing than seeing. Was not Homer, the author of the first travel book, blind like Anchises the father of Aeneas, whom he was to guide on the way from Troy to Rome, in spite of his infirmity?

Or they believed that the eye is a gift of God, and therefore not to be withdrawn, while the ear is the tool and intermediary of the Devil.

Ears were cropped more freely than ever in Lisbon around 1480. They suddenly began falling from heads like leaves from the trees in autumn. Until that time the Portuguese remained attached to their ears, and those who had lost them, by accident or in a fight, hid the unattractive void behind as much hair as possible.

Only one inhabitant of Lisbon showed off his injury with pride: a hidalgo whose mistress, as everyone knew, had bitten him too hard during the act of love. He exhibited his pink orifice to all comers like a decoration won in the amorous fray. Some women would turn their heads away, repelled; but others, after much initial coyness, put their hands up to touch it and finally let the hidalgo bed them.

This climate of amusement came to an end when the entire guild of cartographers was summoned to the market square. Two French merchants were waiting there in chains. A crowd surrounded them, sometimes hurling insults, sometimes mocking their fear and above all their shaven heads. One of them had already lost an ear. Preceded by two drummers and an escort of soldiers, a judge arrived, identifiable by his robe, whose skirts he picked up as women do to avoid too much contact with the refuse scattered on the cobblestones.

The judge climbed to the platform where the merchants stood. The first, trembling all over, was pushed in front of him. Silence fell, so that the crowd could hear and enjoy the reading out of the charges. Master Bouanic, arrested on 3 June 1480 outside the church of St Genevieve in possession of a sea chart of the area off Cape Bojador, which he must have known was the exclusive property of His Majesty King Alfonso V, had been found guilty of theft and *lèse majesté*, and consequently was condemned to …

The judge looked up from his parchment to look at the culprit and revive the interest of the crowd.

"…. to have his right ear cut off."

Applause broke out as the second merchant was dragged in front of the judge.

For the same reason, aggravated by the presumption that this was a second offence, a conclusion drawn from the absence of his left ear, Master Legonidec was to lose his other and last remaining ear, and was warned that the next time he offended against the law on the monopoly of maps prevailing in the kingdom he would die by the rope in this same square.

This declaration was greeted with new applause, which changed to chuckling and shuddering as a giant in a mask, appearing as if from nowhere, climbed to the platform, took a long knife out of his pouch and approached the condemned men.

By some strange trick of human nature, the more terrified of the two was the man who was going to keep one ear. He groaned, begged, even wet himself. No use; soon blood was gushing from the right side of his head and the executioner was holding his ear aloft.

Shouting and raising their arms in the air, the crowd bayed for it to be thrown to them. In a frenzy, they were jostling the soldiers in their way and stopped only so as not to miss seeing the second sentence carried out. The second merchant, a Breton, asked to speak. In spite of having permission refused, he managed to declare that the seashore belonged to no one but those who had ventured to sail the seas themselves. Then he planted his feet firmly on the platform, straightened up, looked at the crowd and lost his final ear without trembling.

What happened to those two ears, and dozens of others, lopped off those who failed to respect Secrecy in the same way?

Were they burnt, buried, thrown to the dogs, or were they embalmed and kept in the archives? Knowing Portugal and its liking for keeping track of things, I am inclined to favour the second hypothesis, although I can't swear to it.

I have often wondered why so much music filled the air in Lisbon at all hours of the day and night. Perhaps God, in his infinite mercy, wanted to give a little comfort to all those abandoned ears?

The next day, and over the following days, a gentleman from the palace went to visit all the cartography studios in the city. As there were 152 of them in Lisbon at the time, it took him a good two months to visit them all. He introduced himself as a legal adviser to the king and his majesty's spokesman on the subject of sea voyages. An escort accompanied him and a drummer went ahead of him to give added solemnity to his declaration.

"Full as he is of paternal love for his subjects, that is to say merciful, the king, a very faithful man, wished to close his eyes to the origin of the maps used by the two criminal merchants Legonidec and Bouanic. However, his patience is exhausted. He hereby warns the guild of cartographers that anyone passing on documents of potential use in voyages to Africa to navigators, other than those approved by the Crown, will henceforward be liable to the same punishment, the loss of an ear."

The royal warning induced our guild to follow the wiser course for only a year. Then our neighbour from the end of the quay, Pedrinho, came out of his house one morning with his head swathed in a turban. We pretended to believe his story of a pine branch that had fallen on him and torn the skin off half of his skull. But as everyone had been discreetly present to see his punishment, we knew that the supposed branch was the executioner's dagger and the reason was his sale to a Pisan of a compendium of anchorages in the Canaries archipelago.

His colleagues came one by one to offer him kind words and sympathy, while privately considering him an idiot. They themselves, even if the necessity of doing business induced them to act just like him and offer their wares to illicit customers, would never get caught.

They underestimated the king's spies.

In the year 1485 alone, fifteen ears were brutally separated from the heads of cartographers. My colleagues' capacity to think up reasons for their sudden affliction taught me much about the duplicity of human nature. These men, who were capable of spending a fortune on a very slight improvement to some feature of a coastline, could suddenly tell shameless lies. No one wanted to admit to his mistake. I even heard one of the masters of our profession – you must forgive me for not revealing his name – claim that a relapse into a severe attack of leprosy had deprived him of both his ears at the same time.

Secrecy, the *sigila*, was not satisfied by these punishments, although they were increasingly visible in the city. Secrecy required King Alfonso V to inflict harsher penalties and got what it wanted from his successor John II.

Secrecy now thought itself safe. From this time on, the slightest breach of the confidentiality of maps would be punished by hanging.

Do you hear me, Las Casas? Can you turn my story to good advantage? Above all, don't think that distance protects you. The fact that an ocean separates us from Lisbon and its cruel practices is no protection for you at all. Don't forget that the viceroy lives here, just above our heads and that he is my nephew. If you broadcast my confidences, I shall arrange for you to feel an unpleasant void on both sides of your head.

&

Secrecy was the prime feature of Portuguese administration. Not content with tracking down the dealers in illicit information, the functionaries of Secrecy investigated and searched the city on a permanent basis. They would walk into our studios without warning and search them.

"Are you sure this is all?" That was their standard question. Or when they were overcome by fury at finding nothing, "What is it that you dare to hide from the king?"

I should explain better. The heart of Secrecy was in the depths of the royal palace, better guarded than any other treasure on earth: the entire body of knowledge about the Discoveries accumulated since the time of the first voyage financed by Henry the Navigator.

In other words, it was a map. The Perfect Map. This Perfect Map had been called *Padrão Real,* the Real Image.

No one was allowed to see this Perfect Map. The ushers of Secrecy took great care to protect it. And the Perfect Map drew nourishment from all other maps made daily in Lisbon. How could it still have been perfect if it had not integrated the progress of Knowledge as the Discoveries were made?

The Perfect Map was an ogre. It cried out to be fed every day.

The notaries to be found on every ship brought it its daily fare. As I have told you, they were the first to disembark from the caravels and take their records to the king.

But the Perfect Map was never satisfied. Who ever heard of an ogre who has eaten his fill?

The Perfect Map could not bear the idea that some cartographers kept certain facts to themselves. Even though they might not pass them on to anyone else, they were still guilty of concealment and deserved punishment.

I have just learnt from you, Las Casas, that the Spaniards have copied this system of the Perfect Map and refined it.

So it seems that in Spain, too, all the royal maps are kept in a great chest that will open only when two keys are turned at the same time. One is kept by the Chief Pilot, the other by the Chief Cosmographer. And all the maps derive from a mother map, *El Padrón Real*, hidden in Seville in a cellar of the Casa de Contractación de Indias.

This news has delighted me, giving me fresh strength to continue my story.

So the kingdom of Portugal set an example and those of us who had chosen to assemble there to teach the world were not wrong.

❧

Master Andrea still thought we were drawing our maps on too small a scale.

"Enlarge them!" he kept telling us. "What use is reproducing the world if you have to ruin your eyes to see it?"

It took me some time to understand the reason for his obsession. Like all old people, he had deteriorating eyesight; and like all old people, he refused to admit it. Year by year he had to stand further back to escape the haziness blurring his vision, and when he stood further back he could not read the details. Then he would fall into a rage. Trying to calm him, it was Javier who mixed our colours who came up with the idea of the wall. We could clear the far end of the studio of all the casks, remains of handcarts and heaps of tiles piled up there, reveal a surface on the wall of the shed beyond as large as the gable end of a two-storey house and whitewash it. Then it was a case of pinning up the largest sheet of vellum ever created in our studio; it took the skin of eight calves, and as I had the reputation of a man with a good hand for working on a small scale, it was my task to stitch them together well enough to earn compliments on the invisibility of the joins. We began, working in total secrecy, by tracing the extensive coasts of Morocco on it, enormous capes, beaches, reefs, river mouths taking up five or six times more space than they were allotted on ordinary maps.

Then, and only then, Andrea was invited to see it.

With the distrust common to master craftsmen, he immediately claimed all the credit for devising this incipient masterpiece.

"At last," was all he said, "at last you've listened to me. At last you're giving Africa the size that continent deserves. You're good lads! It's only a pity you're so slow to do as you're told!"

At this time, I remember, the line of the Equator had long since been passed and the outline of the continent where the black men lived stopped at the mouth of a river that appeared enormous, not to be compared with any other waterway known to man. The seamen who reached it had not explored it any further. They had brought back from their voyages in those parts only one certainty: a southern bank to this river, a river the size of a sea, had been discovered, so Africa went on.

We could not imagine what repercussions our idea would have on the history of the Discoveries, and indeed on the life of Master Andrea.

His wife, with whom he had been engaged in long-running hostilities, had just died. She used to come into the studio full of recriminations at any time of day, flinging abuse in a shrill, loud voice at a husband who was as absent as any sailor, indeed more so, and expressing her hatred, her utter hatred of maps, which were worse rivals than other women because they attacked not a man's body but his dreams. Maps were worse than the sea, because there was more variety in them. Curses on them, she would say, may they all be reduced to ashes! Several times we had to prevent her from putting her incendiary plans into action.

Now that his best enemy was gone, Andrea didn't know what battles to fight or with whom. The project of the gigantic map gave him a new interest. He devoted himself to it body and soul, day and night, with an ambition that increased daily.

"We'll create a map to outdo the Catalan Atlas!" he cried. For those of my guild, as I have told you, that work by the Majorcan Jew Cresques was an incomparable marvel.

Who betrayed us?

And can I really call a scrupulous respect for the law, in making all progress in knowledge known to the Palace, by the name of betrayal?

No trumpets preceded the eminent visitor, no advance warning was sent to us, no escort arrived that previous day to "make the place secure", as soldiers like to put it in their lofty but unambiguous manner. One fine day, a little before noon, the door opened. Since it was often left ajar, if only to let out living creatures – dogs attracted by the smell of glue, seagulls who will eat anything – none of the cartographers paused in his work.

Someone finally cried, "Hello there!"

As one man, we raised our heads and saw a gentleman with his feet in the dust of our studio and his head lost among the skins hanging from the ceiling to dry. This gentleman, incredibly, seemed to be … the king himself, flanked by two men, one richly and one severely dressed. With one and the same movement, we rose to our feet, while Andrea, red with confusion, approached this apparition stammering, "Sire … oh, sire, what an honour!"

He took the king's hand and bent his right knee.

"Your work," announced the illustrious voice, "has done great service to the cause of Discovery. We are pleased."

"Oh, sire … oh, sire!"

To our astonishment Andrea, whom we knew as a lion, had turned into a lamb. The king raised his right hand as if in blessing.

"I have heard tell of a masterpiece."

"Which one would that be, Your Majesty?"

We were relieved to see our master recover his pride: he would never let any but perfect maps out of his studio. He thought himself the equal of the great masters of the art of painting and thus he never produced anything but masterpieces.

The king ignored this proud remark and made himself clear, "I have heard tell of a very remarkable map of Africa."

"The maps sent to Your Majesty take into account all the progress made in the state of knowledge."

"I have heard tell of a wall …"

"You have been imperfectly informed: it is only a sketch meant to concentrate the thoughts of my young employees."

"Exactly. To understand the reality of the world, my mind requires a good, large view of Africa. Come along, I don't have much time."

Andrea became enmeshed in apologies for the untidiness, dirt and smell in the studio; why hadn't he been told in advance, he would have seen that the place was more worthy of …

The king wasn't listening. Followed by his two companions, he walked some way towards the back of the room. Andrea hurried to guide him between the inkwells, tables and trestles of the shambles in the studio.

"Bartholomew!"

"Yes, sir."

I had to run next door and borrow candles from our neighbour. Already rumours were going around. "The king is with the Genoese." The jealous were already grumbling, "Why in his studio and not ours?" A crowd gathered. I made my way through it, answering none of the questions put to me, with the haughty bearing of a man who knew that he was superior to these people.

The king went up to the huge map, eyes round and wide open, and murmured, "Good God, what a long continent! Where does it end?"

"Every ship tells us that it goes on further south."

"Could it be that it never comes to an end?"

And he put out his hand slowly, like a man afraid. Afraid of burning himself, or of harming a fragile reality.

He followed the line of the coast with his forefinger and asked questions. Andrea himself held the candlestick to give him light as he traced the outline.

"Am I still in the kingdom of Morocco?"

"Yes, sire."

The royal finger moved lower. "And is this the port of Sale?"

"Yes, sire. Well known for its pirates."

"So the desert is not far away. We should be approaching Cape Bojador, so famous for holding us back so long!"

"There it is: a tiny excrescence protruding from the shore."

"Why in the world were we so afraid of it? A forebear of mine told me: no sailor dares to round that cape. They all believe that there is a great gulf beyond it lying in wait to swallow them up."

"Everything unknown is a gulf."

"All honour to our seamen who overcame their fear."

"Without Your Majesty's support, no ship would ever have left Lisbon for such distant horizons."

At that moment a chamberlain appeared, or anyway some other person of equal importance, with gold lace all over his clothing and a powdered face. To reach us he had to get across all the untidiness in the studio, and as his haste prevented him from looking where he was going he had knocked over a jug of red ink and stained his hose.

"Sire, the Spanish ambassador is getting impatient."

"Who cares? Let him wait! My God, I had no idea there were so many of the Fortunate Isles! What precision in the drawing! And look at the pretty fish around the edges of the map! Master Andrea, what I heard about you is true: your studio is full of artists!"

The chamberlain reminded him of the ambassador again and the king, though grumbling, had to give way. He saluted us with great graciousness and left. The gentleman in the severe clothing stayed behind for a moment to tell us to protect our masterpiece from indiscreet eyes better. From his tone, that of a man who would brook no argument, we all recognized him as a functionary of Secrecy.

And so the first royal visit to our studio ended. We got back to work as best we could, with our minds elsewhere and our hearts full of pride. Quills began scratching on vellum again. A little later we heard Andrea's furious voice.

"Who let the cat out of the bag? I'll find out. That map is mine, all mine."

A month later the king came back, accompanied by the same two men, the richly dressed one and his austere companion. Two weeks later he was back again. By now he knew the way. As soon as he entered the studio he made haste towards the old wall of the shed at the back. The king always asked the same question.

"Well, how is Africa doing?"

"Africa is getting longer, Your Majesty."

"Let's see!"

And pushing everyone else aside he hurried to the giant map and, like a father amazed by the growth of his child, examined the improbable size of Africa.

Andrea showed him the latest discoveries about the continent as reported by the caravels coming home: a huge lagoon here, a new archipelago there. And always that interminable coastline which, after hesitating and going east, plunged due south again.

"When will it come to an end?"

"How can we tell, Your Majesty?"

The royal conclusion was always the same. "I shall send out twice as many ships."

One day we were entering the latest information that had reached us from the port on the giant map – rather good news, to the effect that Africa was still getting longer, but beyond the huge forests a desert of burning sand began. In view of the fact that the explorers were still going south, the desert could not go on for ever, and soon there must inevitably be an icy cold that was incompatible with burning sand. As we worked, we heard a noise that came from the entrance of the studio.

We immediately abandoned our wall to go to the aid of Master Andrea, who was shouting frantically. We saw him grappling with a man we knew only too well, the royal confidant whose clothing was invariably severe, the functionary of Secrecy. He was accompanied by some soldiers.

"Never!" shouted Andrea.

"It is the king's will," replied the austere man, "and the mark of his confidence in you."

Andrea walked up to him and would no doubt have hit him hard but for the intervention of the troop of soldiers. I have to acknowledge that at no point did the king's envoy lose his calm demeanour.

"On the one hand, it is considered that despite our repeated warnings, the security of your studio is not adequate for Secrecy."

Master Andrea's anger had not died down but had entered a new phase. From being scarlet, his face had turned as pale as plaster.

"And on the other hand the king, in his inexhaustible wisdom and with his passionate concern for the Discoveries, has decided to give your gigantic map a home in his palace, in return for which he repeats his gratitude and will pay you a sum the amount of which will not disappoint you."

Master Andrea shrugged his shoulders, leaving anyone to guess whether he was expressing derision for the functionary's pompous manner or for the pecuniary recompense. The shrug was his last expression of displeasure. All at once he became affability and helpfulness in person. He cooperated directly and usefully in the taking down of the map, indicating the safest way to handle it without tearing the vellum. He paid great attention to the packing of the masterpiece, after having it covered with silk fabric and delicately rolled up. Then he wished good luck to the austere man, his escort, and the never-ending continent of Africa.

Once the door was closed, the studio seemed to fall into a void.

We returned to our pens and inks, but how could we set to work with energy now? We had been deprived of our *Padrão Real,* our Perfect Map. It was to make it more and more perfect that we took so much care with our work, all of it adding details to the great masterpiece.

When evening came, someone went to call Andrea to discuss tomorrow's work with him. Silence. We took it in turns to call him, raising our voices louder and louder. Still no response.

We searched for him as best we could, first in the studio, then in the city. Not a sign of our master.

We carried on for a month without him, jumping whenever the door creaked, quivering with expectation whenever a figure resembling him came along the quayside.

Then one of us left to go and work for one of Andrea's competitors.

Another left next day, two more the following week.

That was the end of the studio.

I never heard anything but fragmentary and contradictory news of Andrea later. Sometimes he was said to have been seen in Pisa, invited there to revive the art of cartography that had once been among the glories of the city; sometimes there were rumours that he had gone to Majorca, the home of his master Cresques, to search for the source of his genius there; sometimes he had been seen in Venice, a city that has no equal for buying people's souls; sometimes back in Genoa sitting in a tavern by the harbour doing nothing but watch the vessels putting in and going out. In fact he had disappeared in the same way as his studio, scattered to the four quarters of the compass.

There are many cartographers who have to struggle against such centrifugal forces. A map not only defines the frontiers between land and sea. It also gathers separate pieces of information together and reassembles them. Or rather assigns them to their proper place.

In essence, every map is a skin. Like a skin, it confers identity. Like a skin it is also a container; it keeps the reality contained in it from escaping.

The Grim Reaper had visited Porto Santo. Christopher woke up one night to find Filipa groaning beside him. In the morning she was dead. It seems that at the moment when her body was lowered into the grave, the wings of all the miniature windmills began to turn. As there was not a breath of wind in the air, this remarkable event was taken as a last greeting from Filipa, wishing the Enterprise good luck.

After her funeral, father and son left the island at once. They were never parted in Lisbon. They walked only side by side, they slept only side by side, they talked only to each other, with their words intermingling. They had become so close that you couldn't tell them apart; Filipa's death had changed them into a single person, one and the same, devastated at the same moment by the same sudden access of grief, shaken sometimes by the same smiles and laughter, paying for it next moment with even worse distress because they were ashamed to have laughed, to have forgotten her.

I took care of my brother and my nephew as best I could. I listened to their memories. I talked about other matters. I managed to make them laugh, and to make them cry as well when I felt that keeping back their tears threatened to stifle them. And we returned to our old reading habits of the time when, in the footsteps of Marco Polo, we were bound for the realm of the Grand Khan, pen in hand.

Except that this time Diego, although still very small, came too. Sometimes on the knee of one or the other of us, sometimes nestling between us, sometimes on the other side of the table trying to scribble himself, although he usually fell asleep over it.

It was as this crew that we navigated the *Ymago mundi*, exploring its most hidden nooks and crannies, trying to elucidate its many – too many – obscure areas.

And so the future viceroy was initiated into geography – the viceroy who today, from the room just above my head, rules the affairs of half the world.

The parts of the book he liked best dealt with wild beasts and the many different peoples of the world. He kept asking us to read the sixteenth chapter, about the wonders of India:

It is clear, from what has been said before, that India covers a vast area. From what follows, it will be seen that the country is no less vast in the variety of its marvels. Its forests are very tall; there are pygmies to be found in its mountains, men two cubits tall who hunt cranes. These people bring forth children in their third year of life and they die in their eighth year. A white pepper grows in this country that acquires a dark tinge from the fire put on it to chase away the snakes who live in these forests.

The Macrobians are found there, men twelve cubits in height, who make war on the gryphons, lions with wings and talons like those of eagles.

There are Agrathes and Brahmans who throw themselves into braziers for the sake of love. There are barbarians who kill and eat their parents when they are worn out by old age; those who refuse to practise this custom are considered impious. Others eat raw fish and drink the salt water of the sea. Certain monstrous humans have feet the wrong way round, and there are eight heels to their feet; others have the heads of dogs and wear animal skins. They also bark like dogs.

There are women in this country who bear a child only once, and these children are white when they are born and become black in their old age, which lasts only one summer; others have children five times, and those children live no longer than their eighth year.

There are men who have only one eye, called Carismapi; and there are others called Cyclopes who have only one foot to stand on, but move faster than the wind. When they sit down on the ground they make shade for themselves by holding up the sole of their foot in the air.

There are others who are headless and have their eyes in their shoulders. Instead of a nose and a mouth they have orifices in their chests, and in the manner of certain beasts their bodies are covered with a silky fur.

There are men living close to the Ganges who live solely on the odour of a certain fruit, and when they travel they take that fruit with them. If they happen to smell a bad odour, they die of it.

There are snakes so large that they will eat stags; these serpents can cross the ocean by swimming. Other remarkable creatures of monstrous form have also been reported.

Eels one hundred feet long can be seen in the Ganges. There is also talk of a worm which, like a crab, has two arms, each six cubits long, with which it can clasp an elephant.

The Indian ocean brings forth turtles with shells large enough for a human dwelling. The authors have spoken of a great many other marvels. It would take too long to enumerate them all, but I refer the reader to authors such as Pliny, Solinus, and above all Isidore who, in his Book 1, Chapter 3, writes of these marvels and others as well.

Dear little Diego!

He knew how to keep quiet when we were discussing matters that he guessed were particularly important. I remember his eyes, round with surprise, when we expressed our enthusiasm for Chapter Eight:

Et dicit Aristotiles q mare paruu est iter fine Hyspanie a pre occidentis 2 iter principiu Indie a parte orientis ...

Aristotle states that the sea separating the western extremity of Spain from the eastern part of India is only small. In that theory, this mention does not denote Nearer Spain, known today simply as Spain, but Farther Spain, known now by the name of Africa, of which good authors such as Pliny, Orosius and Isidore have spoken. Furthermore Seneca, in Book 5 of his *On Nature*, says that this sea can be crossed in a few days with favouring winds.

Reaching India from the west!

Christopher's old fever was back. It burned even more fiercely, if possible, because Filipa, as he was always reminding me, had been the first to support him. The Enterprise was relaunched.

Two geographical facts, and two alone, could stand in its way.

One was that extreme heat might make it impossible to pass through certain parts of the earth. Pierre d'Ailly had reassured us on that head: life was possible everywhere on our globe and the seas all over it were navigable.

The other was that the Ocean Sea might be too wide between

Europe and India, and for that reason the crossing would be impossible. But the *Ymago* said the voyage could be made "in a few days".

Christopher's expression was radiant, like the face of a prisoner seeing the door of his cell open. He kept repeating the Latin phrase: *paucis diebus, paucis diebus.*

It must have been at that moment and on that day that his dream changed to decision.

We went on reading – the *Ymago* is not a slim volume and describes the planet as a whole. Christopher filled its margins with notes in black ink. But our minds were not on the book now. They were already at sea.

⁂

Christopher would interrupt our reading from time to time and take Diego out to give him a change of scene and a chance to stretch his legs. Their favourite destination was the village of Cascais, from which you could look far out to sea. They shared the same mule, Diego seated securely on it in front of his father.

Rather than accompanying them, I kept my ears open and heard this unlikely dialogue.

"Diego, tell me what Customs and Excise do. Diego, how would you draw up a budget?"

"Father, don't you think I'm a little young to learn all this?"

"On the contrary. I began very young myself. On the route to the west that I am going to open up, I shall discover new lands and I shall give you the task of administrating them."

"Father, what does administrating mean?"

"You know that we mustn't waste time. You still have many, many things to learn."

"Don't you have those lands yet?"

"You know very well that Porto Santo is all we have."

"When will you have them?"

"When I've discovered them and the king has entrusted them to me."

"Do you think Mama is still alive in one of those lands?"

"I can't swear to it."

162

"Then we'll have to go further, and in the end we're sure to find her."

"I can promise you this: we will never stop discovering lands while I have the strength to go on."

"Father, does it take long to discover things?"

"As long as it takes for you to prepare yourself." And my brother returned to his interrogation. "Diego, what is a land register? Diego, what is the difference between high and low justice?"

While he tried to answer, the poor child looked around for anyone who might rescue him, but the world was empty. His mother had been the only person able to moderate his father's educational fervour.

Hernán, Christopher's other son and Diego's brother, never spoke of any of this, although he was his father's official biographer. How do you come to terms with the fact that your father paid more attention to your elder brother than to you?

Instead of laughing at Christopher and his deranged obsession with teaching Diego, I would have done better to listen to his lessons myself. Perhaps that might have made me a less disastrous governor of Hispaniola.

Christopher had brought more back from Porto Santo than his grief. Besides his son, he also had a story to keep him company. It took him some time to agree to tell me that story. He kept saying that he would, promising to tell it, beginning it and then stopping short.

At last he did launch into it:

"It was one evening in Madeira, when stormy gusts of wind were blowing from the east. I'd gone out to look at the waves. As usual, I thought I was alone in the world, when I heard someone passing by behind me. With a start, I turned round.

'Who are you?'

'A pilot glad to have survived.'

"I suggested what one always suggests to sailors: why didn't we immediately repair to the nearest tavern, where he could describe his glorious and terrifying adventures over a glass of wine, then two glasses of wine, then several more? The pilot said no. He did not like noise, he told me, he would rather walk. So it was as we walked along that he told me the news he had. Westward beyond the ocean, he said, there were lands where the people lived naked. I bombarded him with questions, hoping to find out more and above all to keep the pilot with me although he seemed close to fainting with exhaustion. But all he did was to keep repeating the outline of his story. 'Five years ago, as we were sailing due south to Africa, a stormy east wind rose and carried us off course for weeks and weeks on end. One day we saw a coast. I assure you, westward and beyond the ocean there are lands where the people live naked.'

'Why did you tell me this?'

'Because you deserve to be told.'

'How can you tell that?'

'From your way of looking into the distance.'

'So how did my way of looking into the distance attract your attention?'

'It goes on and on.'

"It was useless for me to insist; the pilot would say no more. I couldn't get another word out of him. All he did was shake his head when I asked where he was lodging on the island. Night came to his aid and he slipped away."

Christopher always kept this story of the unknown pilot to himself. He never told anyone else, never let it be widely known, never used it as a weapon. Not even at the most difficult moments, not even in his most solitary hours, when no one placed any faith in his claims. Not even in front of the Committee of Mathematicians, if only to put a stop to their sarcastic digs at him. Not even when the realization of his Enterprise was at stake, which meant his life.

And he told me the story only once, in a low voice, after making sure that no one else could overhear it.

After making me swear by our mother that I would not pass it on to anyone else, for any reason at all – "Swear again, Bartholomew, repeat after me, I swear by our mother, not for any reason at all."

He was afraid to talk about it. Afraid that his story might go away, vanish into thin air.

I was annoyed. I didn't understand his fear until much later: some stories are as frail as phantoms. And if my brother had lost that story of the unknown pilot, no doubt he would have collapsed at once, like a man with his skeleton snatched away.

Perhaps one evening in Madeira a man really did introduce himself to my brother as a pilot and told his story. Perhaps that man was lying. Perhaps he spoke nothing but the truth, without adding another word or any details to cast light on it.

Perhaps the unknown pilot never existed at all, at least in human form as described by my brother.

Perhaps the unknown pilot was none other than a word of God to which Christopher gave a human face and a seaman's voice?

Perhaps the story was a present from his mother-in-law, Senhora Perestrello, née Moniz, who was so anxious to see her son-in-law do great things. Perhaps she gave it to him as a kind of dowry.

I can imagine Christopher making it his own.

Stories shamelessly give themselves to the latest person to hear them. You say that you have heard a certain story from someone, who had it from someone else, who in turn had it from yet another man, who himself ...

Perhaps he heard nothing either in his mind or outside himself. Perhaps Christopher never met anyone but fishermen on Madeira. Perhaps he invented the pilot because he needed him. Perhaps the confidence his brothers had in him wasn't enough.

Perhaps a lie offers stronger support than the truth, because it comes from deep within you and the reality comes from elsewhere.

All I know, and I am even more certain of it now that, with hindsight, I can identify the real part played in the success of the Enterprise by everyone and everything, is that my brother's treasure, his strength and his sanctuary lay in that story told by the unknown pilot.

The story never failed him. He could always cling to it, even in his worst moments.

I remember ... all the time the king's mathematicians were pouring scorn on the Enterprise, one after another, I never took my eyes off my brother's face. It always wore a smile, and I knew the source of that smile: the unknown pilot's tale. What does adversity matter to a man who has a secret buried deep within him, a secret against which nothing can prevail?

What I can say is that I did not keep my word. I took advantage of all Christopher's absences to look for the pilot.

No seaport ever laughed more at anyone than they laughed at me in Lisbon.

"Who are you looking for did you say, Bartholomew? A pilot? A pilot who says he sailed to the other side of the world and was ready to tell his story? Come, come, Bartholomew, you know perfectly well that *all* pilots reach the other side of the world some time or other, and they are *all* ready to talk about their discoveries, just as long as you'll open their mouths with a glass of beer or wine. For a start, what does your pilot look like? Is he tall, fair-haired, a Viking? Or small, stocky and olive-skinned, the Greek or Cypriot type? Poor Bartholomew, always embarking on impossible tasks for your brother's sake! Poor Bartholomew, when you brother comes back we'll promise not to tell him about your crazed inquiries. We like you. We'll protect you from his scorn."

As Andrea had abandoned us, we had to find some means of live-lihood. We would not have felt it worthy of us to accept offers of employment from his rivals. The master who had taught us so much of the art of cartography did not deserve such an insult. We decided to set up on our own account, giving preference to selling books. We had come to that decision in reading, re-reading and annotating the *Ymago*. It seemed to us that words told richer and more varied stories than the outlines of coasts.

And I still had useful contacts after my journey to Strasbourg and Louvain. I told myself that printing, that new invention, was itself like a wave of the sea: you only had to let it carry you away.

✢

Does a man deserve the noble name of bookseller if he works only in a tiny, shabby little shop that can't hold two human beings and a hundred books at the same time? If my brother and I happened to be there together, we had to push the two crates where books waited to find room on our three already over-populated shelves out into the street, and pray to God, author of the Bible and thus an ally of book-sellers, to keep rain from falling. The one advantage of this rat-hole was its situation, next to the Corpo Santo church, a place that sea captains were bound to pass, since like animals they always went the same way to the water they wanted (in their case, the harbour).

On days when the sky was cloudy, however, and as two precau-tions are better than one, we did not forget to give a boy a coin to tell us the moment the first drop of rain fell. Everyone knows about the bitter hatred of water for the written word. It never misses the pleasure of drenching a volume, dissolving the sentences as if writing were its rival. I suspect that water thinks its own flux and flow are worth more than all the stories in the world, rendering them useless.

Fortunately Christopher seldom honoured the bookshop and me with his presence.

I did not waste much time mourning for our collaboration. My brother was clearly the kind of bookseller who is death to a prosperous business and has chosen that profession only to read as much as he wants at his leisure, without paying for it.

I wouldn't wish a brother like mine (or an associate, or yet worse an associate who is also his brother) on any bookseller.

He came in to choose his daily dose of reading matter in the morning and brought it back to me, with his comments, in the evening. He gave me countless orders for works of which he had heard, I have no idea how, but which he assured me were indispensable to him and he needed them urgently. I could almost have spent my whole time satisfying this one customer.

And when I did manage to procure him such rarities – the necessity of them is a mystery to me to this day – of course paying for them was no part of his plan.

"Where's your brother?"

That was always the first question asked by our faithful customers who came to buy maps and books, when they opened the door of our shop. And they always looked disappointed to find me alone.

At first I tried telling lies. "Christopher took ship for Flanders yesterday." Or, "Christopher's asleep."

But how do you hide the truth in a city as small as Lisbon, with a harbour as its central hub?

"You liar, Bartholomew! No ship has set out north for the last week!" Or, "Don't you take me for a mooncalf, Bartholomew! Everyone knows he's murdered his ability to sleep – that's how he got his red hair, from the weariness burning him up."

I was soon left with no option but to confess the shame of our family: for several months, my brother had been spending his days and nights reading. I became the butt of insults and mockery.

They all wanted to take his mind off his new passion, claiming that he was running great risks.

"Tell me where he is, so that I can teach him a thing or two about life."

"I don't know where he is. When my brother is reading he disappears."

"Don't you do anything to stop him? For heaven's sake, Bartholomew! Books are gulfs, like the gulfs waiting to swallow up imprudent sailors on the other side of the horizon. One of these days your brother won't come back."

There was a general fear of books, apart from the Bible, and it was kept alive by the priests. If maps were reassuring, being satisfied with drawing the best possible portrait of all Creation, books appeared to seamen to be works of the Devil, evidence of his desire to lead human beings astray and drag them down to hell.

These fears ending up contaminating even me. As there was nothing I could do to stop Christopher reading, I tried to understand the reason for this mania of his.

"Why are you always wearing out your eyes on a book?"

"Because I can't always be at sea."

"Just how do books console you for not being at sea? How do they replace ships in your mind?"

"Reading is like looking at the horizon. At first all you see is a black line. Then you imagine whole worlds beyond it."

"Oh, very well. But why your mania for writing in the margins of all the books you read?"

"If I'm going to read properly I need to write things down. Writing guides and safeguards all the thoughts set off by reading. Without a guide and safeguard, my ideas – and I know them well – would go off heaven knows where and never come back again."

Another remark of my brother's:

"Writing is like navigating on terra firma. The white page is the sail you hoist, and the words are the wake that the ship leaves behind."

Another remark of my brother's:

"Every book invents its own route. It travels from destination to destination, as free among all the stories it might tell as a ship is free to sail the sea."

※

And yet another remark of my brother's:
"When I write in the margin of a book I am mingling myself with its author. I give myself up to the flow of its logic until the course of that river reaches its mouth."

※

Another (and very frequent) remark of my brother's:
"Oh, leave me alone!"

※

Another (and even more frequent) remark of my brother's: nothing at all. A persistent silence, broken from time to time by an exasperated grunt.

※

Mine and mine alone was the job of running the shop, which while tiny was also supposed to bring in enough income to keep us from dying of starvation. Since dictionaries had always been my favourite books, I had decided to compile one.

You will know that since the time of Prince Henry, blessed be his name for his inexhaustible capacity for invention, Portugal had adopted the custom of sending not only a notary on board every caravel but also a convicted criminal taken from prison. Once our ship was sailing along the coast of an unknown country, the criminal was put ashore. Then it was up to him to find a way to survive.

When the caravel turned homeward it went in search of him. Sometimes only his bones were found. No one grieved for him. It had been God's will for the wicked man to pay for his sins.

Sometimes he was standing on the shore, frantically waving his arms to attract attention. That showed that he was still alive. And how had he escaped death if he had not induced the natives to accept him? In that case he would know their language. All that had to be done was to harvest knowledge from the castaway's head, as a bee-keeper harvests the honey from his hive.

Other booksellers in search of new words merely went down to the port to ask the homebound criminal summary questions. They presented him with the hundred most common words and he translated them into the native language he had learnt. If he was an intelligent man, that worked well. If he was short of both intelligence and memory, the "dictionary" would be full of mistakes and omissions, formidable barriers for travellers to surmount.

All good cooks go to market to buy their own ingredients. I went visiting prisons, to choose future castaways. Before paying my visit I had studied the files on the criminals and conscientiously examined the reasons for their conviction. Long experience allows me to say that the best castaway to recruit for a dictionary is a swindler of violent inclinations: his violence will enable him to stand up to attacks by the savages, at the same time as his fondness for words (and what swindler doesn't like to talk about his prowess?) will make him want to use them and to remember the words that he hears.

All other castaways have turned out less efficacious in carrying out their mission. They include men who commit crimes of passion. They have disappointed me more than criminals of any other kind; as soon as the object of their adoration is dead they turn as meek as lambs and as a result they are easy prey for the Moors and even the blacks. As for words, they hate them. Words have been used to tell them lies, that's all they know.

I am Genoese and therefore a businessman. What is a compiler of dictionaries if not a merchant? He exchanges things for words that describe those things. Or he exchanges a word for another word, provided that both mean the same. You need the patience of a bridge-builder to undertake the long search for corresponding meanings.

It will be objected, in reply to my recriminations, that in making his discoveries, Christopher too built a bridge, a bridge across the Ocean Sea. How can I quarrel with that? My own bridges are tiny, hardly visible, always shaky. Who can tell whether there is real equivalence between the word *baay* in the Wolof language and what we mean by "father", when among the speakers of Wolof *baay* also means a father's brothers, his male cousins, even his friends? Who is sure that in using the word *God* for the Supreme Being we mean exactly the same as the speakers of the Lingala language when they say *Nzambe*?

⁊

Once again, I groan and I pull myself together.

My little dictionaries did bring in some money, but it was mainly Christopher's doing that we survived those years of 1481 to 1484. And we had his sea charts rather than my unlikely dictionaries to thank for it.

His knowledge had roots going far back in time. Yet again I think of Genoa. Genoa was our genesis, the teeming seaport where we were made. Since our Genoese childhood we have really only been repeating events.

My brother wasn't ten years old when he was struggling for the permission to go to sea that our father still refused him. Seeing him scribbling on a sheet of paper one day, I went over to him.

"What are you doing?"

"Starting my sea chart. It will be the first real one!"

Accustomed as I was to my brother's boasts, I didn't usually react, but this one, I laughed, was going too far.

We had already wandered around the harbour so much, bombarding the sailors with so many questions, that they had finally told us some of their secrets and shown us their documents. We had marvelled at those portolan charts with their accounts of harbours and islands. I pointed out to Christopher that, since the dawn of time, countless cartographers had been at work before him. This reminder did not deflate his arrogance.

"Their charts show only the coasts. Their seas are empty."

"So how are you going to fill in that empty space?"

"By showing the direction of the winds and the currents – they are the roads of the sea. I'll add the strength of those winds and currents that give ships their speed, because at sea it's the roads that carry you forward. I'll put in the colours of the water, showing how deep it is. I'll put in the shape of the clouds that say when a storm is coming."

"How will you get to know all this?"

"I'll have sailed everywhere. I'm just wasting time staying on land."

My brother was as good as his word. Having spent his life on all possible kinds of ships, carrying all imaginable cargoes in all weathers to all conceivable destinations, near or far, he had memorized the whole of the sea. His knowledge had been accumulated in the course of his own voyages and thanks to the tales of other sailors, at least those whom he respected.

Here his mind, otherwise so forgetful, had the dual power of a sponge and a bolt: it absorbed all information about the sea and never let go of it again.

This was the feat that made us a living during our last years in Lisbon after the death of Filipa, when her family, especially her mother, had given us up as hopeless.

Every morning, for two hours, I managed to bring Christopher out of his daydreams with a problem. I gave him a place, for instance the west of the island of Ireland. I gave him a date: the month of May.

He would say nothing for a few moments, frowning. You would have thought he was walking through his brain. He soon found what he was looking for and I drew the map to his dictation.

"A current moving at a velocity of half a sea mile comes up from the south-west and passes along the coast. The winds blow from the west one day out of three and often exceed twenty knots."

That was the reason for our success: the maps and charts produced by the Columbus brothers described places and seasons, winds and currents more precisely than any before them. They were also cautious in never claiming to be perfectly accurate. They presented only the probability: "Sailing along the Portuguese coast in the month of December, you have a three out of four chance of facing winds from the west, north-west or south-west, of a strength which has a two out of three chance of exceeding twenty-five knots ..."

Those who have never been to sea will be surprised to find that people can be satisfied with such uncertainty, but sailors know that their element moves, and in that element there are only modest truths, frail assurances.

Then, and only then, my patience was rewarded, and Christopher was kind enough to explain the mystery of the *volta* which had been on my mind ever since his visit of 1473.

"Nothing simpler, Bartholomew. A north-east wind blows along the coasts of Africa almost all the time. So the ships have no trouble in going out on their voyages; they sail down the coast easily, as if pushed along by the hand of God. Going back is more difficult; they have to face the same winds, and those winds are now against them. This is where we have to praise the courage and perspicacity of our Portuguese friends."

It was so unusual for Christopher to pay tribute to anyone but himself that I jumped in surprise.

"They dared to sail further out from the coast in search of another wind direction."

"I suppose they found it."

"Going north-west, they sailed before the north-east winds instead of fighting them. And on reaching the Azores archipelago they found favouring west winds again. Then they had only to let the west wind carry them back to Lisbon. They had performed a turn, the *volta*. I shall do the same, but on a larger scale."

That evening, in spite of our usual temperance, we drank happily to the *volta*. I congratulated my brother in a voice growing ever thicker. I had never before understood so well that navigation entails knowing when to make a detour, knowledge that is the daughter of humility and persistence. You do not fight what is stronger than yourself, but that is never any reason to abandon the ultimate destination of your voyage.

☙

I can assure you, without bragging, that we worked hard all through those years; and our little map-making workshop might have grown and prospered, if Christopher's dream hadn't swept all that away.

In the same way as there are men of peace and men of war, generals without their equal on the battlefield who prove incapable of governing a domain, there are certain mariners who should never leave their element. Their feet, so good at helping them to keep their balance in a pitching sea, set off catastrophes as soon as they step on land.

That was certainly the fate of the Columbus family. Why didn't my brother content himself with the title of admiral and the work it involved? He would have made more discoveries than anyone, leaving it to others to administer the lands he found.

And his glorious reputation would have remained intact.

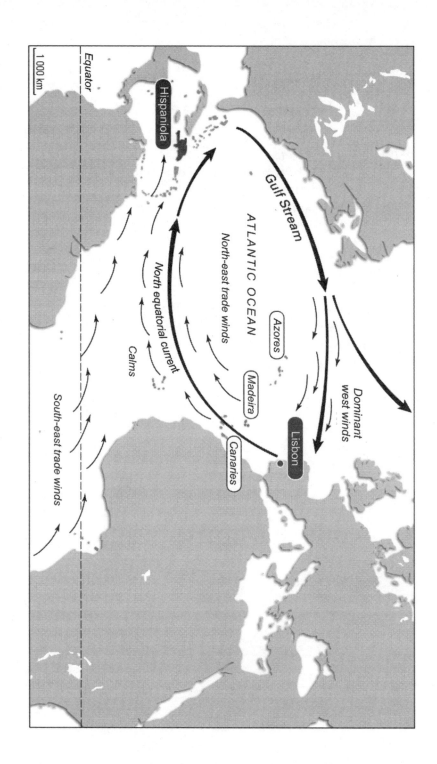

What does *aplomb* mean?

Taking advantage of the wealth of leisure time I have at my disposal, I have had all the dictionaries available on this island of Hispaniola brought to my room.

And since the state of my legs prevents me from leaving this palace very often, I wander from page to page like a fat old bumble-bee intent on gathering pollen, if without much taste for flowers left or indeed much sense of smell. But from time to time a word rouses me from the weariness with life that God, in His wisdom, has devised to make the approach of death less cruel, indeed wholly desirable.

Aplomb. What do my dear dictionaries say?

The verticality of a line, as indicated by a plumb-line. Figuratively, a person's self-confidence, his certainty of his destiny and thus of his rights.

All my life, that long life now coming to an end, wherever I have met, for better or worse, a crowd of my fellow humans of all races, both sexes and all conditions, I have never come across anyone with such great aplomb as my brother.

I recollect a little story which is not, perhaps, without significance to the great history of discovery, beginning one day in 1473 in Florence. It illustrates aplomb as little else could. Calm down, Las Casas, calm down. Restrain your impatience. Stories are much like rivers or human beings: to understand their origins you have to give yourself time to trace them back to their source. The impatient who do not make this journey upstream will never, never understand the twin nature of stories and flowing water. A Portuguese canon by the name of Fernão Martins met a man as distinguished for his knowledge as he was discreet in his way of life. Paolo del Pozzo Toscanelli divided his time between three activities: medicine, which paid badly; the spice trade, which paid better; and cosmography, which paid nothing at all but explained everything through the movement of the stars in their courses.

This man, whose work kept him in one place, regretted not having travelled. So he was happy to talk to Martins, who came from a country of navigators. Toscanelli told him that he felt sure the Portuguese were wrong to show interest only in the east. If they set off west they would reach India more quickly and easily, instead of having to sail along the interminable coast of the continent of Africa. He showed him maps and calculations. Martins left with his mind troubled. He told Prince John, the future king, who was in charge of exploration. The prince asked the Florentine for a report. On 25 June 1474, Toscanelli replied:

> Here is a map that I have drawn with my own hands, thanks to which you can undertake the voyage west, indicating the places that you must reach, at what distances from the pole and the equinoctial line you must change course, and how many places you will have to pass to reach those regions, the most fertile of all for every kind of spice, rich in jewels and precious stones. Do not think it wonderful that I call the west the land of spices, while it is generally claimed that spices come from the east, for all who sail westward in the lower of the two hemispheres will always find the aforesaid sea routes to the west, and all those who travel east by the land route in the upper of the two hemispheres will always find the same land to the east.

The Florentine's letter was submerged in the notaries' reports telling tales of marvels along the African coasts that were certain knowledge. So why take any interest in new routes to India of such a tenuous nature? The king shrugged his shoulders. And when a document did not interest the king, no one even took the trouble to classify and file it. It disappeared into the bottomless pit of the royal disdain. Or it immediately ceased to exist.

Four years later, however, in some dusty corner, the Chief Curator, guided by his superhuman memory, which as the members of his guild often remarked must have shelves in it, went to look for the letter to pass it on to a man who had become a friend of his, Christopher.

Never fear, Las Casas. In spite of my age my mind is perfectly clear. Unfortunately. It seems to me that a wandering mind would have exorcized my ghosts. Contrary to your present opinion, I have not lost the thread of my discourse. We are back to the subject of aplomb.

For as soon as he had read and re-read the letter from the Florentine, Christopher decided to write to him, despite the Curator's protests. They were not without logic: if a letter from a foreigner had been scornfully dismissed by the king of Portugal then by virtue of that fact the letter had no right to exist. And if the writer of a letter that no longer exists receives a missive asking him for more information about that non-letter, it is incontestable proof that the letter does still exist. This contradiction could give rise to harmful consequences for the unfortunate Curator.

My brother did not care about these fears. In his usual way he never thought of the ruins, human or material, that he left behind him. All that mattered was coming closer to his goal.

As I never had the leisure to go to Florence, I have not seen my brother's letter. But I have consulted Toscanelli's reply:

"I take note of your great and noble ambition to go to those lands where the spices grow.

In reply to your letter I send you a copy of another letter that I had written before the wars of Castile to a friend then in the service of His Serene Majesty the king of Portugal who, from his elevated position, wished me to be asked about my observations. I send you also, at this same time, a map similar to the map that I drew for this friend, hoping that this will satisfy your request."

Shamelessly and without a scruple – yet another instance of aplomb! – Christopher wrote straight back to the Florentine.

The Florentine replied, but in a drier tone, clearly annoyed to be troubled again.

"I am not surprised that you, a man of such great courage, the same being true of the Portuguese nation that brings together noble persons always ready to undertake great ventures, should be full of enthusiasm for the idea of this voyage, and anxious to bring it to a happy conclusion."

He ended by wishing Christopher good luck.

A word in praise of aplomb.

Without it, and its sister impudence, my brother would never have received written confirmation, illustrated by cartography, of the figures we had derived from reading Marco Polo, Pierre d'Ailly and many others. Ptolemy had seen Asia as smaller than it is. Thirty degrees of longitude had to be added to his figures.

Consequently, the western sea was curtailed by that amount.

What information could be more useful to us?

One evening our father Domenico came home with an expression of unusual gaiety, which was not of the kind engendered by glasses of red wine drunk in the tavern.

"I know why we're not rich!" he said.

We looked at him, baffled less by the announcement of this magic formula, for the whole earth runs after riches, than by his confession of entertaining such ideas. We thought that he had long ago admitted his inability to make money in spite of being Genoese, and that he was resigned and past feeling ashamed of it.

He now solemnly declared, "A man who does not love figures cannot expect them to love him."

Our mother Susanna shrugged her shoulders. She thought little of her husband's flashes of inspiration, which were both frequent and of no practical use whatsoever for improving the family's frugal daily life.

My father was delighted by his sudden discovery that figures were persecuting him. He thought that it both explained and excused his failures. But how could he keep the figures from passing on this animosity of theirs to his descendants? The question weighed on his mind for weeks before he came home with the solution.

"I've found the answer!"

"So by what miraculous means are you suddenly going to make figures love you?" Susanna asked him.

"It's too late for me. But I've found a man who will teach our children about them."

This man was an Algerian Arab, Master Haddad, a former pilot who had suddenly suffered a bad attack of sea-sickness. He had been put ashore half dead and nothing would induce him to go to sea again. The mere sight of the harbour filled him with terror. He was living by his wits, including the ability to give lessons in mathematics, which he drew from long knowledge of the subject in his family.

A group of fathers as poor as ours and, like him, sure that their failure to make a fortune came from the ill will of numbers, had clubbed together to pay the old sailor a few coins to teach us.

My mother protested. "Another of your nonsensical notions! Paying a penny to that brigand is out of the question."

My father slammed the door behind him and came back a little later with the former pilot.

"It's up to you," he told him. "Convince this dragon my wife and the deal is done."

The gentle and almost fragile demeanour and voice of our potential teacher made a good impression. But my mother still held out. She could not believe that mathematical exercises were any use.

"Daily life doesn't need such complications!"

"Once upon a time ..." began the candidate for the post of teacher, and the entire family, including three cats, fell under his spell.

"Once upon a time, in Baghdad, ten centuries before the birth of Jesus Christ, that is to say about four centuries before the present day" – as he said "about" a glint of malice briefly lit up his old face, showing that a still youthful spirit was only waiting for life to prove itself less cruel – "Once upon a time there was a caliph called Al Ma'moun. This caliph, like all caliphs, had his ferocious moments, but the rest of the time he wished for the welfare of his people.

"The caliph's reasonable anxiety was the same as yours, Senhora," he said, bowing his head in our mother's direction. "He was not prepared to respect – and to finance – mathematicians unless they could prove that they were useful. He summoned the man who, his councillors had told him, was the most capable of them all, al'Khwarizmi. As his name suggests, he was from Khwarizm, a region in central Asia south of the Aral Sea. The caliph charged him with 'making what was obscure clear, and what was difficult easy'. Al-Khwarizmi bowed, thanked the caliph for such an honour and went away to shut himself up in the cell allotted to him in the heart of what was called the House of Wisdom. He never left it for two years and no one was allowed to disturb him. His meals were left on a window-sill.

"At last he came out, with his eyes dazzled by the sunlight after so many days shut away from it. He was holding some sheets of paper and lost no time in presenting them to the caliph, who was waiting with patience of a kind unusual among the powerful.

"'You certainly took your time,' said the caliph. 'I hope for your sake that you're not going to disappoint me.'

"'My book,' replied al-Khwarizmi, 'is an account encompassing the finest and noblest methods of calculation that men need for managing their inheritance and making their donations, for the division of their goods and their judgements, for their trades and for all transactions between themselves, such as tilling the soil and building canals, as well as other aspects of human life and other techniques.'"

The former seaman fell silent, while his audience, the Columbus family, came back from Baghdad and that distant century.

"I propose to teach your children a summary of that book."

My father took both my mother's hands. "Think of that! There's the knowledge that I never had! At last our family will occupy the place that it deserves!"

And so it was that our mother agreed, not without suppressing a final misgiving. Wouldn't calculation, a Muslim invention, contaminate her offspring and lead them in the direction of either madness or excommunication? She went to see her confessor, who reassured her: for a long time, he told her, all merchants of any importance had used these methods and were very much at ease with them, to the greater glory of the true God.

I remember the first lesson. Our master spoke only about the word *algebra*.

"Do you want to be strong, children?"

"Yes, of course, master!"

"Do you want to impose your will on others?"

"Yes, yes, we'd like them to be our slaves!"

"Do you want to know how to deal with fractions?"

"They could always come in useful, master!"

"Do you want to know the law of time?

"We don't know exactly what that means, master, but why not?"

"Very well: the Arabic word *Jabr*, which gives us the word *algebra*, is all that: strength, constraint, the reduction of fractions and the order of events."

I remember the way in which al-Kharizmi put his problems. He always took them from daily life. You would have thought they were riddles. Some of them are still firmly anchored in my memory, I don't know why.

"*Take a fortune. Subtract one-third of it plus three dirhams. Then multiply what remains by itself. And you have a fortune again.*"

Or:

"*Take a triangular plot of land. Its two sides measure ten cubits and its base twelve cubits. What would the side of the square measure?*"

When our master felt that our attention was straying, he caught it again by telling another story about Baghdad.

"One day Caliph al-Wathiq called all the astrologers of the House of Wisdom together.

"'How long do I have to live?' he asked.

"The astrologers did their calculations, did them again and settled on the number of fifty years.

"The caliph rewarded them with presents of horses, precious stones and other valuable gifts. He died ten days later.

"And now, children, back to work! *A man dies. He leaves four sons. He makes a gift to a neighbour equal to the share of one of the sons and a gift to another equal to a quarter of what remains of one-third of it ...*"

Our father worried at regular intervals: had our relationship with numbers really improved? He still considered them a powerful tribe, one that he almost believed dominated Genoa. With the support of that tribe we were sure to make our fortunes. Without it, we would be doomed to mediocrity.

Our enthusiasm delighted him, all the more so because we used words that he didn't understand.

"The hypotenuse has no secrets from us now."

"We must tell you all about cubic roots some day."

Then he raised himself to his full height, which was not very tall, took us by the shoulders and led us into the city.

"Do you know my children? This is Christopher, the elder brother, and here is Bartholomew. Look at them well. They're going to do great things. How can I be so sure of that?"

He laughed heartily, amazed to think that anyone could doubt such an obvious fact.

"Do I really need to explain?" Then, with a casual air, he looked at anyone who didn't seem to believe him and confided in an undertone, "They are making friends with numbers."

Unfortunately we didn't have long enough to learn much. All the same Master Haddad taught us certain truths.

For instance, the multiple nature of time.

"The time of the farmer who sows and harvests is not the same as the time of the merchant who buys and sells. Nor is it the time of the banker who lends and then waits to be repaid. Do you know what numbers are for, children?"

"No, master."

"They're for changing all these different kinds of time into a time common to them all and measurable by money."

"We don't understand, master!"

"And yet it's simple and necessary, if you want to be good Genoese, which means good merchants. Tomorrow I'll explain what a rate of interest is."

"We hope that will be less obscure, master."

He also invited us to marvel at another miracle, *the beauty of triangles.*

"Do you know what the first triangle is, children?"

"No, master."

"The triangle formed by your two eyes and the thing or the person you are looking at."

"Then what, master?"

"Close one eye."

"Done it, master."

"Don't you notice anything?"

"No, master."

"You've lost your sense of distance. You don't know whether the thing or person you are looking at is close to you or far away."

"You're right, master!"

"Among other powers, the triangle allows us to calculate distances."

It was also this Master Haddad who taught us why the globe is divided into 360 degrees. The question occurred to me one morning, and I thought it urgent: why not a simpler number, like 100 or 400?

Master Haddad, our teacher, smiled. As if the habitual sweetness of his own manner were not enough, he was now about to speak of beings for which he felt especial affection.

"Numbers are a people apart, Christopher and Bartholomew, a distinguished and mysterious people. Human beings use them, but they do not trust them. They are always trying to attach them to visible, concrete reality. That is why we like the number 10 so much: because we have ten digits on our hands. It is the same with 360. What kind of shape does a year look like? A circle: the seasons pass, the seasons return. How many days in a year? 365. What is the closest round number? 360. In choosing it we are making the measurements of space and time correspond. You will find out later, when you are older, that echoes or correspondences of that kind are soothing. And there's more besides. Tomorrow I will explain ..."

There was no one like Master Haddad for leaving us in suspense. It was a small form of torture, he had explained, that would help us to understand. The mind uses the time of waiting to hear more to go back over what it has learnt, for instance looking at the ten digits of our hands with a new eye.

And impatience to know the rest sharpens the brain.

I didn't even let him sit down the next day before I asked, "So why is it 360?"

As always, he went a long way round in approaching the subject.

"Once upon a time, long before Jesus Christ was born, there was a group of wise men, who were called wise because they liked to look at the sky and foretell the future from the movement of the stars. They lived between two great rivers, the Tigris and the Euphrates. It is likely that this proximity to flowing water also contributed to their deep understanding of time. These wise men liked nothing better than solving problems, and that passion of theirs, which may seem strange, is at the heart of their character. Thus, in exploring the capacities of numbers, they came to *sixty* and marvelled at its powers: it is *divisible* by one, two, three, four, five and six. No lower number has those powers. Among all the useful qualities of a number, that of designating a *quantity* is the most obvious. And the more easily the quantity thus designated can be divided, the more useful the number will be. That is why the Babylonians saw *sixty* as the most useful of all numbers . Delighted by their discovery, they applied it to all sorts of purposes. In order to measure time, for instance: the hours were divided into sixty minutes, and the minutes into sixty seconds ..."

I opened my mouth to interrupt this flow of words, as clear as it was relentless, but Master Haddad had already guessed my question.

"You are going to ask: why not *a hundred* minutes? Because *a hundred* is not divisible by *three*. The Babylonians set the circumference of the earth at 360 degrees."

"Six times sixty."

"Well done, Bartholomew!"

But before a year of lessons was up our master disappeared without trace. Perhaps he had gone east, towards the native land of *Jabr*? He spoke of a pilgrimage that he wanted to make before he died. In those parts, he said, in the direction of Baghdad or even further east, in the middle of the lands there and of the Silk Route, on the way to Khiva and Samarkand, there was a clarity in the air that helped you to see behind things. And it was that light that had brought *al Jabr*, algebra, into being.

I have seen such a light only very rarely, and for no longer than you see the famous phenomenon of a flash of green light over the sea. But our father was right. The friendship of numbers brightens the light and so increases your abilities; behind disorder you see an order that others, those who have not made friends with numbers, do not see.

Those mathematical memories from long ago came back to us one day when a man walked into our shop.

"I'm from Nuremberg. I've heard about two brothers called Columbus. Are you the Columbus brothers? I need your knowledge."

Christopher looked at the newcomer with amazement. "Who are you? You don't look like any other cartographer."

"My name is Martin Behaim, and I am a cosmographer by trade."

"Behaim, Behaim …"

Christopher took a childlike pleasure in names, particularly when they referred to places. He turned them over and over in his mouth like something delicious to eat.

"Behaim means Bohemia, doesn't it? Is that where you come from, as we come from Genoa?"

"I expect so," replied our guest. "Bohemia is part of our family legend. Even if one always comes from further away than might be thought. I live in Nuremberg, and Regiomontanus, whose real name is Johannes Müller, taught me algebra and geometry. Do you know *De triangulis omnimodus*?"

Christopher shrugged his shoulders, like a man who has no time to waste on German lucubrations.

Behaim said he was wrong to disdain triangles. Once they were tamed they became incomparable measuring instruments.

We assumed haughty expressions, and assured him that no one knew better than us how powerful those geometrical shapes were. Now we'd be glad if he would hurry up and tell us what he had come for. We had work to do. Behaim apologized for troubling us. He had heard, he said, of my brother's reputation as a navigator. Since it was his ambition to create as complete as possible a terrestrial globe some day, one summing up all the knowledge acquired by mankind, the contribution to it of a seaman like Christopher would be invaluable. In exchange, he suggested providing the most useful mathematical and cosmographical information for a ship sailing the high seas, when there was no coast in sight and the vessel could be steered only by the stars.

Christopher muttered that while he might not be German, reading the skies was a skill not entirely unknown to him, as anyone could tell from the fact that he was here in Lisbon, not lost and going around in circles somewhere in the middle of the ocean. Moreover, this idea of a globe appeared to him far-fetched.

A wide-ranging discussion ensued, and here I call on my poor head to report it faithfully.

"A globe? What a strange idea! There's nothing more inconvenient than a ball when you're at sea. I was once stupid enough to take a ball on board, and however hard I tried to keep it in one place it kept rolling from side to side of the deck."

"Knowledge of the earth is not solely reserved for seamen."

This piece of ordinary common sense, delivered in the same soft voice that he used for everything he said, stupefied Christopher. He looked at Martin with his jaw dropping, as if he thought he must have gone mad. Christopher's mind could not imagine travel without navigation. As he saw it, the Silk Road itself was navigated by captains whose ships were camels, and Marco Polo had not walked but sailed from Venice to the court of the Grand Khan.

Martin fell silent. He gave my brother all the time he needed to adjust to the improbable idea that sailors were not the only human beings capable of showing intelligence.

After a long pause, Christopher nodded. Once, then twice.

"All right, let's suppose it isn't. Then what?"

Once again our Bohemian visitor let some time pass before returning to the attack.

"All maps are flat. However, all the flat maps are wrong, because the earth is round."

To my surprise, my brother agreed without turning a hair.

"I know, but what size will your globe be?"

Martin spread his arms.

"You think you can fit everything we know about the planet into that small space?"

"I shall at least give a faithful image of it."

Christopher thought about it. "Fundamentally, yes, maps are wrong but useful. Globes are true but no use."

They talked on and on. It's very likely that their discussion went on all night, although I can't swear to it, since not being as impervious to slumber as my brother I fell asleep. In the morning Martin Behaim, or Bohemia, and Christopher were still debating the matter.

I ventured to interrupt them by pointing out that certain duties necessary to our material survival awaited us.

Once again Behaim apologized profusely, but my brother waved all that aside, assuring him that he had seldom enjoyed himself so much. He would like them to meet again as soon as possible, he said; why not this evening?

As we walked to our place of work at a brisk pace, I heard Christopher thanking God for sending him this opportunity to exchange ideas.

"Didn't you tell me, Bartholomew, that Eratosthenes of Alexandria measured the size of the earth by drawing triangles?"

And so Alexandria – and triangles – assumed new importance in life of the Columbus family.

※

For relaxation between two lessons, Behaim often told us about the life of his master, the inexhaustible Regiomontanus.

He had been born in a village near Königsberg, which in the German language means "the king's mountain". That explained his Latin name. After learning astronomy and making astrolabes, teaching optics and translating two books by Ptolemy, he had fallen passionately in love with triangles.

On Sundays, to calm his mind, he used to build automata. His masterpiece was a wooden eagle which can be seen on the spire of the church of St Elizabeth. It leaves its nest when an important person arrives. "It will do the same when you arrive," he said, "flying towards you and flapping its wings."

※

"Once upon a time there were the winds," said Christopher.

"I would like to explain projection to you today," replied Martin.

"Once upon a time there were the currents," added Christopher the next day.

"Do you understand about the magnetic north?" asked Martin.

Sitting in his corner, little Diego was drawing. He often drew dragons.

When Martin left us late at night, he would thank us for the ideas we had exchanged with him, bowing very low and including me in his gratitude, although my own contribution was solely to listen. I was so happy not to be considered a negligible quantity, as our visitors usually thought me, that I did not notice his infirmity at once: the man never smiled. His face was fixed in gravity as if he had been forbidden, by who knows what superior and jealous authority, ever to show the slightest pleasure.

⁂

Six months after Christopher's death, at the end of that dismal summer when I went from town to town, never finding anywhere hot enough to melt the ice in my heart, a letter finally caught up with me. It came from Nuremberg. I opened it with my pulses thudding, as if it came from a country where my brother was still alive. I was not entirely wrong. Martin offered me his condolences, recalling our youth, when Christopher and he had divided the world between them.

Your brother chose the better part: the unknown. What is known, as I have found out from experience, is not worth the sacrifice of one's life, even less so when it is always outflanked by the unknown. In the year when your brother was making discoveries, I contented myself with reproducing what was known.

During my stay in Lisbon, you were always asking me why I never smiled. Today I will tell you what I have never confessed to anyone; checking the facts brings one no merriment.

I ought to feel the most bitter and lasting hatred for your brother. Ah, the accursed year 1492! His voyage of discovery falsified my globe at the very moment when I was finishing it. I was glorying in

191

presenting the whole of our planet, at the same time as he was proving the existence of new lands. I was very angry. Anger is worst in scholars because if you cannot express it in blows or brawling it corrodes you from inside. I shut myself away. I was suddenly overcome by a strange malady: I had become deaf to all sounds, rumours and tales concerning the west. I recovered a little peace of mind by thinking again about our wives, his wife Filipa and my wife Martha. It seemed to me that we had chosen similar women, the daughters of islands: his from Porto Santo, mine from the Azores. Women are in the vanguard, they are like ships themselves, and the love they give you is a voyage. You encounter storms. You smell rare scents. You walk among plants that you never knew before.

Perhaps it was on that day, thinking of those islands and our wives who were of similar origins, that I shook off the curse you noticed and for a moment I smiled.

Those two women are dead, lying still in the earth, and so is your brother, who in his life was always moving. And I have dragged myself to moulder away in Nuremberg, further from the sea than any other place I could find in Europe. Life is over for us. The best part of it was our friendship in Lisbon. Each of us was following his dream and paying just enough attention to the dream of the other to draw material from it to nourish his own. No passionate man can feel enthusiastic about a passion that is not his. But we reduced that indifference, a constituent part of our natures, as much as was possible.

He concluded with two sentences that failed to hit their target.

Dear Bartholomew, do not mistake your sadness, as a survivor, for his. As I knew him, I know that his advance towards death expressed his last and strongest curiosity.

I never replied to him. You owe a man like Martin Behaim, Martin of Bohemia, the truth. I would have had to tell him about Christopher's final terrors, his fears, his delirium, his anguish in the night. It was not in the least like the feverish exultation of the navigator hastening to discover unknown territory.

One day in June 1484, Christopher said he was ready. His

conversations with Behaim had filled those few gaps in his knowledge to which he would admit. The time had come to face the Committee of Mathematicians, that formidable body of men who had the king's ear. Without the favourable opinion of the said Committee, we could not hope for money to finance the voyage.

King John II loved knowledge. And like all who are racked and thus alarmed by that passion, he had surrounded himself with scholars to whose advice he listened.

Among all the disciplines of knowledge, he showed a preference for mathematics. He saw that science as more than a matter of simple games to entertain the mind, more than a language, more than a secret order of things that nature seems to obey: he saw it as an arm of government.

He said more than once that a country as small in size as his kingdom of Portugal had no option but to become mathematical.

When he was asked, with all possible respect, to say exactly what he meant by that, he explained that intelligence was the only resource of the weak. Consequently, as mathematics was the supreme manifestation of intelligence, the kingdom should be allied to that branch of knowledge.

Such was the logic that had induced him to set up the Committee of Mathematicians.

Forgive my memory; I cannot recall all its members. I remember only the most eminent of them, that is to say the most formidable, those who attacked our project most fiercely when the time had come to present it to the king.

There was a churchman among them, Diego Ortiz de Vilhegas.

There was the Jew Rodrigo, so famous that he needed only to give his first name in order to shine brightly, a cosmographer, and also astrologer and physician to the royal family.

There was the other Jew, José Vizinho, also a physician from time to time, but principally recognized all over Europe as a master of algebra, one of the most famous professors at the University of Salamanca.

એ

Diego Ortiz de Vilhegas, unofficial co-ordinator of the Committee of Mathematicians, believed with all his heart in God and marvelled daily at his Creation. That is to say, he had a relationship of confidence and even affection with reality, unlike most of his colleagues, who liked nothing so much as to take refuge in the peace of equations and the neat order of demonstrations, and always cursed the stinking, noisy and imprecise chaos of daily life. Vilhegas had therefore suggested the idea, which the king thought excellent, of going for walks. Yes, simple walks by the Committee through the city or over the nearby fields.

"Believe me, friends, to avoid the worst of evils, the evil of madness, it is better to verify the fact that certain material things exist outside our brains," he said, "and that such information is not necessarily a threat or bad news."

The first walk, confined to the centre of Lisbon, was a nightmare to the mathematicians, confirming them in their view that the only tolerable company to keep was the company of numbers.

As soon as they left the royal palace the pallor of their faces, their resemblance to the living dead, their abstracted expressions and clumsy gait, in a word, their oddity, attracted the attention of first two, then ten, than a hundred street urchins who would not leave them alone. Wishing to recall the material diversity of the world to his mathematical friends, as well as certain aspects of creation that resisted imprisonment in equations – for example scents and colours – Vilhegas had imagined that they would pass through Terreiro do Paço square and thus the market place. This exposure to material reality did not last long. As soon as the group entered the labyrinth of stalls it was bombarded by one, then ten, then a hundred over-ripe projectiles in which, if their minds had been on observation and classification that day, they would have recognized pears, figs, pomegranates, guavas and even a few eggs. But their minds were bent only on escaping. A patrol of soldiers, noticing the disorder, rescued them from their plight.

Diego Ortiz was not going to admit defeat. He tried the experiment again in quieter surroundings.

And gradually the city became used to those little processions of absent-minded scholars ill at ease in their own bodies. Furthermore, fear now protected them. Their role in the councils of the king had become known.

That day, a Sunday, when we had just handed in our report for discussion on the following day, we ourselves had a lesson in reality. I had persuaded Christopher to give his brain a rest and go out with Diego and me to the cape where certain families were watching the sea. They had gone to the very edge of the cliff; one more step and they would have fallen off. They were like a black line drawn along the coast of the kingdom of Portugal.

I jumped – the Committee was coming our way. Christopher turned. The mathematicians passed without so much as glancing at us. They were deep in discussion. One of them was asking what brought this crowd of women here, blocking the view.

"We did," another of them told him. "Yes, we did. With our inconsiderate backing of voyages of discovery."

The Committee stopped, obviously astonished by this response.

"By our recommendations to the king, we send thousands of sailors far out on the seas, and less than half of them come back. As a result we are making an equivalent number of weeping widows or future widows."

"What does it matter?"

"What are women for?"

"By the way, who can tell me the chemical composition of tears?"

I did not hear the rest of it. The Committee had gone on with its walk.

Listen, Las Casas.

Take note of this, Jerome.

The day that I am about to describe to you is of prime importance in the history of the Discoveries: it was the day when Portugal turned down my brother's gift. It was the day when Portugal deprived herself of the New World.

I opened the little window, hardly more than a slit, looking out over Lisbon harbour. Far away, at the bottom of the hill, ships were emerging one by one from the darkness. It seemed to me that I had never heard the seagulls call so much. There is a kind of obsession in the Columbus family: we have a tendency to believe that every other living creature is preoccupied with us. I therefore told myself that these birds had guessed the importance of the day and were wishing us good luck. I thanked them with a sweeping gesture, never doubting that our feathered friends would see and appreciate it. Behind me, Christopher was waking up. As always, he had slept with his fists clenched, unlike me. And he had kept muttering the words of his introductory presentation: "Sire, my noble masters of the Committee …" As soon as I felt myself falling asleep he would start again. "Sire, my noble masters of the Committee …"

We dressed as if for the holiday procession on 15 August, the feast of the Assumption, and feeling sorry that our mother could not see us in our best clothes, we set off for the royal palace with our hearts beating fast.

Mocking children escorted us. Christopher didn't even notice them. He was reciting Seneca's prophecy, one of his most recent finds. Who, or what mysterious forces, had made him immerse himself in the tragedy of *Medea*?

He had found some lines there that excited his fervent interest.

Venient annis
Secula seris, quibus Oceanus

Vicnula rerum laxet, et ingens
Pateat telus tiphisque novos
Detegat orbes nec sit terris
Ultima tille

He gave me a somewhat more explanatory translation of these lines, as was his wont. He bent not just his family but also words and numbers to his will.

In the distant years of the world, there will come a time when the Ocean Sea will cast off the moorings of things and a great land will open up. And a new sailor, like the helmsman Tiphys who was Jason's pilot, will discover a multifarious world, and the island of Thule will no longer be the last of the lands.

At first I didn't understand the reason for his enthusiasm. He had looked all around to make sure that no one was paying us any attention and then lowered his voice.

"Tiphys was Jason's pilot, as I shall be the pilot of the king of Portugal."

Those six lines had never left him since that day. He recited them whenever he felt threatened. This was his new strategy for making himself invulnerable. What did a man whose coming was foretold by Seneca have to fear from an ordinary Committee of Mathematicians?

Soon he was devoting himself body and soul to this quest, searching books, and first and foremost the sacred texts, in which with a little imagination you could read that someone resembling him would come to earth to do the will of God. In this way he had also recruited St Thomas Aquinas, Nicholas of Lyra, St Augustine, the whole of the Bible and the evangelists to justify his ambition.

One day, a little while before his death, he would publish a collection of those notes of his: *The Book of Prophecies*.

I, having no such shield and no belief that Holy Scripture announced my coming, was worried to death. My brother's calculations had never entirely convinced me. Although I took care to bury it deep in my mind, in case any mathematician heard it, a little voice kept telling me that the earth was larger than Christopher claimed.

197

And the fact that he was boosting his own stature did not change that.

First we were received very courteously by the king, with only his chamberlain in attendance. A large table was waiting, but he offered us chairs in front of the hearth, as if for a conversation between friends. As soon as we were seated, I was wishing myself a crab, a worm or a flatfish, one of those creatures that can hide underground. For my idiot brother, as soon as the usual compliments had been paid, protestations of our respect proclaimed and the aim of our voyage called to mind ("to discover large countries, islands and terra firma by sailing west, to reach the western coast of India, as well as the huge island of Cipango and the kingdoms of the Grand Khan"), shamelessly went straight to the point: his own demands.

"In return for undertaking this Enterprise, I wish to be honoured and armed as a knight, with the right to wear golden spurs ..."

The chamberlain gave a start. The king narrowed his eyes. My brother went on:

"I want the title of Grand Admiral of the Ocean Sea ..."

Here the chamberlain got to his feet.

"This Genoese has taken leave of his senses."

The king calmed him with a gesture. It seemed to me that a glint of amusement had come into his eyes.

" ... and to be granted the position of viceroy and governor in perpetuity of all the islands and the terra firma that I may discover in person, or that may be discovered as a result of my industry."

By now the chamberlain had been infected by the king's mirth.

"Is that all?" he asked.

My brother did not seem to notice these reactions. As so often, he was living on another planet, in the world of his dream.

He took out a piece of paper and began to read it, raising his demands on the debit side all the time.

"I want one-tenth of all the revenue deriving from all the gold, silver, pearls and precious stones found, and deriving from all the metals, spices and other lucrative items, and all kinds of merchandise bought, exchanged, found or conquered within the bounds of my admiralty ..."

He took a breath.

"... as well as the right to contribute a one-eighth part of the expenditure of all the expeditions to the newly discovered lands, in return taking one-eighth of the profits drawn from them."

"You are asking a great deal," said the king.

"I am offering even more!"

The king nodded his head and raised his right hand as if to pacify a man getting carried away.

"Perhaps you will allow us to look at your project first."

He signed to an usher. One by one, eleven black figures slipped into the room and took their seats at the large table: the Committee. Without waiting to be asked to do so, as if in a hurry to oppose them, Christopher sat down opposite. I joined him. The king had not moved from his armchair and did not leave that retreat all though the debate.

Master José Vizinho took charge of the interrogation. Of all the mathematicians, he was the one we most feared. Everyone knew that he had been a student of the very learned Rabbi Abraham Zacuto, a leading light at the university of Salamanca. Who could argue against such an authority? Master José's opinion would be the deciding factor in forming the king's judgment.

All the more so in that his mind was incomparably clear.

"Before we come to the heart of the business, please remember, Messer Columbus, that we have no opposition in principle to your Enterprise. Our part is solely to asses its possibility. Let us begin with the most important point: according to you, what are the dimensions of the Ocean Sea that you propose to cross?"

"Pierre d'Ailly has replied to that question in his eighth chapter, at the end of a long inquiry: it is a narrow sea."

"To say it is narrow is not a measurement, Messer Columbus. We cannot content ourselves with vague feelings. Let us come to the figures. And to assess the size of the ocean, let us first try to agree on the extent of terra firma. We will begin with what is obvious: as our planet is round, the further the continent of Europe and Asia extends to the east, the shorter will be the way to reach it going west ..."

The heads of all the Committee were bent in unison. You would have said that reasoning was music to which they were beating time. No one looked at the speaker, Master Vizinho. Their eyes converged on the face of my brother, who for the moment seemed to be controlling his tension. Only I, who knew him better than anyone in the world, had noticed his right eyelid beating faster than the left lid. Master Rodrigo too was burning with unrestrained fire. The fingers of his left hand were tapping the table and his lips were raised at the corners, showing the points of his teeth; he was an impatient man who liked to draw blood.

Master Vizinho began again. Where, in what parts of his throat or stomach, did he find the formidably dulcet tone that he gave to his voice?

"Let me repeat my question. Take our globe, the circumference of which extends, by definition, over 360 degrees. What part of that 360 degrees do Europe and Asia together occupy?"

"262 degrees. Consequently the Ocean Sea that I am suggesting you help me to cross occupies only 78 degrees."

Master Rodrigo could not contain himself. "Nonsense! How did you come to that number of degrees?"

Christopher's first mistake: he was too quick with his reply.

"360 minus 282 equals 78."

Master Rodrigo's eyes flashed.

"Thank you, we can all do subtraction. I am talking about the figure of 282 degrees."

"According to my own work, which agrees with the conclusions of the very knowledgeable Greek Ptolemy, whose work in its own turn is confirmed by all accounts of travels, beginning with the authoritative writings of the Venetian Marco Polo, the number cannot be less than 282."

"Nonsense!"

Unimpressed, Christopher added that, as he planned to begin his voyage from the Canary Islands, he would be taking ship over 9 degrees further west. The extent of his navigation therefore would not be greater than 78 degrees minus 9 degrees, which equals 69 degrees.

Dom Diego Ortiz had his work cut out to restore peace. He asked Master Vizinho to go on. The king never took his eyes off Christopher.

"We will return to the number of degrees. Let us go on to the dimensions of each of them. To what distance does a degree correspond?"

Christopher was already opening his mouth. Master Vizinho interrupted him.

"For those who are not, like us, versed in these matters, I will recall
…"

And he delivered a clear, brief lesson in all the kinds of degrees then in force. It was at that moment that I saw our Enterprise about to founder.

"Well, Messer Columbus, what do you say is the measurement of a degree?"

"56 and two-thirds miles!"

"Ah, the Christian degree! As if by chance! If you could have found an even smaller one, you would have chosen it. Have you never heard that the best cosmographers assess it at 62 and a half miles?"

Much hubbub ensued, punctuated by sarcasm that no longer hurt us, we were so inured to it by now. Reference was made to our Genoese dishonesty, our Genoese impudence, our Genoese ignorance.

Once again Dom Diego had to speak up if the meeting was to continue. Master Rodrigo was the worst of them. You would have thought him a hound kept on the leash too long and finally allowed to fling himself at the stag.

Only the dulcet tones of Master Vizinho succeeded in calming tempers to some small extent.

"Let us look at the last and perhaps most important point, Messer Columbus, in assessing the extent of the voyage you are suggesting to us. How much, would you say, does a mile measure? Wait, wait! I will guess. Something tells me that yet again you will have chosen the shortest, the Italian mile, which is less by a quarter than the Arab mile. Am I wrong?"

My brother could only agree. He did so with arrogance, despite the sarcasm: yes, of course, the Italian mile. What kind of Christian would he be, he asked, to put his faith in the calculations of unbelievers?

This time Dom Diego had to mention the presence of the king before any semblance of silence could be restored.

"Our Committee now appears to me sufficiently well informed. According to Messer Columbus, then, and under his control, the sea that he proposes to cross in a westerly direction is … narrow. Because first, a restricted number of degrees separates us from India: 78. And because second, each of these degrees, as he sees it, covers a distance of 56 miles plus two-thirds of a mile. And because, third, these miles are Italian, that is to say the shortest miles. If you have nothing to add," here he paused for a moment, "then I declare this meeting of our Committee closed. The said Committee will report to Your Majesty within a week."

His Majesty rose and, entirely unexpectedly, went over to my brother, all smiles, and even more surprisingly took both his hands before, in the total silence that had miraculously fallen, speaking yet again of his affectionate regard for him, as well as his interest in the Enterprise, "of which [and here I remember his exact words] I hope you will speak to me again soon."

Remarkably enough, the expressions of the faces of the Mathematicians changed as soon as they heard these warm royal words. The contempt they showed for my brother turned to amiability. I even heard the most terrifying of them all, Master Rodrigo, murmur encouragement.

"It will be sufficient, Captain, for you to revise certain calculations for us to deliver an entirely favorable opinion on your fine project."

Such is the nature of the human ear: it hears the voice of power more distinctly than the voice of conviction.

It was with those two expressions of goodwill in mind, the spontaneous words of the king and the diplomatic words of the Committee speaking like courtiers, that we waited for the verdict.

Unfortunately for us, the Mathematicians had the souls not of courtiers but of scientists. Away from the presence of their king, they retrieved their dignity by saying what they really thought: "The calculations of the seaman Columbus may serve his personal ends but do not in any way serve the truth. Consequently, if by any chance Your Majesty were to give financial support to this voyage, you would stand every chance of losing not just your stake in it but also the respect of reasonable men."

King John II summoned my brother, showed him the conclusions of the Committee and said that he was very sorry, but given the high reputation of these scholars he could not disregard their opinion. Repeating his regrets, he gave Christopher many signs of his high regard and affection. And as he accompanied him to the door – a signal honour – he asked my brother not to hold this decision against him and to remain faithful to the crown of Portugal.

These noble and sensitive words, instead of mollifying Christopher, fanned the flames of his anger. That evening his decision was made. For himself, but also for me.

The Columbus family, not the kind of men who will put up with insults, could not stay a day longer in the kingdom of Portugal, closed as it was to the spirit of the True Discoveries.

I must admit, however, that all the same it took us another week to sell what anyone would buy from us, close the shop and pack up ready to leave.

And so we left my beloved Lisbon on 17 October of the year 1484. I like to think my impression of that day is well-founded: the city seemed as sorry as the king to see us leave. But it is true that Lisbon takes pleasure in affliction. We travelled together to Coimbra and there our horses went different ways. Father and son were going to Spain. I was to take the road to Porto and then north. I felt a pang in my heart as I cast them a last glance.

My brother was holding the hand of little Diego, who was now nearly five. I was holding nothing. Christopher had given me the mission, not a very clear-cut one, of defending the cause of the Indies Enterprise at the royal courts of England and France.

And so my story ended. I can assure you that my two Dominicans had heard it with bated breath. They had not interrupted me once. Every day for the three weeks that the account had taken me, Las Casas and his scribe Jerome had arrived at the appointed hour, as if they lived only for the story. Every day they had come through the chapel to reach my room, where they sat down to listen to me, as motionless as corpses. Only Jerome's fingers moved as he made notes.

To tell a story is to navigate. You need inspiration as the navigator needs a good wind and then it carries you along. I had found my inspiration in Christopher

I waited some time for one of them to ask questions, at least for the sake of civility, about my eight years in England and France.

No questions came. I was not surprised. They were interested only in Christopher.

Then I rose to my feet.

"I have no more to say. You know the rest better than I do: how my brother finally persuaded Queen Isabella and King Ferdinand to support him. Then the famous departure on 3 August 1492 from Palos de Moguer."

The Dominicans had risen in their turn. Las Casas took my hands. He told me how grateful he was several times, with warmth and, it seemed, with conviction.

Then he wished me good health. He was leaving for Spain. He and Montesinos were going there together to plead the cause of the Indians. When he returned, he said, he intended to continue "our conversations", as he called them.

"We have not answered the question, have we? Why did that curiosity, that fevered desire for discovery, suddenly turn to the worst of cruelty?"

I made him a double promise: to try to get somewhere in casting light on that mystery and to try to survive until his return.

They left, two white-robed figures respectfully saluted by the passers by. I followed them with my eyes for a moment, and I was just returning to my retreat when Las Casas came back.

"I have been thinking: Brother Jerome is staying on the island. I would recommend you to take him as your confessor. I know you well now. A haunted soul like yours needs company in preparing for death."

I declined this offer. I could not avoid it any longer now: it was for me, and me alone, to confront the torments of memory.

III

Cruelty

I have decided to give myself a breathing space. For seven days I will try to forget my past. The present is sweeter.

My tomb is built already; I am living in it. The Alcazar is a huge box with tiny square windows, perhaps to show the world that a palace can know what goes on without seeing it. There is a short gallery half way up on the eastern and western sides. This gallery has arcades. No one ever goes there. The soldiers stamping up and down outside the heavy door must think they are guarding an empty palace.

The Alcazar is made of the local stone, which consists of pieces of coral. That is why they look eroded; they were once sunk in the devouring sea. I often pass the palm of my hand over their rough surfaces and express my gratitude to them: living among you, I say, I feel as if I have not left the ocean and my great sadness is that I cannot navigate now. Even better, when no one is looking at me – so as not to add yet further to my already well-established reputation for eccentricity – I put my ear close to one of those eroded stones. And then, as with a shell held to the ear, I hear the sound of the waves breaking.

I have no reason to complain. My dear nephew is very considerate. Whenever his duties as governor leave him the time, Diego comes in person to ask how I am.

Out of respect, which I appreciate, Diego wanted his own apartments to be exactly like mine: an anteroom, a large chamber, a study to work in. We both live in the north wing of the palace: he on the first floor, I on the ground floor. Our lives overlap, except that he rules the Indies and governs our island, while I am of no importance any more.

The other difference between his floor and mine is the presence of a woman, his wife Marie, whom everyone says he loves. Her own apartment is next to his on the western side. Perhaps it was he who wanted the similarity between our apartments – did he also want to remind me of the double gulf between us, the power that I no longer have, the love that I never had? Good actions are often shot through with malicious intentions.

Why do I feel this sudden bitterness? Old age is a bad counsellor, no doubt of it. Ever since his birth on Porto Santo, my nephew and I have been more than friends; we have been allies. What did the twenty-seven years between us matter? We were bound together by the same instinct: those who were close to a man like Christopher could survive the permanent violence of his energy only in league with one another.

Don't think that I am bored. I do not lack for distractions over and beyond the daily work of my memory.

Every Friday, for instance, I accompany the Viceroy on his visit to the new buildings. We go to trudge through sand and mud, to breathe in copious amounts of dust, to risk breaking our bones at every step we take by balancing on unsteady rafters and drystone walls in order to admonish, one by one, all the groups of labourers who are capable of any kind of impudence, first and foremost by arriving on the site late. You should see the governor and his predecessor (Diego and me, uncle and nephew) taking each other's arms in turn, bumping into one another, pointing our forefingers at a view and then another and yet another, both of us delighted to see the beautiful, beautiful city of Santo Domingo rising. Ah, we exclaim, the military Tower of Homage! Anyone who tries to attack us will need courage. Ah, the elegance of that façade! Don't you think it a little too attractive for a monastery and a Dominican monastery at that? Diego, did you know that the house you see over there was the first in the city? I knew the man who lived there, Francisco Garay, one of your father's servants. These foundations promise a gigantic building. You must tell your friend Las Casas that his order has something to worry about: the Franciscans will soon have a monastery of the first importance! Dear Bartholomew, do you feel strong enough to go down into the sewers? The network designed by Nicolas de Ovando is no longer adequate. I've given orders to have it extended ...

Of all the viceroy's activities, building is his favourite. I knew that same enthusiasm when I myself created a city. It is intoxicating to see an idea become an outline traced on a sheet of paper, to see that outline become stones and the stones become churches, palaces, a hospital; and then to see life, to see the place teeming with people who have moved in where, not long before, there was nothing but grass and trees. Madness lies in wait for the man who tells himself, I am the cause of this chain of metamorphoses, the madness of feeling that he is the Creator Himself, or at least a member of the Creator's guild.

And these walks give me another pleasure, which I must, unfortunately, admit is even greater than that felt by the builder of cities.

It is a flame that turns in my guts, much as I used to feel in the past when I desired a woman; it is also a fit of sardonic laughter that makes me clench my jaws. It is a luminous gaiety that both floods the inside of my head and tells my legs, for all their weakness, to dance. It is, let me confess it frankly, the incomparable pleasure of revenge.

Do not forget that I had only just been appointed *Adelantado* and Governor of this island, on 5 March 1496, when a troop of Spaniards, greedier and with fewer morals than the rest, rebelled against the rule of law and order that I intended to prevail in the island in future. They were led by a formidable man called Francisco Roldán – whom Las Casas describes in his history as the worst kind of bandit.

Civil war ensued.

The rebels, I don't know how, had pled their cause with the king and queen, and even more improbably had convinced them that I must be replaced. My successor arrived in the summer of 1500, and his first act was to put both Christopher and me in irons and throw us into the hold of a caravel. And so, like malefactors, we were taken back to Spain, where we lost no time in explaining the true facts to the two monarchs. But the damage had been done.

So you will understand my jubilation today.

What could be more delightful than to return in triumph to the scene of one's greatest shame, the viceroy's beloved uncle, benefiting by the official and constantly renewed favour of royalty?

I take pleasure which is never sated in my old enemies' protestations of eternal friendship. And I shall seek out, one by one, those who are impudent enough to avoid me and force them to swear allegiance.

I would like to forgive, but I have too much rancour in me and no doubt I am too petty to attain such magnanimity.

Only three openings link me to the outside world.

The first is no more than a little slit of a window high up above my bed. I have only ever seen it shut.

The second is the door. No one uses it except the servant who brings my meals, my confessor and sometimes my nephew the viceroy.

The third is a friend whom I can reach only at the risk of breaking my bones: a window with two seats made in the thickness of the wall. To reach this wonderful lookout post I have to climb on a chest and, from there, reach a marble ledge as slippery as ice. I know that such exertions are not fitting at my age and one day I shall hurt my head and break both hips. I know that I ought to shake off, once and for all, the curiosity that seems to be the worst part of my nature. But a force inside me always proves stronger than prudence and reason.

The reward once I am up there is worth my efforts and the risks I run. From that vantage point, I can see the entire harbour.

In Genoa no one told anyone's legs to run, yet everyone met down by the harbour. It is true that all the streets had a steep slope and they all led down to the water.

"What use is the rest of the city?" Christopher asked me one day.

We were still under twelve and we came to the conclusion that the rest of the city was no use for anything.

"Do you think there are any cities without a harbour?"

"I don't think anyone could survive in a city like that."

"Nor do I."

Santo Domingo is not Genoa or Lisbon, if only for one reason: in Lisbon and Genoa it was impossible to count all the vessels moored by the quays. In Santo Domingo you can count them on two pairs of hands. I have never seen more than twenty caravels at a time enter the mouth of the Ozama river.

Santo Domingo is only a very small seaport, still in its infancy. The main quay is just a pontoon. As for warehouses, with the best arithmetical will in the world I cannot count more than five of them and the fifth has no roof yet.

Finding me up on my perch one day, Las Casas had asked, "What is it about seaports that you like so much?"

"You see the whole spectacle of life there as you see it nowhere else."

He reflected for some time. Then he nodded. "Just as I thought.

Ports are worth nothing to you." And seeing my baffled glance, he explained further. "You told me you wanted to prepare for death. Ports, I realize, attach you to life, so you ought to break off your contact with them."

I didn't try to work it out. I have met thousands of human beings since my birth, including cosmographers and mathematicians; but for logic there's no one like a Dominican.

Crestfallen, I climbed down from my lookout post and promised myself I would leave more time between my visits to it.

I now wait for night to resume my observations. I watch the port asleep. The tide rises and falls below the motionless caravels. The water reflects the faintest gleam of moonlight. Without hearing it, I guess at its murmuring, which stimulates my bladder. These days I take a container with me so that I need not leave my high window.

The dogs, fierce attack dogs, never stop barking in their kennels. They are given just enough food to keep them alive, but not to quell their ferocity.

Long, dark processions, probably of rats, scurry under the doors of shops. Down outside the gate soldiers are playing dice.

In a low voice, I speak to Christopher. I would like him to give his permission. I was not expected to tell his story; as I said before, it was to his second son Hernán that he entrusted that task. Would I be able to convey our fever of all those years ago?

This morning, as on almost all mornings, Mass was said for the Discoverer. Throughout the service, I wondered what my brother would have thought of the title of Discoverer. He thought his coming had been announced in advance. He thought himself a man appointed. And for him, his work was not a discovery but the accomplishment of a task. I am sure that in his own eyes, he was content to carry out God's plans.

Letting my thoughts wander on, I reflected that the Indians of these islands shared the same universe as Christopher. They too lived in signs from the past. Seeing us arrive on their shores, they did not *discover* us. They *recognized* us. That is why we triumphed over them so easily. How do you find the energy to fight events foreseen since the origins of your history, since the time of its dreams?

When the night is oppressive, and my legs are too heavy for me to climb to my perch, I walk along the walls of coral stones with a candle. I see shells in them, dragonflies fixed there, the skeletons of fish, the branches of sponges, miniature forests. I am truly jealous of those stones: they know how to tell a story without words and the tales they tell fear neither the erosion of libraries, nor floods, nor fires. They are written to remain there for ever and ever. I have no such ambition for my own account.

Well, my seven days of rest are over. I must keep my promise to Las Casas and set off again, cost what it may, in pursuit of the truth.

Perhaps the worm was always in the fruit. Perhaps the violence of the Discovery was already foreshadowed by the violence of our departure.

Friday, 3 August 1492.

Where does that date stand in God's calendar?

To celebrate what secret anniversary did He provide Himself with two spectacles of such intensity on the same day? Being all-powerful, He could have put off one of them to keep them from overlapping. He could have taken a more refined pleasure in each.

But that was not His will.

So He must have had some design. I am still looking for it today.

It is better, it seems, to purge yourself twice before dying: to empty both your bladder and your memory. Then you feel lighter as you leave this earth. At the moment I have emptied my stomach. Now it is the turn of my memories.

The third of August ... the Jews thought of nothing but that date. They were all to have left the kingdom by then. Such was the decision of Queen Isabella and King Ferdinand.

The third of August.

Why did my brother choose the same day to put out to sea? Had he received orders, and if so, from what authority?

I could tell you about the battle that Christopher and his crews had to fight to fend off Jews in desperate search of a ship. I could describe the now legendary Santa Maria, Pinta and Niña leaving the port of Palos in a glorious sunset. I could tell you in detail, and with feeling, about the fleet slowly going down to the sea, with the three caravels lost among other vessels of all kinds; vessels bought by the Jews who had to leave and paid a fortune for them. I could make you hear, through the raucous calls of the seagulls, the weeping and singing of the exiles. I could ... yes, it is a great temptation. This daily confession has aroused a taste in me that I never knew before, a taste for narrative, the pleasure of casting a spell with words, not always respecting the facts.

This time, heroically, I will resist temptation.

This time I will not lie to you.

I arrived too late – yes, you heard me correctly – *too late* to see my brother leave. It was his fault; he didn't think to tell me. And sailors, as I know, do not always make their decisions by the calendar; they leave when they feel like leaving.

It was also the fault of Queen Isabella and King Ferdinand; their decision meant that the roads were clogged. Some of the Jews had decided to take refuge in Portugal. Most of them were making south.

It was impossible to move fast; whole families and yet more families, laden like mules, had crowded on to the roads.

It was useless, and dangerous, to go across country; the farmers would be waiting with pitchforks and dogs.

I had no option but to adjust to the pace of the others on the road with me.

For two days I was a prisoner of my wrath, constantly blaming the whole of this earth for making me miss witnessing the real start of the Enterprise. And then I began to feel interested not just in my own distress but in the distress of others, my travelling companions.

"How many years have you been living in Spain?"

All around me competed to reply. A little girl with a shrill voice won. "Ever since the first destruction of the Temple in Jerusalem!"

Imagine my amazement.

An old man whom I was supporting now and then as he walked along gave me more information. "My granddaughter means the year 585 before the present era. We belong to the tribe of Benjamin. We lived in Toledo. Do you know where that name comes from?"

I confessed to my ignorance. We had had time to talk a little and I had told him about my interest in the origins of words.

"From the Hebrew word *taltelah*, meaning 'tribulations.'"

❧

The third of April had come and gone. With my crowd of Jews, I finally reached Palos, where another crowd of Jews had been on the move for days and days.

Coming, going, assembling, drifting apart, losing each other, finding one another again … human beings had never walked so

And he began lamenting.

He had a voice as thin as the trickle of water that winds its way between the pebbles of the river bed in summer, as frail as all that is of the river itself.

My throat is hoarse from lamentation. My tongue cleaves to the roof of my mouth. My heart beats wildly because of my great sorrow ...

The woman swiftly rose to her feet. "Oh, my God, my God, why You send me a husband like this? My God, my God, why am I always alone in the world in times of war?" And she turned to me. "..., we need bread. Thank you."

※

When I came back with the bread I had got from a baker, threatening at sword-point, I could have sworn that the children had been spruced up for me, their hair combed and almost all the dust brushed off them.

"Thank our friend," said their mother.

The children flung themselves on me, and it was then that I saw, a little way apart from the others, a little boy and a little girl lying in each other's arms. They were embracing. They seemed no older than ...

I asked the woman if she knew these children, and why she did nothing to interrupt their indecent caresses.

"They were married yesterday."

"What, at that age?"

"A rabbi united them in marriage. The wife is my daughter."

I could not help telling her that her religion was a very strange one to authorize such unions between children.

"It is written that the husband must care for his wife, and the wife must care for her husband. Sir, you know everything, what do you think the future holds for us? Nothing but separation and solitude. When they have no one left to look after them, and nowhere to go, their marriage will be the country where they live."

The man had gone back to chanting.

My throat is hoarse from lamentation, / my tongue cleaves to the roof

many steps before or raised so much dust. August is the middle of summer, when the drought is worst. No rain had fallen for months, and as it is water that joins the elements together, the soil was only sand. Mere contact with a foot would send it flying towards the sky.

God, whose greatness is enhanced by contradictions, all praise to His name throughout the centuries, cannot have wanted the spectacle of the distress here to be too visible, even though He Himself had allowed it. Hence His command to the wind not to blow.

It was in this yellowish fog that final and terrible transactions were taking place.

"I want a boat. There are eight of us."

"Hey, this one's a real joker! Why, there's not been so much as a plank available for the last week."

"How much will you give me for this silver dish?"

"Five pesos."

"But it's worth a thousand."

"Take it or leave it."

"Would a house in Madrid interest you? I have the title deeds here."

"I can offer you my donkey."

"Could you repeat that? With all these negotiations going on, I'm afraid I didn't hear you."

"You Jews must have skin over your ears. You'd better circumcise them! Ha, ha! My donkey for your house, that's what I said. Take it or leave it."

"Take it or leave it," "Take it or leave it" – such was the refrain all over the market place in Palos, regularly interrupted by another refrain loudly proclaimed by a soldier, always the same soldier, who was obviously enjoying himself as he forced his way through the crowd again and again.

"Jews! What you stole from Spain will stay in Spain!"

He added to this reminder of the law personal comments, more and more elaborate as time went by, with more and more details and practical suggestions.

"Jews, don't try to hide anything; we know you, we'll search you before we let you leave – your clothes and your bodies, your mouths and your arses. Jews! By order of the king and queen you're not allowed to take anything with you."

Similar chants heightened the ferocity of the negotiations, as if there were any need for that.

"Hear that? If I buy something from you out of the kindness of my heart, I'm conniving at a crime. So take it or leave it. Take it or leave it."

❧

How could that soldier have guessed that one of these Jews, cursed by God, had embarked at his leisure on the Santa Maria?

My brother had written to tell me about his plan. He was going to hire a Jew to act as interpreter when he reached unknown lands. According to him the people of that race, since they do business everywhere, can speak all languages. Ever since the days of Babel, and no doubt to punish them, God has bestowed that knowledge on them. It rends the linguist's mind apart and ends by sending him mad.

And I went to sleep.

I am ashamed to say so, but I went to sleep all of a sudden, just after sitting down on a pile of old rigging.

I know why I fell asleep only too well, and I will tell you in spite of the very poor opinion you will entertain of me when you have heard it.

The cause was not fatigue. Besides, how would I dare to excuse myself by personal exhaustion, when all these families had been milling around here for weeks, and before that had had to walk for weeks to reach the sea here?

I have thought hard about that sleep, that sudden loss of consciousness when all the noise, the pestilential odours, the constant jostling ought to have kept me awake. And I realize that my liking for cartography was a form of the same slumber, arising from the same refusal to see the world as it really is.

What is a map? A piece of the earth, reduced to a small size and pacified. What is a cartographer? A man who manages to live at one remove from life and its horrors. He prefers the portrait to the original, or even better and to preserve even more tranquillity, he prefers the sketch of the portrait. What is a man asleep? A man in flight.

❧

What new courage, gained I don't know how, or
me from that lethargy? I opened my eyes. The
colour. Yellow a little while ago, it was now blac
the night was clearer than the yellow of day. T
full, cast light on hundreds and hundreds of famil
on the quaysides. When they had stopped walk
raised by their feet had fallen on them. Hence th
sand covering them all like a shroud, and the so
"merchants", all of them vanquished by exhaustic
together, victims and executioners alike.

I tore myself away from this sordid connivanc
bodies, I went away from the port. And what is
filled with water when there are no vessels left or

❧

I met shadows. A family of shadows. I counted s
shadows and four child shadows, sitting on a lo
as if they had collapsed on it. They were slowly
then back, all six of them. This is the way that Je
but perhaps they were only swaying with wearin

I went closer. "Have you come a great distanc

The tallest shadow slowly raised his eyes to i
from somewhere very far away. A face appeared,
Two eyes studied me. I can still see them tod;
such astonishment in a pair of eyes. "Anyone m
speaking to me. Anyone might think he was tall
me without barking. I thought all mankind ha
Yet this man is speaking to me. I thought that th
forbidden anyone to talk to Jews!"

Above those eyes, his brows were frowni
someone making an effort, searching his memo

I repeated my offer: could I help them? I re
man's gaze was no longer one of surprise. He i
examination and concluded that it was an illusi
for a non-Jew to approach a Jew offering help.

"Leave us, please, sir."

of my mouth. / My heart beats fast because of my great sorrow and pain, / my sadness is great and prevents / slumber from giving rest to my eyes. / How bitterly I lament, how bitterly! / My anger burns within me like a fire. / To whom shall I tell my sorrow? / If there is any comforter, if he will / have pity on me, take me by the hand, / then I will place my heart before him, / I will tell him some part of my sorrow. / Will I perhaps, in speaking of my grief, / soothe and compose my feelings?

The woman took him by the shoulders, shaking him so hard that I thought he might break to pieces.

"Stop that! Can't you stop it? Stop it just for once! Just for a change, can't you help me?"

The man bowed his head and went on chanting. His only concession was to lower his voice again and the words came out of his mouth without a sound.

I never forgot that lamentation heard on the terrible night of the fifth of August. I thought for a long time that the man had made it up himself.

I did not find out who its real author was until I arrived here on the island of Hispaniola. One day, as I was walking along, recalling those words under my breath, a passer by, hearing me, gave a sudden start and turned around.

"Where did you get to know ..." Afraid, he looked around in all directions. "Where did you get to know the work of Solomon ibn Gabirol?"

My great age and distracted expression must have reassured him enough for him to tell me more.

Solomon had been born shortly after the year 1000 in the Spanish city of Malaga. Orphaned young, he found support in the head of his Jewish community, who was vizier to the Caliph of Saragossa. Child as he was, he enchanted the vizier with his poetry. Unfortunately the vizier was assassinated and many of the community killed. He had to leave Saragossa at the age of nineteen. It was then he composed the lamentation that I had heard murmured almost five centuries later.

Having told me this story, the passerby went on.

And then a reflection occurred to me, one that has accompanied me ever since. As olive trees live through the centuries, so do laments: their roots go deep, deep down into the earth, right to the heart of the human race.

What is a Dominican?

Strange ideas occur to me these days with increasing frequency: for instance, the notion of cutting the body of Las Casas in two when he comes back from Spain, taking out the soul hidden there and examining it at my leisure. It would also be desirable to cut off his head to observe the way his brain works.

What is a Dominican?

When my brother died in the middle of spring 1506, I was devastated. He left me a world all the emptier because he had enlarged it. I was wandering without a destination. Having never really talked to anyone else, I went on talking to him.

People thought me mad.

An idea came to me that before making the great leap into the next world, Christopher had taken refuge in Lisbon. Had it not been in that city that we prepared for his voyage together?

I made haste to go there. I had sent a letter to Samuel, the dear friend of my youth in Master Andrea's studio, the one who liked drawing the faces of his children better than the shores of continents. I had often thought of him. I missed his humanity; I told myself that it alone could bring me a little peace.

Travellers warned me when I reached the frontier of Portugal. Still terrified, they kept saying that the city was stricken by the plague, it was raging there, and to save his life King Manuel had fled to one of his country estates. But I still went on my way. Despair arms you against fears. You are indifferent to misfortunes and even maladies. Perhaps you even wish for them? No doubt, deep inside you, someone is calling on death, which alone will deliver you.

The travellers had told the truth; I found an epidemic rife in Lisbon. But not the plague I expected, something worse, an epidemic of savagery. I had hardly entered through the Levant gate before I met three men pursuing a fourth. They held him against a wall and cut his throat. Turning to me, they looked at me for a long time. When I think back to that scene, I still remember the two knife-points scratching my throat. One of the bandits decided that I "didn't look like one of them." The others agreed and let me go.

Further on I met a howling crowd led by women, who hammered on the closed doors of the church with their fists, shouting, "Open up, hand them over! The fires are waiting to burn them at the stake!"

One of these Furies was brandishing a torch and looked as if she would use it.

The air of Lisbon, which I had known as so sweet, calm and musical, echoed to the sound of shouting, explosions, dull thuds, the hasty footsteps that tell you a man is on the run, and the only scent in the air was the stale, acrid, warm smell of fires.

I quickened my pace, understanding none of this brawling, but beginning to fear for my friend Samuel.

He must have given orders, for as soon as I arrived outside his house the door opened. An old man welcomed me in. "My name is Luis and I serve Master Samuel." And as I was going towards the little courtyard garden I heard three bolts being shot into place behind me. My friend was waiting. We embraced, and without delay, without even waiting for the refreshment of a glass of water, I asked what madness had descended on Lisbon.

"It's a long story," said Samuel, "and we fear to think what the end will be, since each day is followed by one that is even worse.

"Since 1492, Spain has been pressing Portugal to follow its example and expel the Jews. King John resisted. But his successor, Manuel, cherished an ambition to reunite the two Iberian kingdoms under his own rule. With that end in view, he decided to marry the daughter of the Spanish monarchs Isabella of Castile and Ferdinand of Aragon. The princess, also called Isabella, refused to set foot in a country that she said was 'infested'.

"Rather than expel the Jews, King Manuel decided to convert them all, either with their consent or by force.

"On 6 October 1497 – how can we ever forget that date? – soldiers came to our houses to find us and took us away to the port, supposedly towards the ships. There we were, twenty thousand of us on the Ribeira quay, all the Jews of Lisbon, from babies to old men." Samuel smiled. "And we were all baptised together. You see before you a good Catholic."

224

"Really a Catholic?"

"How could we abandon the rituals of our ancestors?"

"Then I can understand why people don't trust you."

"They hate us mainly because now that we are Catholics we share their rights. They used to have their own preserves, they used to have professions exclusively their own. Gradually we have gained access to these privileges. How can they accept competition from us without a struggle?"

Suddenly I was ashamed of myself. I had forgotten the most important thing.

"How are your children?"

Over twenty years had passed since we worked in Master Andrea's studio. Of course they would have grown up and left their parental home. But I looked in vain for any sign of them in this house and suddenly I sensed a great void there.

My eyes went back to Samuel. He was sobbing.

He sobbed for a long time, without shedding tears. I laid my hand on his shoulder.

Some turtle doves approached him. You might have thought they felt his grief.

Finally he went on with his story. "In 1493 our captains discovered land in the middle of the Gulf of Guinea. They called it Lizard Island before it was named Saõ Tomé. In fact the lizards were crocodiles. None the less, King John II decided to populate this new colony. He sent slaves there, with convicts who had been serving their sentences in the galleys, and two thousand Jewish children snatched away from their families. Most of them are dead. I don't know what became of mine. Forgive me." He rose to his feet. "Luis will take you to your room."

And he left me. I had not noticed before how much he had lost of his once sturdy, almost stout figure. His footsteps left no prints on the sand of the path. The turtle doves followed him. I left that shadow of a man to disappear, and then asked Luis what had happened to my friend's wife.

"She died of waiting."

I had to get my breath back after this new blow.

"And Lisbon, usually such a calm place – what's the reason for its present madness?"

Luis told me the story in a low voice, as if he did not yet dare to give his words reality.

A month earlier, on the nineteenth of April, a woman praying in the church of Saō Domingo had seen golden stars come out of the great crucifix. Hundreds of people had run to see the miracle. There was a convert from Judaism among them. He had been foolish enough to mutter that it was impossible for an ordinary cross, in effect a piece of wood, to work miracles.

He was instantly beaten soundly, struck dead in the church forecourt and then burnt on an improvised pyre, along with two of his brothers who went to his aid.

Since then the city had been given up to fire and the sword.

Next day, to the great alarm of my host Samuel – I even had to fight him – I pushed back the three bolts and slipped out.

Peace and quiet had not returned. I went towards the loudest source of the noise, the church of St Mary Magdalene. The crowd was so dense that it was spilling out beyond the forecourt and into the square. Although, like all seamen, I feel I am stifling in a large crowd of people and I hate being in very close contact with human bodies, I forced my way on and managed to reach the transept. In the pulpit, a man robed in white was shouting, "Heresy! Heresy!"

The crowd struck up the same theme in chorus. "Heresy! Heresy!"

"Purity! Purity!" cried the man in white.

And the crowd proclaimed, "Purity! Purity!"

The preacher took advantage of these surging cries to shout, in an even louder voice, "Destroy them! Destroy this abominable people!"

"We will destroy them! Yes, we will destroy them!"

Here the preacher, with a wide-ranging turn of his head, scrutinized his congregation. "What are you waiting for?"

There was a moment of silence. People looked at one another, briefly taken by surprise.

"He's right. What are we waiting for?"

And the crowd rushed to get out of the church, shouting louder than ever. "Heresy, heresy, to the stake with them all! Purity! Purity for Lisbon! Kill them, kill them!"

I let the human tide carry me along, feeling both terrified and shaken by disgust.

There had been violent episodes staining our Spanish island with blood during the years when I governed it and I had not been able or willing to prevent them – and now I found them again here, the same gestures, similar victims, in my dear city of Lisbon. I saw the door of a house broken down, a human hunting pack race inside. I saw a woman dragged out by her hair, still clutching her baby to her. The baby was snatched away, passed from hand to hand as they spat on him, then a man took him and, holding him by one leg, whirled him around in the air while the crowd bayed, before smashing his head on the rim of a well.

Montesinos had asked me, why? Why is there such hatred in mankind? And who is that strange being whom we call a Dominican, capable of both risking his life to save the Indians and calling for the murder of all Jews?

God alone knows how I loved the work of a cartographer in which dream and precision mingle. But in another life I know I would devote myself to dissection, with a preference for the bodies of Dominicans. What could be a more edifying task than to search for the origin of violence in the carcass of one of these holy men? It must be some tiny organ shaped like a pair of scales, an internal balance allowing him to pass without previous notice from the greatest benevolence to the worst savagery.

And now I must turn to dogs.

I never knew anything about them before, and hardly noticed them.

I thought they were good at herding flocks, tracking down stags and wild boar, keeping the lonely company, and sleeping in the sun the rest of the time.

I have come to know them better on this island of Hispaniola where I am preparing to end my days. When Christopher had just discovered it, he made me its governor. I created a city here, relishing my new power.

One night I was woken by the barking of dogs.

I thought it was a nightmare. But I found myself sitting up in bed, eyes wide open, fully awake and the barking was still going on.

It seemed to come from the river and was so violent that it made my head ache. I called my guards, without any success. I know from experience that no one sleeps more soundly than a soldier who is supposed to be guarding you. I got up, dressed and went down to the harbour. I walked past the caravels; the noise came from the last ship to put in here. I called. There was no reply from anyone but the dogs. I couldn't see them, but they could sense my presence and it was sending them wild. I went back to the hut that was my palace at the time.

Next day I summoned the captain of the caravel. "Why that cargo of dogs?"

"Those were my orders."

"Ridiculous orders. We see ships from Spain make the voyage so seldom and there's so much else that we need."

"Orders are orders. My job is to navigate."

"And who are you delivering these dogs to?"

"Ask the soldiers."

Ernesto Alvarez, who was in command of my troops, looked down his nose at me.

"Each to his own trade, Bartholomew. You govern the island; I keep the peace. And since you don't give me enough men I've had to find auxiliaries. Do you want to meet them?"

The "auxiliaries" had been brought ashore and shut in cages.

A man came forward, smiling broadly. He told me that he was "Vasco Balboa, breeder and trainer, sent by Their Most Christian Majesties." He showed me his animals.

"A separate cage for each, Governor! And plenty of food or they'll eat one another."

At first glance I thought they were calves. No doubt my ears had deceived me the night before, and led astray by I know not what fears, had confused mooing with barking. I was pleased. We would not go short of milk.

Of all the missions of the Conquest, God surely charged us with bringing cattle here. In twenty years' time, or a century hence, who will be able to imagine that before our arrival the native inhabitants not only knew nothing of the existence of cows, they could not imagine an animal presenting them with so many good things?

Then the calves opened their mouths and I saw their teeth.

Vasco Balboa was very proud of his trade. He told me about his work of dog-breeding, following in the footsteps of his father, a man who was enthusiastic about ferocity. They had carefully selected the fiercest of herd dogs, had mated them with each other and so from generation to generation had created a new breed of mastiffs from which great things could be expected.

"Look at that one – I've called him Leoncico. He's the most active."

Alvarez and his friends did not hide their satisfaction .

"The Indians giving us so much trouble will get a surprise."

Three days later we set off on campaign. A village near La Vega had rebelled. Some ten of those huge dogs were at the forefront of the troops. Balboa had difficulty in holding them back. They were straining at the leash so hard that he had to run.

※

The worst terror begins with surprise. I saw the astonished eyes of the Indians as they looked uncomprehendingly at the pack.

I had often walked around the island villages. I had seen dogs there. Normal dogs of moderate size, with docile natures. They shared the life of the community. Now and then the Indians ate their dogs. How often had I been offered dog meat at a meal? But they asked the dogs to forgive them before killing them and the dogs bowed their heads. They knew that the necessity of eating sometimes leads to regrettable violence. These unfortunate incidents did not disrupt the good understanding between men and dogs.

So what was this breed of animals, growling as they moved forward, showing their fangs, slobbering with fury?

The Indians did not have much time to wonder. Our men let the raging dogs off the leash. The Indians ran. One by one they were brought back. Torn to pieces. Then slowly and meticulously eaten. The dogs even ground their bones to powder.

"Well, what do you think of that, Governor?"

Alvarez and his men had watched the scene, laughing uproariously at the terror of the Indians. "Why go to any trouble ourselves, when these good dogs will do all the work for us? Did you see that? A few good dogs are better and faster than an army."

The good dogs, their chops bloodstained, came to be praised by their master for carrying out their mission.

The huge Leoncico had not been a disappointment; he alone had torn out the throats of three savages who looked like resisting. Then, no doubt to reward himself, he had flushed two children out of their hiding-place in some hay and had eaten them.

Shame on me, in my gratitude I patted his head.

On the way back I said repeatedly how pleased I was. The news, particularly the bad news, spread around the island at lightning speed. All the Indians would soon know what terrible allies we had been sent. Peace was quickly restored. The dog-breeder boasted of his prowess. Pride had raised him to some point not far from the sky. He replied to questions as the powerful do, in an offhand tone.

"My monsters? I told you, they started out as ordinary herd dogs."

"How did you breed that … that ability into them?"

He looked at me scornfully, as if I were an idiot.

"That, Governor, is my secret. A secret for which many of the courts of Europe envy us, believe me!"

"And the taste ... the particular appetite they seem to have for Indians?"

"Nothing easier. Ever since their arrival I've fed them on nothing but the flesh of these savages. You kill enough Indians, there's no shortage!"

After six months of similar campaigns, all victorious, in which Leoncico and his companions had worked wonders, Balboa came to see me.

"I hope you appreciate my work, Governor?"

"I think I have shown you that I do."

"Then wouldn't you agree that such work deserves a reward?"

I reminded him how low the financial resources of our colony were, as a result of the laziness of the Indians when it came to prospecting for gold.

He shook his head. "I don't mean money." And he made a brusque movement, as if I had insulted him. "Like everyone else, I'm thinking of my children, my family. I may spend my time breeding dogs, but I'm going to war. More successfully than many soldiers."

I suddenly understood. "You want a noble title?"

"That's what I had in mind."

Shame on me again, I agreed to his request.

The dog-trainer bears a longer name today: Vasco Nuñez de Balboa.

That was the kind of man I was.

We were all like that, blind and inhuman, before Montesinos opened our eyes.

The captains have never forgotten me. They know that I shall always give them a warm welcome. As soon as they come ashore they make haste to the Alcazar Palace, where the viceroy is waiting impatiently for them on the first floor. But once they have delivered the official report on their mission, they never fail to come down to the ground floor to visit me.

These seamen bear such names as Ponce de León, Nicuesa, Ojeda, Esquivel, Velásquez ... all of them valiant explorers, all of them Christopher's heirs. Who will remember them when I am gone? I know that a legend is being constructed and it will veil the truth. We shall build an official history which retains only one or two names.

Those visits take me back to the time when I was twenty. I listen avidly to the tales told by sailors, as I did in the good old days in Lisbon; and I set down their discoveries on a little map in my own way. What does it matter if my fingers, twisted like vines today, do not hold the pen as firmly as they used to? What I draw tells the tale of the progressive enlargement of the world. The islands of Cozumel and Margarita, the Pearl Coast, Castile of Gold, Honduras, Yucatán ...

Christopher died convinced that he had succeeded in his Enterprise: as he saw it, all the territories where he landed were parts of the Indies.

Doubts surfaced in those of us who survived him and the great progress made in exploration only adds to them.

Nothing here is like Cipango, still less the empire of the Grand Khan: not the landscapes, the architecture of the buildings, the faces of the native inhabitants. Could it be that Christopher discovered a continent entirely unknown until his time? I remember the laughter of the Committee of Mathematicians: "The Indies, Messer Columbus of Genoa, are much further to the west than you say."

So either my brother made a mistake, or he lied to us.

But in any case, does he not deserve even greater honour? What

232

can be nobler than to find a previously unknown way to what is known, or to invent what is unknown?

I have other visitors whose subject is also exploration, but who are not seamen.

Soon after the notorious sermon, as if Brother Montesinos had revived audacity and the need for truth, a man who would not give his name came to see me. He was tall and thin, and his face was almost skeletal. When he told me that he was an engraver by profession, I could not keep from thinking that the acid he used in his daily work must have eroded his cheeks, they were so hollow. He told me he had left his native country, the Netherlands, because he needed bright colours. The grey and black of his works, which were also those of his country, made him too sad.

I asked him if our island of Hispaniola had met his expectations.

"Unfortunately not," he replied, and he took the first of his engravings out of a haversack. "It is my misfortune that the ravages of old age have spared my eyesight. I see only too well. I cannot console myself by taking refuge in blindness."

I began to feel indignant as I looked at the engraving. "Who told you these fantastic things?"

"Reality. Would you like to see more of them?"

I almost sent him packing in my anger. I stopped myself just in time.

He came back the next day. I bought all his engravings, twelve of them. Ever since, I have forced myself to look at them every evening, as a form of penance, while the question asked by Montesinos, always the same question, turns in my head like a bat in the air: why?

I finally showed the viceroy those engravings. Cautious as always, and easily disgusted, he grimaced. "What's this about?"

"It's a theatrical show that may serve me as my last confession."

"What show?"

"The show of our cruelties."

After much hesitation he put out his hand, picked up the sheets and began looking at them, first one and then another. He gave a start, brought the collection closer to see it better, murmured, "How horrible!" He almost dropped all the engravings as he pushed them away, then drew them close once more. This sequence of advance and retreat went on until he reached the last engraving, accompanied by horrified comments.

Then the viceroy raised his head. "What business of ours are these abominations?"

"I was governor. A bad governor. Christopher was wrong about my capabilities; I had no authority over anyone, not even my Spanish troops. Half of them rebelled against me. I saw these tortures. I allowed them. Perhaps I sometimes instigated them? I laughed at the terror of the Indians. Perhaps I even took pleasure in the sight of their sufferings? I am responsible."

Diego shrugged his shoulders and went away.

I was left alone with the twelve engravings.

In the foreground, a Spaniard brandishing an axe. An Indian is waiting with his forearm laid on a block of wood. A woman, already mutilated, is waving her stumps in the air. Another is firmly held by a soldier as he puts out one of her eyes with the point of his knife. Dogs chase the fugitives. Those whom they bring down are eaten. In the background, Indians are being pushed towards the edge of a sheer cliff and fall from it. (*Plate I*)

A noble conquistador wearing a ruff and trunk-hose is standing with half of a child cut in two down the middle held proudly in each hand. A woman, no doubt the mother, follows the scene with dead eyes; she has been hung from a tree. In the background, grey hounds are running and catching any Indians who are left. (*Plate III*)

In the foreground, on the right, a baby is cooking on a grill. A soldier is tending the fire. To the left a stall, like a butcher's stall, displays legs, thighs, arms. Indians carrying heavy burdens, anchors or cannon, are whipped to make them go faster. In the distance, we can see another group of Indians being dragged towards a cannon. A ship is waiting to take its cargo on board. (*Plate X*)

At the centre of the engraving, a conquistador in fine clothing is directing events with a baton, like an orchestral conductor. But the music he is conducting is torture. An Indian lies on his back. Fire is burning the soles of his feet; there is a ligature round his neck. A soldier is pouring boiling oil on his chest and stomach. (*Plate XI*)

When, at the pressing request of Queen Isabella and King Ferdinand, I put to sea in April 1494, and on my arrival on the island of Hispaniola my brother showed how pleased he was to see me after our long separation – when he had shown his confidence in me by appointing me *Adelantado* of the Indies and governor of the island, I said that my first wish was to get to know the territories of which I would now be in charge.

Others were surprised. They pointed out that there were countless urgent questions for me to resolve, and such a journey would not only delay answers to them and diminish my authority when I had only just assumed it, it also entailed great risks for my safety.

I did not listen to these arguments. I set off to explore, protected only by a small escort.

I was not yet forty at the time and my body had the strength of youth. It did not suffer any of the infirmities afflicting it today.

God rewarded me for my decision. Perhaps He was particularly proud of His Creation in this part of the world. During those two weeks of travelling, I never ceased to marvel at it.

All I had ever seen before in the way of the colours, shapes and sizes of plants was surpassed here a thousand times. We passed through a joyous profusion where the boundaries between the natural kingdoms were not always clear. What looked like a flower turned out to be a frog when you came closer. Something winding along the ground or hanging from a tree might be a liana or a snake. Animals added to the festive sense, whether leaping from tree to tree like the monkeys, or scurrying through plantations like the wild pigs, whether long-nosed rodents, the zagoutis, or crocodiles basking on the sandbanks.

In these Indies, Noah had finished the work he began before the deluge. His ark had landed more wonderful creatures here than those of the Bible.

And when the eye tired of the jungle and its abundance of diversity, you found a clearing to give immediate rest to the sense of sight, or a little field carefully cultivated, the very image of peace, of miraculous harmony between nature and the presence of humanity.

How could I not like the island of Hispaniola, when you saw life itself in more variety than anywhere else, with more freedom and tranquillity?

It is no good for me to explain that fact again and again. People still ask: why did you choose to come back here?

One last time, I repeat that it's a case of love. I must be one of those who fall in love more intensely with places than people. Hispaniola was dear to me from the very first day.

We were approaching the high mountain about which I had been told and which I had made the object of our expedition. It was as we climbed it that I began to understand the death-dealing tyranny of gold. The clouds dispersed. The mountains came into view one by one and we saw the cordillera gradually unfurling all the way to the horizon, like a gigantic monitor lizard.

This magnificent spectacle did not interest any of my escort, not even the two supposed experts on natural science. They had eyes only for the river winding its way along the bottom of the valley down below. They talked excitedly, saying that in its muddy waters you could find nuggets; and many more would have been found if the Indians were not naturally lazy, adding that a month ago a lucky *encomendero* had found a chunk of yellow ore as big as his fist.

I had to threaten my companions to make them go on to the summit. Gold drew them to it body and soul, like the most powerful of magnetic stones. I watched human beings suddenly changed by gold into frenzied animals. It struck me that part of my task would be to govern these wild animals and I shivered. With fear and revulsion. The future was to show how right I was.

I think about gold very often, over and over again.

You were severely blamed for greed, Christopher. But I, better acquainted with you than anyone else, know that unlike so many other conquistadors, in fact almost all of them, you were not interested in accumulating wealth. Your only fever was for the Discovery. And gold, finding gold, was the only guarantee that your dreams of distant voyages would continue to cast a spell on kings and queens.

Perhaps gold meant even more to you. Perhaps it was a sign, a message like your beloved prophecies. In setting you on the way to gold-bearing lands, God was showing that He looked with favour on your Enterprise.

Every morning, Sundays included, two soldiers carry me down to the mouth of the river. They are more than considerate of me. They suggest other routes, different expeditions. Why not go into the forest for a change? If you were strapped to a horse, we could take you to Lake Xaragua. You love birds and there are many of them there. Frigate birds, ibises, flamingoes. And all the way to the lake the sea has three colours. Far out it is dark blue, almost black; then greenish; finally white as you approach the shore.

I say neither yes or no to them, I thank them. They know they must hurry up. I like to arrive at the same moment as the rising sun.

They are always joking, and it's always the same joke. "Oh, Governor. You're getting heavier and heavier, do stop eating so much!"

And we all three laugh, to be imitated next moment by the cockatoos. These good fellows know better than anyone that I weigh less and less all the time. I eat very little. Old age is a separation. You are gradually leaving yourself. That is why I have chosen this place, beside two expanses of moving water, the river and the sea. I do not want to leave anything behind. I like the idea that day after day the water is carrying away the parts of me that I shed.

Often, just before mid-day, I am joined by some girls. Of the thirty young ladies brought here from Spain to start families, twenty-six have found husbands. The four left on the shelf go on walking up and down the Ladies' Road. They are increasingly impatient. They go all the way down to the ocean and look out to sea. Perhaps the next ship to come in will bring Prince Charming at last.

I have seen two kinds of women watching the sea: those who feared it would make them widows, and now these who are pining for a husband.

As they watch, they talk. I like their chatter, the modest nature of their dreams.

I think again of my brother's three caravels: the Santa Maria, the Pinta, the Niña. In fact the Santa Maria was really called the

Marie-Galante. The name of the Pinta means painted, wearing cosmetics. And Niña means girl. The caravels that discovered the New World were named after whores. I am amused whenever I remember that.

Then the wind dies down. The birds settle on the water. It is the time of day when the heat becomes unbearable. The motionless sea burns more strongly than the sun. The young ladies surrender to it. They go away, not without some anxiety for my health: you will bake in this heat, Bartholomew, or worse, you will melt, you are sweating so freely! This is the moment I like best. The soldiers have retreated; they are sleeping in the shade of palm trees or playing cards. I can hardly hear what they are saying. They are talking about women, what they do to women at night and what women do to them, and also about me, still clinging to life. "Do you think he'll last much longer?" They are right to wonder. I can feel my strength draining away. I must warn Las Casas. I shall not keep my promise. I shall be unable to finish my account. I shall be dead when he gets back. What does it matter? He doesn't need me for his *History of the Indies*. He knows that I was not expected to be telling the story.

The fishermen are beginning to come in from the open sea in their long canoes.

And I am talking to my brother.

I know that I have little time left; I confine myself to a few key questions.

Why?

Why go discovering if it is only to kill those you discover?

Besides, Christopher, who discovers whom in a discovery? The man who makes the effort of crossing the sea makes a discovery, but the man he has discovered also discovers him as he advances towards him.

I have to pester him, I keep returning to my other obsession: what is gold, Christopher? The sum of everything? A universally equivalent factor? All is sacrificed to gold: countries, plants, animals, men, women. And once the gold is gained it is exchanged for other countries, plants, animals, men and above all women. Where is the profit in that? Christopher, Christopher, if our eyes could immerse themselves in gold and look deeply enough, do you think they would find the answer to that enigma, the imbecility and cruelty of mankind?

I do not let his silence deter me. I go on.

Christopher, Christopher, forgive me for pestering you. Where you are now, you must have many other things on your mind. How many Indians were there, Christopher, when you disembarked? And how many are there today? Look, listen: we have murdered so many that the island of Hispaniola there behind me is almost as deserted as the sea.

Christopher, Christopher, are you sure you discovered the Indies? On the other hand, what does it matter, Christopher?

Christopher, Christopher, don't you think it is part of the law of discovery to be thrown off course by what you discover?

Christopher, Christopher, don't you think we should escape the prison of Reality to enhance Truth?

If you had not lied, first and foremost to yourself, would you have dared to set out and sail so far west?

My questions must displease him, because he never replies.

I know I am departing from my appointed role; I was not expected to be telling the story. Still less was I expected to ask questions.

Bibliography

Christopher Columbus must have been the subject of as many books as the Second World War, which is saying a good deal. Out of this vast number, I will mention:

Attali, Jacques, *1492*, Paris, Fayard, 1991.

Bellec, François, *Tentation de la Haute Mer*, Paris, Seghers, 1992.

Besse, Jean-Marc, *Les Grandeurs de la Terre, Aspects de savoir géographique de la Renaissance*, Paris, ÉNS Éditions, 2004.

Boorstin, Daniel, *Les Découvreurs*, Paris, Robert Laffont, 1988. Original English edition, *The Discoverers*, New York, Random House, 1982.

Broc, Numa, *La Géographie de la Renaissance*, Paris, Éditions du Comité des travaux historiques et scientifiques, 1987.

Columbus, Christopher, *La Découverte de l'Amérique* (tr. Soledad Estorach and Michel Lequenne), vols. I and II, Paris, La Découverte, 2002. Various English translations of the journals kept by Columbus exist, e.g. *The Four Voyages of Christopher Columbus*, tr. J. M. Cohen, Harmondsworth, Penguin, 1952; *Journals and other Documents on the Life and Voyages of Christopher Columbus*, tr. Samuel Eliot Morison, New York, Heritage Press, 1963.

Columbus, Christopher, *Livre de prophéties [Libro de las profecias]*, text ed. Michel Lequenne, Grenoble, Éditions Jérôme Millon, 1992. English version, tr. Blair Sullivan, ed. Roberto Rusconi, University of California Press, 1997.

Debray, Régis, *Christophe Colomb, Le Visiteur de l'aube*, Paris, La Différence, 1991.

Djebbar, Ahjmed, *L'Algèbre arabe, Genèse d'un art*, Paris, Vuibert, 2005.

Ikor, Olivier, *Caravelles*, Paris, Lattès, 2010.

Las Casas (de), Bartolomé, *Historia de las Indias*, French, *Histoire des Indes* (tr. Jean-Pierre Clément and Jean-Marie Saint-Lu), vols. I, II and III, Paris, Seuil, 2002. English, *History of the Indies*, Harper & Row, New York, 1971. (A reissue of the first English version published 1699.)

Las Casas (de), Bartolomé, *Brevísima relación de la destrucción de las Indias*, published in Spanish 1952. French: *La Destruction des Indes*, tr. Jacques de Miggrode), Paris, Éditions Chandeigne, 2000. English version, *A Short History of the Destruction of the Indies* (tr. Nigel Griffin), London, Penguin 1992.

Lequenne, Michel, *Christophe Colomb, Amiral de la mer océane*, Paris, Gallimard, 2005.

Morison, Samuel Eliot, *Admiral of the Ocean Sea*, Boston, Little, Brown & Co., 1970.

Munzer, Jérôme, *Voyage en Europe et au Portugal (1494–1495)*, int. and tr. Micel Tarayre, Paris, Les Belles-Lettres, 2006.

Polo, Marco, *Il Milione* [The Travels of Marco Polo]. French: *Le Devisement du Monde*, text ed. A.-C. Moule and Paul Pelliot, vols I and II, Paris, La Découverte, 2004. First English version tr. John Frampton, 1579. Many later versions in English.

Todorov, Tzvetan, *La Conquête de la Renaissance*, Paris, Éditions du Comité des travaux historiques et scientifiques, 1986.

Géographie du monde au Moyen Âge et à la Renaissance, ed. Monique Pelletier, Paris, Éditions du Comité des travaux historiques et scientifiques, 1989.

Voyage d'Eustache Delafosse sur la côte de Guinée, au Portugal et en Espagne (1479–1481), ed. Denis Escudier, Paris, Éditions Chandeigne, 1992.

And all the books of Gilles Lapouge, including *La Légende de la géographie*, Paris, Albin Michel, 2009.

I must give a special mention to *Voyage aux pays de nulle part*, ed. Francis Lacassin, Paris, Robert Laffont, 1990. This very rich collection shows that we travel in our heads as much as by sea and on land. It was here that I found the tale of St Brendan, the work of one Benoît, adapted by Jean Marchand.

Acknowledgements

Embarking on so great and uncertain a voyage meant taking an exceptional crew on board.

First, to pay credit where credit is due, my thanks to Cristina Castel-Branco. Year after year, this wonderful friend has given me the keys to Lisbon one by one.

My thanks to my daughter Judith. She was studying history while I was writing this book; she told me the tale of the Spice Road and put me on the track of the *Ymago*.

My thanks to Jean-Baptiste Cusinier. He succeeded, if with some difficulty, in helping me to make progress in the (delightful) science of mathematics.

My thanks to Claire Guillemin, a meticulous explorer of the secrets of Santo Domingo.

My thanks to Admiral François Bellec, thanks to whom I quickly learnt to read the skies, an essential skill for all who put out on the high seas hoping to return.

My thanks to Michel Chandeigne, whose publishing imprint (10 rue Tournefort, Paris Ve) produces works that are treasures of erudition and elegance.

My thanks to Professor Jean-Paul Duviols. No one knows more about the 15th and 16th centuries in Spain and Portugal.

My thanks to Luc Ferry, who initiated me into some of the secrets of the sacred nature of ignorance.

My thanks to Mireille Pastoureau, curator and librarian of the Bibliothèque de l'Institut de France and a great expert on the Discoveries, who was kind enough to give me her invaluable aid.

My thanks to Marie Eugène, the good fairy who has watched over countless versions of this book.

My thanks to my faithful and greatly valued team of readers: Jérôme Clément, Thierry Arnoult, Philippe Delmas, Élisabeth and

Bernard Achard, Isabelle de Saint Aubin, Joël Calmettes, Christophe Guillemin, Michel Sauzay, Claudine Pons, Catherine Clavier, Bertrand Goudot, Christian Dargnat, Emmanuel de Fontainieu and Emmanuel Macros.

My thanks to my wife, who could hardly believe that a writer is away from home even more often than a seaman.

My thanks to Claude Durand.

My thanks to Jean-Marc Roberts.